Murder Live

Also by Frank Palmer

MURDER LIVE
Frank Palmer

Constable • London

First published in Great Britain 1997 by Constable & Company Ltd,
3 The Lanchesters, 162 Fulham Palace Road, London W6 9ER
Copyright © 1997 Frank Palmer
The right of Frank Palmer to be identified as the author of this work
has been asserted by him in accordance with the Copyright,
Designs and Patents Act 1988
ISBN 0 09 477650 4
Set in Palatino 10pt by Pure Tech India Ltd, Pondicherry
Printed and bound in Great Britain by
Hartnolls Ltd, Bodmin

A CIP catalogue record for this book
is available from the British Library

For Miles and his team

1

EIGHT DAYS TO CHRISTMAS

For *Friday the 13th Blues*, the usual off-screen continuity announcer was dropped.

Rounded vowels were judged too churchy, like a curate impersonating the archbishop, for a programme that promised uncensored shots of crime on the streets, life in the raw. Now ... As it happens ... Live.

They replaced him with a darker voice of doom and picked *Friday the 13th* for the title, because, like walking under ladders, it's supposed to be unlucky.

It was certainly unlucky for the chief constable who gave the fly-on-the-wall documentary the go-ahead and is now the subject of a high-powered Home Office inquiry.

Unluckier still was Clive Voss, the TV personality. He got shot. Now ... As it happens ... Dead.

Couldn't have happened to a more caring or a vainer man, according to which paper you read over the weekend. In the view of the printed press, annoyed at being scooped, and backwoodsmen MPs, anxious for any publicity, it shouldn't have happened at all.

With a general election looming, crime and punishment near the top of the agenda, the Home Secretary was unlikely to pass up the chance of appeasing leader writers while, at the same time, loosing off a warning shot at TV. He stood up in the Commons yesterday and, to drowsy hear-hears, announced an immediate, thorough and independent investigation.

It's being called the Cameron Commission after the head of the Inspectorate of Constabularies who is leading it, under the supervision of the Police Complaints Authority.

You won't find my name in the Hansard account of Parliamentary Proceedings; nor my assignment.

While Sir Donald Cameron's brief is to draw up guidelines on the limits of police co-operation with the ever-expanding electronic media, I'm using the cover of his Commission to find who murdered Clive Voss and why.

As I reluctantly packed my bag, I blamed my wife. She's a breakfast TV newscaster and I suspect that someone somewhere wrongly thought this would give me an insight into a profession that's marginally more insane than my own.

As she drove me through the fog to the train, she claimed I'd lumbered myself by making no secret of a liking for cop shows, *The Thin Blue Line* best of all because it's more fun than the rest.

Anyway, here I am, stretched out on a hotel bed, miles from home, lumbered, so sit back in your armchair (a bum on a seat, they call you in my wife's trade) for the reprise.

Lying here, I close my eyes and repeat: Reprise.

To American TV, it means a quick update, the story so far. Musically, it means a gorgeous passage is repeated; moments of sheer magic returning. Reprise. I love that word.

I open my eyes. Nothing very lovely about the video I've already played over twice after unpacking a change of suit and shoes and a week's supply of shirts, underpants and socks, including the lucky black-and-white pair.

I look up at the high cream ceiling, using it as a wide screen as I run it again through my mind.

Previously – here you can select your own music. The frenzied beat of jungle drums, perhaps. Or a plonking piano that breaks into baroque. A shaky camera, however, is obligatory.

Previously, on … Damn it. No title. Can't pinch *Friday the 13th Blues*. Been done. Besides, ever since *Hill Street*, every other programme featuring an emergency service has been called Something Blue.

Let's think. How about *Murder Live*? OK? OK then. Cut. Action, if that's what you can call lying here, waiting for the phone to ring while digesting a lunchtime toastie of Wensleydale cheese and pickle from Room Service.

Previously, on *Murder Live*, the normal Friday night schedule was shelved, apart from the immutable *News at Ten*.

In the hour before and for two hours afterwards, a dozen outside broadcast crews had been granted official *carte blanche* to go with the police responding to 999 calls anywhere in the county.

No force, not even the Met, can guarantee non-stop thrills and spills. To fill any boring blanks, cameras were at a greyhound meeting before ten. A panel of experts had been lined up in the

2

studio to field questions on law and order from an invited audience after the news.

The show opened with a rather desultory drugs raid in an inner city bedsit, then switched to the dog track for the 9.15 which was no more exciting.

Back on the cold streets, a joyrider was chased and breath-tested, his face hidden behind a series of dancing dots.

After a commercial break, which I fast forward through my mind, came a call to an explosion in offices above a bank. The fire was dying when the cameras returned to the greyhound stadium for the 9.45, a sponsored race.

Immediately after the presentation to the winning owner, Clive Voss appeared, rocking in the front seat of a truck, dark, handsome face tense, reporting in the usual clipped fashion that he was on his way to trouble outside a city centre nightspot.

The usual shaky camera filmed his back as he jumped out, *Starsky and Hutch* style, before the vehicle had stopped. When the camera eventually caught up with him in a dark alley, he was lying in a spreading pool of blood, beyond famous last words.

With their on-the-spot commentator speechless, the voice of doom took over, stating the obvious. 'We're not quite sure what's happening, but we'll be back.'

More ads are mentally zipped through to *News at Ten*, heavy stuff; the single currency, the government losing its majority, more food poisoning, but no mention of what had just happened virtually before viewers' very eyes.

The regional news that followed managed only an 'and finally' with the desk man's head down over an unrehearsed piece of late copy. 'Reports are coming in that a TV journalist taking part in a live police programme being shown earlier this evening and due to continue after the next break has suffered head injuries and been taken to hospital. More details after the weather.'

But the grave-faced compere of the studio discussion had no more details after the weathergirl had forecast a cold and windy Saturday.

He introduced his experts, an anxious-looking chief constable among them, but allowed only a couple of tame questions and answers before pleading technical problems.

3

The show came off. On came *All the President's Men* which my wife blames for every succeeding generation of journalists who investigate everyone's shortcomings but their own.

It was left to the newspapers to try to sort out the story over the weekend, a bit at a time, as more details emerged, the main fact being that Voss was shot in the forehead at close quarters and was dead on arrival at hospital.

The grey phone on the bedside cabinet rings.

The chief of the inspectorate calls.

I'll be back after this short break.

2

'Out of courtesy,' the Chief Inspector of Constabularies decrees without the courtesy of consultation, 'we're seeing the chief constable first.'

For the highest ranking officer in a modern police service, the top cop, as he's often called in the press, Sir Donald Cameron has a remarkably old-fashioned air, well suited to the sumptuous surroundings of the Royal York Hotel.

He's sixtyish, very tall, slim, with a ramrod straight back. His suit is an immaculately fitted pale grey which makes my own darker shade of more coarse grey material look what it is – something out of M&S. His hair is short and a paler grey, not quite white.

He is waiting at the foot of a sweeping staircase beneath twin chandeliers of frosted glass, perfectly at home. He puts me in mind of the sort of police chief my grandad used to rail about in his days on the beat in the '50s and '60s. 'Ex-Indian army wallahs,' he called them, but only because 'wanker' wasn't in common usage in those days. 'Jobs for the old boys. All airs, graces and not a clue.'

He shakes my hand firmly. 'Room OK?'

'Splendid, sir,' I reply.

'Splendid. Splendid,' he repeats absently, eyes on the stairs down which is descending a petite, middle-aged Asian woman in an eastern sari of subdued green silk.

A huge Christmas tree with red and gold trimmings stands in

4

the well of the stairs reaching up thirty or so carpeted steps. She looks like the fairy climbing off the top branch.

She smiles warmly when she reaches us. Above the hubbub of a dozen different conversations in the crowded foyer, Cameron introduces me to 'our supervisor from the Complaints Authority'.

My, my, I think, taking her small, soft hand. If she doesn't like the way he conducts this inquiry, she has the power to bounce back his report, marked: 'Must try harder.' The old Empire has been turned on its head.

A youngish, dark-suited man rises from a stool in front of a highly polished grand piano. He is carrying a thick black coat, three-quarter length, which he holds out for our supervisor. She slips her arms into it, smiling her thanks.

Only when his task has been completed am I introduced to 'our clerk'. These three alone, and about the same number in the Home Office and on my own force (and my wife, of course), know of my real mission here.

At the revolving front door, Cameron stands aside for the supervisor, but not for me or our clerk. Waiting at the foot of red-carpeted steps is a black Daimler with a uniformed chauffeur to whom I'm not introduced.

Cameron opens a rear door for her, not for me. It seems I'm last in the pecking order 'cos I'm riding up front.

Suits me, I think as we purr out of the hotel's lawned grounds. The morning fog has lifted. There are splashes of blue in the sky. The three towers of the Minster are a creamy colour in the weak sunlight.

I'll take in a bit of an ancient city I last toured in an open-top bus with my grandparents when I was ten – three-quarters of my life away.

Saves me from having to nod solemnly while Cameron waffles in the back in an educated Scots accent about Chief Constable Johns – 'splendid CV, good record in his previous shire force...'

That's not what I've heard on training courses from officers who have served under Johns. They regard him as an incompetent bastard. 'Bastards in the police service,' my grandad once said, 'you must never mind, but you have a right to expect them to be competent bastards.'

Eyes left on the Roman walls on top of grassed banks, I'm

5

beginning to get bad vibes, fearing the old boy network in operation, anticipating a whitewash of a report.

Approaching police HQ, a modern building in deep red brick, next to much larger and older military barracks, Cameron completes his background briefing. 'And, of course, he's thoroughly media-trained.'

Oh, Christ, I groan inwardly. The biggest vibe of all.

My wife reckons you can always spot a police chief who has been media-trained. They begin with Answer No. 1 out of the public relations manual – something on the lines of 'Let me say straight away how deeply shocked we all are and saddened for Mr Voss and his family.' Chief Constable Johns is saying it now.

His brown eyes in contact lenses are on our supervisor, the one he's got to charm. His next sentence will be something like 'Let me assure you of our full co-operation.'

He goes on, 'I want to pledge to you personally...' I fight off a smile through the rest.

Johns is the only one in uniform, a black, smooth material, with the cream, woven emblems of his office on his shoulders.

Once he'd have looked impressive in it, but now a middle-aged spread is straining the silver-buckled belt of the tunic. His temples are greying and he has the jowly look of a fifty-year-old who eats and drinks too much and doesn't exercise enough.

'Thank you, Mr Johns,' says the supervisor, very softly.

'Ronald. Please call me Ron.' He gives her a constipated smile. 'Now how can I help?'

The supervisor looks puzzled. Before she joined the Complaints Authority, she lectured on Asian art at a red-brick university and has probably never conducted an interrogation before. Cameron appears to have forgotten how, if he ever knew, and the clerk has his head down over his notes.

All eyes fall on me. 'Just take us through the background,' I say.

He doesn't invite me to call him Ron.

'Image-wise' – as true as I sit here, on a high-backed armless chair at a polished oval table in the conference room extension to his spacious office, Chief Constable Johns starts like that.

6

Image-wise, he begins, East Yorkshire Police had been having a rather unhappy time. 'Complaints up, clear-ups down, both on the mend now, let me assure you.' He smiles to himself. 'As a result of changes I've made.'

So, when the controller of Ridings TV approached him with the idea of three hours of prime time, he took 'the positive view'.

Yes please, to a free plug, he means.

The station's executives, he continues, never referring to a neat pile of papers in front of him, sat where we are sitting and they hammered out the details – a dozen crews to go with the police anywhere they liked, a producer in the force's control room to direct their operations, faces of arrestees to be obscured, a contract indemnifying the force from any libel writs, full thanks in the credits. He ends a long spiel looking rather pleased with himself.

'And, of course,' says Cameron with an icy smile, 'an appearance by you on the studio panel?'

Johns sits back in his big, comfortable chair. 'Correct.'

Cameron switches off his smile. 'Aren't you aware that a force down south which agreed to fly-on-the-wall treatment got into such hot water over their handling of a rape that the regulations had to be changed?'

I sit up and take notice. Johns doesn't. 'We had an agreement which excluded coverage of sexual assaults,' he replies languidly.

Our supervisor asks her first question, an easy one. 'You will have read the Complaints Authority's latest report?'

'Of course.' A smiling nod.

'Including our stated misgivings about the regular presence of journalists at raids?' She arches a plucked eyebrow.

Another nod, no smile this time.

Cameron resumes in a flat tone. 'The drugs raid which opened the programme gave the appearance of being stage-managed. Is that so?'

'Well,' says Johns, very cautiously, finally looking at his papers, 'it was timed for the start of the programme, but, operationally, it made no difference.'

'Aren't Friday nights, being the beginning of the weekend, covered by unpaid Specials?' asks Cameron.

'Normally, but last week we flooded the patch with full-time officers to demonstrate to taxpayers how professional we are, what value for money we give.'

'Didn't that massively increase the overtime bill?'

7

'Er...' Johns has totally lost that pleased-with-himself expression.

'Notwithstanding which,' Cameron nags on, 'we have had complaints from MPs that police cars were unavailable to escort ambulances on urgent missions arising out of watching the programme.'

'Sorry?' says Johns, looking more puzzled than apologetic.

One woman, he's sternly informed, went into premature labour on seeing Voss lying in his pool of blood. Another, living in an isolated hamlet in the Wolds, suffered such trauma that she, too, had to be rushed to hospital. Neither ambulance could raise a police escort over icy roads. 'As a result, their MPs are complaining,' adds Cameron, with a fed-up face.

'I'll look into it,' says Johns, now looking very sorry indeed.

'I'll look into it,' comes the chilling response. 'That's why I'm here.'

The chief goes silent.

'You see...' Cameron hasn't finished yet. '...it makes it seem somewhat hypocritical for the government to protest, as they did only last week, about screen violence when a public service provides the backdrop for it, as in this case.'

I am sitting silently through all of this, completely changing my mind about Cameron.

He's a bastard all right, but a competent one, a wily old colonial boy who's immediately rumbled Johns's ego.

That, I reflect, is what's got him into this mess – ego. Powerful men, it's always men, think they can control, if not censor, what information they share with the public.

OK, Ridings TV kept its word and a series of juddering coloured dots blocked out the faces of the drug pusher and the joyrider. Pixilation, it's called, my wife tells me. She told me something else. Squint and you can see right through the mosaic, like Cameron had seen right through Johns.

To get himself off the hook, Johns calls in his acting head of CID. A burly superintendent, he moves heavily and slowly, strained face washed out after four days of snatched sleep; most of it, I suspect, in his dark blue suit that makes mine look smart.

Standing, because he's not invited to sit, he begins to bring us up to date on the latest forensics. A .38 bullet entered above the bridge of Voss's nose, the size of a fingernail, and exited from

8

the crown of his head, the size of a fist. The weapon had not been found, no eyewitnesses traced.

He goes back fifteen minutes to the fire which preceded the shooting. I half switch off. My job here is to catch the killer, not the arsonist.

The seat of the fire, he reports, was a wall safe at law offices above the bank. Name of McMichael, he adds, then, after a pause, 'Who happens to be Voss's own solicitor.'

Coincidence or connection? I ask myself, fully switched on again. 'So it wasn't arson?' I ask the super.

'A bungled safe-blowing,' he replies.

'Anything interesting in the safe?'

'If so, it's all gone up in smoke.'

'Anything belonging to Voss?'

A weary nod. 'Videos.'

Johns interjects to order a news black-out on the fact that the solicitor's safe, not the bank vaults, was the target.

'It's out already. We can't stop a solicitor talking to the media,' the super patiently points out.

Johns bristles. 'We jolly well –'

'Quite right.' Cameron stops him in mid-sentence. 'Seek his co-operation. Advise him to say, if asked by the media, that what remains of the contents has been taken away for examination, so he doesn't know if anything survived the explosion or not.'

'Done that,' says the super with a tired sigh.

Johns beams pleasurably, dismisses him and relaxes back in his big chair as Cameron seeks his views on the guidelines he has to produce on police co-operation with the media.

It becomes a debate, in which I take no part, about the videos of road crashes and rescues all emergency services release these days to TV. 'Points up the ever-present dangers and our problems in dealing with them,' claims Johns, regaining some of his composure.

'On the other hand,' says Cameron quietly, 'it could be argued that all we are doing is providing free material – and in Friday's case extra resources – at the public expense to networks to build advertising around; or, in the case of the BBC, help their ratings war.'

God, I like this old bod's sharp mind, pleased he's heading my team, and not Johns who's gone quiet again.

Cameron turns to me and I adopt his brisk questioning style. 'Tell me, Mr Johns, did you know Voss?'

'Not well, no. Met him the once. He came to one of the planning meetings as part of the Ridings team. Saw him occasionally on TV. No time to watch a lot, of course, in this job.' He nods at the door out of which his acting CID chief departed. 'I'm informed Voss presented several things – consumer type programmes, shows about successful local celebrities and so on.'

'Has he touched on police matters before?' I ask.

'Well, yes.' He's extremely uncomfortable again, all but fingering his gleaming white collar. 'He had a *Cause for Concern* programme, something like that, and he raised one of our old cases.'

'Saying what?'

'That a gems thief shouldn't have been in prison. I'm afraid he claimed, in effect, that evidence had been planted and he produced eyewitnesses who put our convicted offender elsewhere.'

'When was this?'

'About two months ago.'

'And what was the upshot?'

'Freed on appeal, sorry to say.'

'And what happened to the officer in charge of the inquiry?'

'Suing for libel.' A thoughtful pause. 'Don't know what will happen now, of course, with Voss dead.'

He gives the name of Inspector Susan Herrick as the officer concerned and I ask where I'll find her.

'Doing a spell back in uniform.' He makes a phone call, brusquely queries her whereabouts and puts down the receiver. 'On at six. Training probationers in soccer crowd control. I can send a car to her home, if you like, if you want to see her now.'

'Tomorrow will do,' I reply easily.

'Yes,' Cameron concurs with a sly smile, 'we've a full schedule today.'

Johns sits back, but only for as long as it takes for Cameron to lean forward with a question that burns within me, but I haven't got the rank to ask. 'Do you mean to say that you gave open access to a journalist who, allegedly anyway, had libelled one of your senior officers?'

'Didn't know he was actually to be on the programme.' Johns

picks up a paper from the pile and waves it like a white flag. 'On their schedule they just had teams designated by initials from A to M, no names.'

He, too, leans forward, slipping a visiting card across the desk. 'My home number,' he says with an anxious-to-please expression. 'Ring for any help you need, day or night.'

Cameron takes the card and rises. 'Please deliver to our hotel, in a sealed parcel, all your control room tapes from Friday night and any paperwork, minutes, agreements with the TV company et cetera.'

'And,' I chip in, 'copies of anything you've got on Inspector Herrick's libel case.'

Well, I think, rising rapidly, buoyed by the performance of my new boss, if his report is as tough as his questioning, Chief Constable Johns will soon be catching up on his telly, especially daytime TV, that sad service whose audiences include the unemployed.

3

The controller of Ridings TV is waiting, as arranged, on the far side of the front foyer at the Royal York, deep in an easy chair, legs outstretched.

He stands for the handshakes, then casually motions to two acolytes, sitting side by side on a facing sofa. Though the bar is just a couple of paces away there are no drinks on the low table in front of them.

In an accent that's more BBC than the other side, he introduces them, without defining their duties, as Clarence and Neil (or, maybe Neale), leaving me unsure whether he's being public school and formally offering their surnames or egalitarian and matily giving their first names.

Today being a low profile whizz round the faces and places, getting the feel of things before I show my hand to anyone, I'm not going to ask.

The combined ages of all three won't, I estimate, add up to a hundred; the way it is throughout the media these days, according to my wife. Hitler Youth, Em calls them, intense young men, non-drinkers, exterminating staff over the age of thirty-five. She frets that she's only got a couple of years to go herself.

Appropriately, Wayne Kirk, the controller, is wearing a black shirt, tieless, under a creased cream jacket with matching trousers that are in need of a clean and press.

Neil (or Neale) is bespectacled and sober-suited; a lawyer or accountant, I guess. Clarence is slight in a blue suit that doesn't fit. He has a bad complexion and a tic in his left eyelid; a behind-the-scenes face, a member of the newsroom, I suspect, twitched up, waiting for us to drop something new and juicy to give him an exclusive for his next bulletin.

Cameron leads the way from the foyer along a warm, wide corridor with expensive goods in glass cabinets and down a short flight of marble stairs.

Just before the rear private exit to the railway station, he turns left and opens a heavy oak door into a conference room, booked for the duration of our as yet unspecified stay.

No expense is being spared to convince our supervisor of the independence of his Commission. No chances are being taken either, for it is not unknown for internal investigators using police premises to have their calls listened into, their office raided and their files disappear. For both reasons, the offered facilities of the local force have been turned down.

Trailing between the reception desk and the porter's lodge down the corridor behind Kirk, the controller, I'd been reminded of an enjoyable, oft-repeated series, *Randall and Hopkirk Deceased*, about a private eye whose murdered partner kept returning as a ghost in a white suit to help him out on cases.

I wonder if he'll be as useful to me; doubt it.

Drawn net curtains across the two long windows make the room very gloomy. Cameron fingers a switch. Two strip lights flicker into life in the high ceiling. Also hanging from it is a large white screen with a pull-down cord. On a metal table on the fawn carpet is a grey-cased projector.

Cameron takes a seat at the top of an oblong table and motions everyone else to pull up grey chairs lined against a gold-coloured wall.

When everyone is finally seated, he goes straight in, but easily. 'How did this programme of yours come about, Mr Kirk?'

The controller more or less confirms what Chief Constable Johns had told us. He prattles on a bit about his decision to take the show off air without confirming Voss's death in public, making himself sound very ethical. 'Have to think of his family, don't you?'

Not from what I've read in the papers who have given the murder 'The King is Dead' treatment since Saturday, page after page of it.

According to them, Voss was a bachelor of thirty-three who lived in a luxury block of riverside apartments.

His parents are dead which, mercifully, means the viewer will be spared the sight of them sitting weeping over a battery of mikes and pleading for the general public to help to catch his killer. 'An emotional appeal', it's always called.

It's such a cliché in crime coverage these days that if next-of-kin decline to submit to the tearful ordeal they automatically become suspect. And, when they do appear, half of them seem to get arrested next day.

Voss's closest relatives are two sisters living in the Home Counties. As the programme was a regional variation, not shown nationwide, they couldn't have been tuned in.

Thus far they have given no more than the standard 'too stunned to speak' stuff to the press. No girlfriends have yet surfaced with kiss and tell tales.

People who have talked, mainly professional colleagues, have disagreed. Named sources praised his commitment to consumer affairs, his courage in tackling difficult subjects. Anonymous sources hinted at a mean, ambitious streak; so mean that, instead of spending his generous wardrobe allowance, he was in the habit of borrowing jackets from shops which put them on display with the advert: 'As worn on TV'.

Cameron immediately moves on. 'Tell us a bit about your business relationship with Mr Voss, his background.'

Kirk's reply is again no more than confirmation of news reports – public school, university, BBC trainee, a radio confessional-type chat show *Clive Live*, head-hunted by Ridings TV as co-presenter on the early evening half-hour programme. 'Then he quit.'

'Why?' asks our supervisor.

A good journalistic question that, I would have thought, but all three seem rather surprised by it. There's a pause before Kirk replies. 'Wanted to stretch himself.'

Believe that if you wish, but I've heard stories from my Em about dual presenters squabbling over who says 'Good evening' and 'Good-night' because it signifies seniority. We're dealing here with egos bigger than Chief Constable Johns.

'In what way?' she persists.

We have to sit through a little lecture on how all channels are compelled to buy in programmes from independent producers. 'They come up with an idea, pick a channel and pitch it,' he explains, making them sound like Hollywood agents on the hustle. He set up Voss Vision and pitched a consumer programme which Ridings TV bought.

I'm going to display a little inside knowledge here. 'So he gave up a staff job on, what, forty-five to fifty thousand a year?'

He nods uncertainly. 'About that.'

'...for the risky life of a freelance agency?' I continue.

He smiles weakly. 'They prefer to be called indies.'

Cameron butts in. 'How did he raise the start-up money?'

Another lecture on how company executives like Kirk fund a pilot or indeed a short series if they rate the idea. 'He might have to pay for a researcher or two but most of his crew, lighting, sound and camera, you know, will have other jobs and be prepared to wait for their money.'

Moonlighting, he means; cash in hand.

'Did he have any financial problems?' I ask.

'Well...' Another worried little pause. 'Some firm of plumbers he accused of shoddy workmanship hit us with a writ. We settled. Twenty grand in all.' He shrugs, unconcerned. 'Any thriving media house is bound to have a few writs flying about.'

Cameron nods him on.

Voss, Kirk continues, came up with his *Celebrities* series – local boys and girls made good – which Kirk also bought. 'Very successful, good viewing figures for summer.'

'Any problems over that?' I ask.

A relaxed beam. 'Lord, no.'

His answer is no surprise. For such programmes the subject has to grant full co-operation. The deal might even include a sneak preview and a bit of vetting before screening.

Kirk names the six celebs who appeared – five are vaguely

familiar, a captain of industry, a couple of showbiz personalities, a sportswoman and a woman politician. The sixth name, Alexander Ball, I query.

'Self-made multi-millionaire,' Kirk explains. 'Golden Globe Entertainments.'

Some distant bell is ringing, can't work out why, decide not to seek an answer here and move on, 'And then we come to *Cause for Concern*.'

His cream trouser seat stirs uncomfortably in his soft chair. He knows where I'm heading. 'Yes.'

'And there is a legal problem with a police inspector?' I prompt.

Neil (or Neale) interrupts. 'Not as far as we are concerned,' he says in a polished accent. 'We're named in the writ as the publishers, naturally, but we're indemnified.'

To double-check that I've pegged him correctly as the station's legal eagle, I ask him what he means.

The company insurers, he answers, footed the bill for the consumer complaint by the plumber, but insisted that Voss Vision's future contracts should include a clause indemnifying Ridings TV in any future action.

'Which means . . .' I say slowly, having to be sure of this, '. . . that should the policewoman plaintiff win her case, Voss would have had to have paid up, not you or your insurers?'

He and Kirk nod solemnly. 'Should she be successful,' Neil (or Neale) replies expertly, 'damages could be awarded against the assets of Voss Vision, or, indeed, Clive's personal estate as he is named in the writ.'

Cameron takes up the questioning, somewhat ponderously, beginning with what seems to be a favourite word of his. 'Notwithstanding one successfully pursued writ against him and another case pending, you nonetheless engaged him to take part in Friday's programme?'

Kirk comes back in with an answer about not having enough staff crews to cover all the potential hot spots that his researchers had identified, making his company sound as short of manpower as the police service. 'We had to hire in a couple of other indies, too.'

Cameron again. 'Whose idea was it – this *Friday the 13th* thing?'

'It arose out of our regular brainstorming sessions,' replies Kirk airily. Off he goes again, explaining that TV wasn't like

15

an author who worked in splendid isolation, but was a collect-
ive, a collaboration.

Cameron persists. 'Even in a committee, someone has to be the
first to say, "What about doing this or that?" Now ...' A heavy
pause. '... whose original idea was it?'

Kirk looks sideways at his legal adviser. There's resignation in
both expressions. They know they can hardly refuse co-operation with a man who, with one memo, can stop every police
force in England and Wales from giving them details of even the
most routine of incidents. He controls a major, perhaps, the
major source of their day-to-day news.

'Well,' Kirk shrugs, 'I suppose it was Clive who first sowed
the seed, tossed out the idea for refinement.'

'Why was he assigned to incidents in this city? Why not
elsewhere in the county, Hull or a seaside resort, for instance?'

Kirk finds that easier to answer. 'Because he lives here, has
lots of good contacts.'

Cameron dries up and I resume. 'We're going to have to look
at the finances of Voss Vision. Had he lost his libel case, couldn't
that have spelt ruin?'

'Oh,' Kirk beams again, 'he had an angel.'

Cameron pulls his head back, querulously, like an old judge
who doesn't know a showbiz name that's just been dropped into
his court proceedings.

'A financial backer,' Kirk explains.

He is beginning to grate on me. That Broadway word 'angel',
those idea-pitching indies straight out of Hollywood. He be-
lieves he's at the top of the showbiz tree, instead of some tinpot,
penny-pinching provincial outfit. 'Who?' I ask.

'Golden Globe Entertainments.'

His face is paler than his cream suit now. He's just admitted
his ultra-ethical station, that would not break the news of Voss's
death until next-of-kin had been informed, had once given a
half-hour plug to the boss of a business who'd subsidised the
programme-maker.

'The investment was offered after the *Celebs* series,' he adds
hurriedly but with an unsure expression. 'There is no connection
to be drawn between the two events,' he goes on, rather huffily.

Clarence, his second sidekick who has been watchfully silent
throughout, nods.

'Clive,' Kirk continues, 'wanted to branch out into fiction.

16

He'd taken out an option on a sci-fi feature film.' He is talking fast to cover his embarrassment. 'Nothing whatever to do with his previous series.'

'Or our company,' the legal eagle puts in.

There's a knowledgeable nod from Clarence and a rather sarcastic 'Really' from Cameron who abruptly closes the meeting with requests for everything filmed on Friday night, all of Voss Vision's videos and paperwork concerning him.

Clarence, the silent sidekick, is lurking around reception when I collect my room key and the sealed parcel Chief Constable Johns was ordered to deliver to the hotel.

He sidles up, speaking softly but nervously. 'I take it you know that Clive's lawyer was based in the building that caught fire?'

After the super's warning that some of the details were leaking out, it's no surprise that he knows. It's an old journalistic ploy, anyway – offer the obvious and the old, take a lot of new stuff in return. I say nothing.

'Was it arson – a bomb, perhaps?' he asks.

I press my lips together, hoping he'll take the hint that they are sealed.

He doesn't, gathering himself for the plunge. 'Or was it a safe-blowing?'

I recall the public relations training my grandfather gave me and beckon him closer. 'Piss off,' I whisper with a pleasant smile.

4

Twice this morning I've watched the video of the opening hour of *Friday the 13th Blues*, but, back in my second-floor corner room, decide to risk what my gran used to call 'square eyes' from too much telly.

It's a toss-up between a first viewing of the allegedly libellous *Cause for Concern* that came in the sealed special delivery from HQ, or a reprise of *Friday*.

Something is nagging at me from that chat with the Ridings

TV trio, something already heard or seen and implanted in my mind. *Friday* gets the vote.

I switch on channel five on the TV which stands on a sturdy wooden chest of drawers. The cassette is snapped up by the remote-controlled recorder, specially installed in what's an otherwise standard room – if you can call accommodation the size of a tennis court standard, and that doesn't include the bathroom.

I take off my jacket and shoes and pad a thick, dark pink carpet, drawing sage green curtains across three windows against views of the city's Roman walls and the Victorian glass roof of the railway station.

From the television comes the pre-nine o'clock jingles – 'The ultimate party album for this festive season', 'In Woolies this Christmas', 'The mix that makes your Yorkshire pud rise and brown'. The amateur dramatics set to music that form the title sequences for *Friday the 13th* follow.

I sit, facing the TV, on the bottom edge of one of two single beds with covers of rust and green leaves and drapes above them which match the curtains.

The voice of doom is intoning, 'Twelve days to Christmas, busiest time of the year on the streets for...' I fast forward the rest of the introduction and the stage-managed drugs raid.

The first of the televised dog races, the 9.15 from a stadium near Doncaster, comes on. Six dogs are already in their traps. The commentator only has time to reel off their names, colours and latest prices before the off.

Just over a lap in half a minute and Desdemona, the theatrically named favourite, romps home at even money a comfortable distance ahead of Feet First, an outsider. Few cheers are raised and there's no presentation or mention of the winner's purse.

No echo, either, of the bell that rang downstairs in the conference room. I feel like a punter with a losing ticket.

A zip through the breath-tested joyrider and the law office fire – around twenty-five minutes' worth of film in about as many seconds – takes me to the 9.45.

'The Golden Globe Invitational,' the commentator announces – and I'm on a winner already.

So Alex Ball's entertainments company was sponsoring a race that plugged a gap in a live show which was Clive Voss's

18

original idea. My, my. The excitement of discovery darts through me.

The coverage is much less hurried – the parade with six dogs in numbered and differently coloured jackets, their current form, their owners and trainers all named. Ball's is not among them, but then, even if he is a dog owner, he's hardly likely to enter for his own prize; a bit like the captain of a golf club winning on Captain's Day, not the done thing.

The camera lingers on a muffled tic-tac man as the commentator gives last-minute fluctuations in prices. Into the traps go the dogs, off with the hare, up with the doors.

High Society wins at five-to-two by a length from even money favourite Jaffa Cake. Only the winner is led back by a kennel-maid to the winning post. She lifts it on to a low square platform.

Behind the flower-bedecked rostrum stands a thickset man in a dark double-breasted suit. It looks a bitterly cold night, but his head is not only hatless, but hairless, completely bald. An off-screen voice introduces the sponsor's chairman, Alex Ball.

He could double for that powerhouse LA lawyer in *Murder One* until he speaks. 'For your collection,' he says in a Geordie accent as he hands over a trophy, a small gold-coloured globe, and an envelope to a beaming woman in a thick black coat.

'Inside is the winner's cheque for ten thousand pounds,' explains the commentator who appears, frozen-faced, on screen wrapping up proceedings.

The voice of doom back at the studio hands on to Voss already speeding to the riot that turned out to be a fatally false alarm.

The rest is switched to mute mode and I fall back on the bed, eyes on the ceiling, and switch to muse.

So Alex Ball, boss of Golden Globe, was not only a financial backer of Voss Vision, but he also stumped up a five-figure sum to fill in a blank in a show that was Clive Voss's brainchild.

Whiffs of corruption you can't physically smell, but my nose twitches all the same.

Cassettes are exchanged and almost twenty tedious minutes of Voss fronting *Cause for Concern* follow.

Sitting behind a curved desk, he wears a dark jacket that hugs his broad shoulders and matches his darkly handsome features.

19

Word-perfect delivery in a neutral voice owes something to his BBC radio training, I guess.

He links and appears in items about a holiday that didn't live up to its brochure promises and a much-delayed operation that left a patient in a wheelchair. When he talks to the holidaymaker and the patient, his brown eyes twinkle. When he quizzes the tour operator and the hospital secretary, his strong jaw sets. It's all well-meaning and socially responsible, more up the Beeb's street, I'd have thought; a bit boring, in truth.

For the final item, Voss stands before a grainy blow-up of a small, wiry man handcuffed to a fair-haired woman in a light, unbuttoned raincoat. 'Now for our "Reasonable Doubt" feature. This picture...' He thumbs over his shoulder. '...was taken fifteen months ago and shows Eddie Tring on his way to prison for a crime he did not commit. Tonight he is still there.'

The photo behind him changes to a country manor, almost a stately home. 'This is Wolds Hall, the scene of the safe-blowing and jewellery robbery which, we say, he could not have carried out.'

Safe-blowing, I repeat to myself, that surge of excitement tugging me upright on the edge of the bed.

On the night of the raid, Voss continues, two passers-by claimed to have seen someone answering Tring's description in the vicinity of Wolds Hall. As a result of those sightings, he was arrested, reputedly saying, 'OK, but you're going to have to prove it.' On the sole of one of his shoes was found earth which, police claimed, matched the soil in a rose bed beneath the study window.

In quick succession, three witnesses are paraded on film, all youngish, powerfully built men, all with bristles for hair. One of them is black. All claim to have been drinking with Tring in his local, an estate pub, at the vital time.

A scientist is interviewed in his laboratory, stating that the soil found on the shoe was fairly commonplace on rose beds that had been recently fertilised.

It is, I recognise, a regional rip-off of *Rough Justice*, nowhere near so professionally researched, and the next bit is positively amateurish.

A circle of light picks out a safe in a wall. Cellos vibrate. The yellow ring rises to rest on an alarm clock, hands at 11.10, on a shelf. 'Reconstruction' appears in white capitals across the foot of the screen.

Strings pluck. Drums roll. The door to the safe comes away with a flash and a bang. The clock falls to the ground, glass smashed, hands stopped.

Smoke clears to reveal Voss sitting with his hands folded at his curved desk. 'But if the witnesses we have produced tonight are to be believed, there is no way Tring could have been there at that time.'

An aerial shot now of a motor cyclist careering noisily from the car-park of a public house through narrow streets and out into the countryside. Voss names some speedway star from Sheffield he'd hired to run the route. 'Even he could not make it in that time.'

In vision again, the original photo at his back, Voss lowers his voice. 'And if they are right, where does that leave the evidence of arresting officer, Detective Sergeant, now Inspector, Susan Herrick...' The thumb is back at work. '...on the shoe and his alleged statement?'

His jaw sets firm. 'Such is the conflict of evidence that we say this case...' His voice darkens. '...remains a cause for concern.'

A curt nod now. 'Good-night.' A smiling pause, head slightly cocked. 'And thanks for being there.'

It's such an insincere sign-off that I feel myself cringe.

The phone rings before the credits roll. I gun Voss off, as someone did permanently four nights ago.

Cameron is already sitting in the back of the black Daimler, engine running almost soundlessly, at the foot of the steps when I emerge through the hotel's revolving doors and down the red carpet.

He beckons me to sit beside him, addressing the driver as I climb in rather stiffly. 'Done your homework, Tom?'

Cameron had explained over the phone that he wanted to familiarise himself with the geography of events before chairing a formal hearing of police witnesses tomorrow.

Tom's answer is to wave a gloved hand at a street map spread out on the seat where I earlier sat.

'Scene of shooting first, I think,' says Cameron. Then, to me, 'Let's just get a feeling for the locations.'

Tom's hand returns to the wheel. We move off down the

narrow driveway with its fine view of the Minster, floodlit against a sombre sky.

A very short trip is followed by a longish wait for a gap in heavy traffic in Station Street, time enough to turn for another look at the Minster. A sporty white Toyota convertible is catching up with us.

It's not the model, an MR2, that attracts my attention. The hotel car-park is filled with trendier, more expensive makes. It's the driver's face below a black, leather-peaked cap, as racy as the car. It's black, too.

Now, in these days of racial equality, equal opportunities and political correctness, a cop isn't supposed to comment on black drivers at the wheels of flash cars. Too many patrolmen have fallen into the trap of pulling them over, as I know all too well from my current duties as head of my own force's Complaints and Discipline Department.

Back home on my patch, in the multi-racial cities of the East Midlands, I might not have noticed. But getting off the train and walking through the station and on that trip to and from police HQ I hardly saw a black face. So I notice, but don't comment, certainly not to the Chief Inspector of Constabularies.

Tom negotiates a busy bridge and several bottlenecks, then turns off a main street into a series of side streets and stops. Without me realising it, we have doubled back towards the river which runs behind what looks like an old three-storey warehouse, a very solid structure on a square island that it occupies on its own.

Not so solid – flimsy, in fact – is a flat roof over a wide glass entrance that has been knocked into the ground-floor front wall. Above it, 'Riverside Shuffle' is written in words formed from shaped glass tubes, different coloured lights within, not switched on. Beside the entrance is a display case advertising a full programme of festive discos and the DJs who will compere them.

My dancing days are long over, but there was a time when I frequented such nightspots, especially in my last year at college when *Saturday Night Fever* was sweeping the country. Studying the Bee Gees instead of Beethoven ended with a degree too poor for a professional career in music and I followed my grandad into the police service instead.

We get out of the car and stroll. It's dark and quite cold. Before the canopied entrance is a cobbled alley roughly running south to north, parallel with the river. We're at the spot where Clive Voss disappeared from his cameraman's view.

It would be impossible to walk down it without squashing a carpet of flowers that cover most of the cobbles. The smell from them is gorgeous. Not so my private thoughts.

Ghoulish. It's bloody ghoulish. God knows why people do it. Years ago, I suspect, a cameraman, short of follow-up footage on a disaster or a murder, talked some angelic-looking child into placing a floral tribute at the scene. He'd charge for the flowers on exes, of course, and probably paid the child, too; a tacky stunt. 'Ahhhh,' sighed the entire nation. Now it's become the done thing for total strangers to hug and weep and solemnly lay bouquets while the cameras roll; another cliché in crime coverage.

Cameron shakes his head. I'm not sure if he's agreeing with my unspoken thoughts or deciding against strolling down the alley; the latter, I expect, because he turns and leads the way back to the car, me walking rather slowly.

I have this gammy right leg, the result of a bad wound three and a half years ago when I was tracking, unarmed, a shotgun killer. It's a handicap that prematurely curtailed active sporting days, but I can't blame it for the end of my dancing days. That was voluntary, before all those flashing lights and ear-bursting noises could blind and deafen me.

My leg needs just the right amount of exercise each day and I haven't given it enough, sitting around in the train and car, at meetings and in my room watching videos.

Cameron must have been briefed on my medical record because he doesn't question my slowness, just slackens his pace to mine on the way back to the car.

More side and shopping streets and another bridge choked with traffic bring us to the back of a block of flats, square and three-storey, but without the solid look of the converted warehouse.

An asphalt path leads to the front where the top two floors have balconies with views over a private car-park and on to the river. A policeman stands guard on a ground-floor door.

Cameron shows him his warrant card and exchanges pleasantries. With fingers either numbed from his chilly vigil or terrified in the presence of Britain's top cop, the officer fiddles for a good few seconds before the cream door is un-locked.

Inside is refrigerator-cold, colder still with Voss's choice of décor and furnishings. White walls and chessboard-tiled floors run throughout. The hall is hung, not with scenic, even family pictures, but framed certificates of media awards Voss had won, all of them sponsored by commercial concerns.

The lounge is furnished with couch and chairs of black leather in steel frames; no books on shelves. The small bedroom has a king-sized water bed. In the kitchen, there's cheese and wine in the fridge, nothing else, and no flowers in any room.

I'd dispute the press's decription of the place as luxury. Soul-less, I'd call it. My room back at the hotel has a more homely feel to it and I haven't slept in it yet.

'No woman lived here,' says Cameron as I gaze, then – startled – stare through the hanging strips of vertical cream blinds on to the small car-park, with a sign that says 'Residents Only'.

'Seen enough?' asks Cameron.

More than enough. There's a white-bodied Toyota MR2 in the residents' car-park. No driver, black or white, is at the wheel.

I nod.

Uncomplaining in stop-start traffic, Tom drives across the city centre close to the Minster for two final calls.

Hall Street is so narrow that not even limited parking is allowed. We pass the bank chambers on our left, then the offices of Voss Vision further down on the right.

Cameron democratically doesn't pull rank on a patrolling traffic warden but orders Tom on a hundred yards into a well-filled car-park on open land behind a row of red phone boxes and a low metal railing.

Tom stays with the Daimler. Throughout our tour, he has spoken only in reponse to Cameron's instructions in a polite, subdued southern accent.

We get out of the back and walk (Cameron leisurely, me stiffly) to the offices of Voss Vision, an old shop. In the window, stills from the proprietor's programmes, most featuring the pro-prietor with microphone in hand, have been mounted in card-board frames.

I look at the window for several seconds, not studying the photos, but seeking a reflection of a white sporty car passing by behind my back. None does.

No policeman stands guard and Cameron has not collected the key from police HQ. He tuts and walks on.

No better luck up the street where the bank is closed, the first-floor windows boarded up and a green door leading up to the offices of Adrian McMichael, Solicitor, and the Minster Calculating Agency is locked.

A notice pinned to the door gives directions to temporary offices at the rear, open from nine to five. I look at my watch. We're an hour too late.

'We've got dinner with the chairman of the regional police authority in ninety minutes,' says Cameron with a sigh, not sounding as though he is looking forward to it.

Neither am I. Besides, I have a better idea which I explain on the way back to the car-park where the Daimler, but no white Toyota, waits.

'Get there before the chief constable can deliver his usual PR pep talk, you mean, say nothing to the detriment of the force and all that,' Cameron says with a smile, catching on quick. He nods agreement. 'Good thinking.'

5

A hot dog is munched on a leg-loosening stroll. It's not very tasty without onions, declined on the grounds that they repeat on me. At least it's sparing me polite chit-chat over a four-courser at the hotel.

I am following directions from a helpful porter in a black top hat and green jacket. No black shadow trailed me along a tow-path beside the wide, dark Ouse. No white sports car could possibly have tailed over a footbridge alongside a railway line across the river.

My snack was purchased from a takeaway on a main road and is being eaten walking alone down a crescent with bay windows, the far end of which is bathed in stronger light than the Minster.

I know, because I follow these things, that the home side was almost relegated last season but they are doing better, particularly in the Cup, this season, so, surely, they attract bigger crowds than this, I think.

A compact soccer stadium comes into view, a dozen or so lamps on tall pylons at each of the four corners. A poster on a newish brick wall of the club house informs me I am bound for a reserve match.

Head of the drugs squad three months ago, Susan Herrick tonight finds herself with the Stiffs in the Pontins League, Div. 2. I shudder, not in sympathy, with the realisation that it can happen to any police officer who has the wrong break – or the wrong boss.

Her file which came in the sealed parcel from HQ gave her CV – university-educated, joined the force at twenty-two, five years on the beat in her home town of Hull, then sergeant at HQ in the crime squad and a year as inspector in charge of drugs.

I walk behind the main stand, which has the look of an Alpine hotel, all glass, wooden slates, triangular eaves and an overhanging upper storey, pay the gateman a pound and go through a stiff turnstile.

Inside the game has already started. Spectators are clustered together in the central section of the stand. There are only a few more of them than footballers on the field or on the benches in two Perspex dug-outs. The players in red and black and all blue are doing all the shouting which echoes round the almost deserted stands and terraces.

Herrick is not hard to spot, chatting to a fresh-faced young constable, both wearing yellow fluorescent coats. They are sauntering together, at the regulation pace set by *The Bill*, between blue crush barriers on which no one leans behind the east end goal.

Now and then she points out things – emergency exits, I assume, so her pupil will know their whereabouts when he graduates to the big league.

I stand close to a corner post, with a limp flag, my back to the wing of the stand, obstructing no one's view. Half a dozen rows of red plastic seats and, above a gangway, about the same number of lines of wooden seats are all tipped up and empty.

Quite close to me now, she removes her natty little bowler hat to reveal smooth corn-coloured hair tied at the back in a bun. She has a pale face and an amiable smile. She walks rather sexily, sort of bowed, shoulders back.

26

Now she is tasty, I have to force myself to concede.

Forty is a dangerous age for a man, they say, but I was half a decade before my time. Five years ago, I'd be thinking, Good job I passed on the onions. I might be doing a lot of kissing tonight. Since Em, I'm safer than Forrest Gump.

I comfort myself with the knowledge that it's not as though I'm into uniforms – police, schoolgirls', certainly not nurses' after three months in hospital with a shot-up leg.

The constable ambles away and I amble up, producing my warrant card. 'Phillip Todd, chief superintendent.'

'Oh.' A startled little smile. 'I thought you were stalking me.'

She'd spotted me, then; observant as well as tasty, I think, smiling back. 'With the Cameron Commission looking into the events of Friday night.'

'Read about him in the *Evening Press*,' she replies, completely underawed. 'They didn't mention your name.'

Good, I think. 'I'd like to talk to you about your legal difficulties with Clive Voss.'

'Oh dear,' she says with a troubled expression that's clearly feigned, 'and I have no alibi apart from my boyfriend.'

'Did you watch it on Friday?'

She wags her head into a No. 'See enough of it on duty, thanks very much.' Pause. 'Did you?'

I shake my head. 'Watching *Frasier*.'

Smiling, she gestures with a hand towards the stand behind me. 'There's plenty of room to sit and talk.'

As we walk up three or four concrete steps, she says, 'You from the Met?'

'East Midlands Combined. Complaints and Discipline.'

All the warmth vanishes from her face. Complaints and Discipline strikes more terror into the hearts of police officers than Criminal Investigation Department does in criminals.

As we sit side by side on red seats, she asks, 'Been called in to investigate me?'

It's routine for a more senior officer from an outside force to probe a serious complaint and, therefore, an understandable question.

I shake my head again. 'My boss on this job, Sir Donald, wants to know what your chief was doing granting full co-operation and open access to police operations to someone who'd libelled a senior member of his own force.'

Relief flows through her face. 'There's a chance you might believe me then?'

Nothing to lose, I nod.

In a homely accent that drops most h's, she goes back fifteen months to her time on the serious crime squad and the safe raid at the country manor, a rare crime these days.

Like redundant bank tellers in an age of computers, credit cards and cash points, safe-blowers are a dying breed. Today's mobs get all they want at the point of a knife or a gun.

Records could produce only one name with the required expertise to match descriptions of the figure seen by a game-keeper and a villager fleeing from the scene – Edward (Gabby) Tring.

Armed with a search warrant, she led the raid on his home on an estate in the city. No jewels were found. She impounded clothing and footwear. On the sole of one shoe was soil which matched a flower bed in front of a ground-floor window.

Gabby, it turns out, is an ironic nickname. All he ever said was, 'OK, but you're going to have to prove it.'

He didn't even go into the witness box at his trial to speak on his own behalf. His counsel did that for him, arguing that the prosecution had indeed failed to prove their case. The jury dis-agreed. The judge, after hearing of a similar, previous convic-tion, gave him five years.

Two months ago, her mother phoned her in a panic. 'Seen that Clive Voss show on telly? Shameful. It was awful.'

She borrowed a video in the PR department next day. 'Seen it?' she asks.

I nod.

Chief Constable Johns called her in. 'What are you going to do about it?' he asked. 'Seek an apology and retraction,' she an-swered.

She consulted a solicitor, a friend. He wrote to Ridings TV. The reply came back from McMichael, Voss Vision's lawyer. 'My client stands by his actions.'

She was called in by the chief again. 'Pending clarification, it's a lower profile for you, I'm afraid.' He took her off the drugs squad and put her back into uniform.

She sighs heavily. 'I'm accused of planting clues and verballing, so what could I do but sue?'

Well, she could have done nothing. I think I would. Look at those two Tory MPs who took action over stories that almost everyone had forgotten, brought them back into the headlines again – and lost. It was the same with those two cricket stars. Civil courts are a bigger gamble than criminal trials – and there's no legal aid for libel.

Professional pride's her motive, I suppose; close to ego when taken too far. I'm going to test her. 'Some would say you're brave, but financially foolhardy.'

A deeper sigh. 'Don't I know it. Two hundred an hour in legal fees, plus counsel's opinion. No help from the force or the police authority.'

Well, there wouldn't be. You can't use public funds for a private case. If she wins, she'll pocket the damages. On the other hand, defeat means disaster.

'Now it's all on hold,' she adds gloomily. 'Tring's got a retrial which takes precedence.'

I query that, recalling what Chief Constable Johns had said. 'I thought he'd been freed?'

'On bail, yes. The appeal court ruled the original verdict unsafe in the light of the fresh evidence. They want a new jury to hear it.' Herrick gives me an amused smile. 'Does that help or hinder?'

I ask what she means.

'Well, there are people who are going to say that if there's any evidence against me in McMichael's safe, it's to my advantage for it to be lost.'

A fair point, I agree. A fairer point is this: If she's not on the *Friday the 13th* job, how does she know that the law safe, not the bank, was the target? I approach it carefully. 'So, it's out on the force grapevine that McMichael's safe was blown, is it?'

'More than that. It was on the local TV news at teatime.'

'Didn't it say that the safe's contents were still being examined?'

'Yes,' she answers.

Cameron's ploy seems to be working then, I think, gratefully. Jocularly, I answer her original point. 'You'd hardly hire Tring, a safe-breaker you'd jailed for five years, to do the job for you, would you? And even if you offered it to him, he'd be a bit too cross with you to accept the assignment, I would think.'

Someone, it occurs to me, might have hired Tring, however, because there aren't many specialists still around in his line of business. I'm going to chase what's becoming a better point all the time. 'Was there anything in McMichael's office of likely interest to you?'

'Doubt it.' Her open face seems free of doubt. 'If and when the case gets under way, there'd be the usual disclosure of documents by each side.'

I nod again, acknowledging a legal requirement to swap statements to save court time. The days of the last-minute surprise witness have long gone, if they ever existed at all outside of crime fiction.

'In any case,' she continues, 'we know from TV and the appeal court what the new evidence is. There's nothing we aren't or won't become aware of before the case comes on.'

A perfectly acceptable answer, so I move on. 'Do you know the three drinking chums Voss dug up to alibi Tring?'

Not personally, she says guardedly. The chief gave strict orders that she should not pursue any inquiries or use police records to prepare a private case.

'But on the grapevine?' I persist, with all but an old-fashioned wink.

She pauses, thinks, deciding if she can trust me. 'A couple of health freaks, bouncers, and a black guy who's supposed to have Yardie connections.'

A Yardie, I think. Hard, often armed and dangerous. 'The black guy,' I prompt. 'Name of?'

'Pepper. Jailed down south. No convictions up here.'

She's briefed herself well on the QT, I realise, despite her chief's orders, but then, in her circumstances, so would I. 'Does he run a white sporty car?'

She shakes her head uncertainly. 'Loads of dough. Changes all the time. Why?'

I shake my head and smile, not quite putting a finger to my lips.

She colours slightly, accepting, perhaps, that she shouldn't be questioning me. On the other hand, she strikes me as a feisty type who, once she's cleared her name, will tell the chief constable where to stick his job and walk out, and who could blame her?

30

Abruptly, she answers a question about the witnesses against her that I haven't asked. 'And, of course, they have that so-called scientist in his lab, one of those experts they often wheel out.'

I nod. I know the type. Self-proclaimed specialists, full of psycho-babble, who will support any theory a journalist has decided to present as fact, provided the fee is right.

She goes silent.

Me too, looking sideways at her, thinking, she must be fairly confident that the juries will find in her favour in both Tring's retrial and her libel action. She looks anything but, downcast, eyes on the pitch, not following the play.

Mine do the same.

Let's think this through. Give her the benefit of the doubt. She bangs up Tring fair and square. Someone wants him out to do a safe-blowing job. Voss helps to concoct the evidence to spring him legally. He accuses her on TV of fabricating evidence, running the risk of a big payout. Then they, whoever they are, silence Voss.

This is mega, telephone numbers in cash at stake, must be. But why not just arrange Tring's escape from prison? Any mob with that financial clout could fix it – a faked illness requiring hospital treatment and an ambush on the way; guns smuggled in by paid visitors for an armed break-out; beamed up from a hijacked helicopter. All have been done before.

Why blacken her name? Why stitch her up? To discredit her? To distract her? From what?

'Tell me,' I say, slowly, eyes still on the pitch, 'what were you working on when you were put back in uniform?'

'A drugs job.'

'Involving who?'

'Golden Balls.'

I cock my head, quizzically.

'Alex Ball,' she says. 'One of the untouchables. Know the type?'

Oh, I know that type, too.

Suddenly, I feel illuminated, flooded in light, wallowing in it; far brighter and stronger than the lights that beam down from the pylons on to the pitch.

Know what annoys me about crime yarns on TV? Mr Big is

inevitably Johnny Foreigner – Mafia and Triad types and, quite recently, a Turk, still suffering the backlash of *Midnight Express*, I suppose; a real pain in the arse, that film.

It's as though writers can't accept that the biggest Mr Bigs are as British as bulldogs.

They live in country manors or brand new houses on executive estates, mock Tudor, triple garage, walled garden, electronic gates, all partly paid for in cash to avoid VAT.

They have wives who decorate the place and themselves in questionable taste and daughters who ride ponies. They don't get invited to neighbourhood parties because their accents and dress sense are so off-putting – until they start giving generous donations to the gymkhana and local charities and then everyone agrees that they're not so bad after all.

They start their careers in businesses with a ready cash flow – scrap, second-hand cars, cabs. Not too much profit gets declared for tax. The rest can't be banked so they have to reinvest and expand. In the early days, fighting to get to the top, they might pick up the odd conviction, small stuff like actual bodily harm or threatening behaviour. Soon they have the money to pay others to put on the frighteners or exact revenge.

Their surplus, unbankable cash is used to fund crime – big payroll robberies or, more often these days, drug deals.

They get known in CID as untouchables, not because they're lepers or lower caste or because we wouldn't love (die, almost) to feel their collars. It's simply because we never get sufficient evidence.

They rise to the top of the pyramid. We often knock off the bottom rung, the musclemen or the pushers, sometimes the fixers on the next level, but seldom get all the way to the top.

Alex Ball is just a typical example, I realise, as Herrick, eyes on the pitch, sketches in his background in her warm h-less accent.

A member of a large travelling show family, he tired of life on the road and bought a sea-front amusement arcade, the start of a chain that grew into funfairs down the east coast.

Eventually he went into pubs – big pubs packed out by the young – and clubs. It was easy to acquire an interest in those he didn't actually own. 'Get down to that place near the pier,' he'd order his bouncers. 'Cause a bit of a ruck.'

Next day a lieutenant would turn up while the landlord was clearing up. 'We can offer you security against this sort of trouble.' The day after his bouncers are on the doors. Control the doors, of course, and you control the drugs that are sold inside.

I interrupt her flow. 'Does Golden Balls own the Riverside Shuffle?'

She nods.

I'm positively swimming in light now.

Untouchables like Ball buy into legitimate businesses. Launderettes, they call them, where they can wash through the proceeds of their crimes.

They always keep some cash ready for the sudden spec deal. Once we raided a house on a council estate looking for stolen video recorders. Wrong house, as it turned out, only one VCR, but fifty grand in the loft. The occupier was a champion body-builder and part-time bouncer. In return for free steroids, he was minding the cash for his supplier. He claimed it was contest winnings and side bets. We couldn't establish it was the proceeds of crime. We had to hand it back.

The local CID nicknamed Alexander Ball Golden Balls because he's so lucky, she explains. To stick two fingers up at them, he changed it to a more acceptable Golden Globe and adopted it as the company's title, complete with circular logo.

Back in September, Herrick got a tip that a big drugs consignment was coming ashore. 'Really good inside info,' she adds tantalisingly.

A boat from Holland was to switch the stuff to a fishing smack in the North Sea, she continues. 'Got the day, but not the name of the boat or where it would land. That's last-minute stuff. He personally decides the destination.'

'What day?' I ask.

'Friday the 13th.'

I frown, puzzled.

'There was one in September,' she laughs. 'Didn't you know?'

I shake my head. Once I've reached Saturday the 14th of any month in safety I tend to forget. 'How did you handle it?'

'Put a tap and a tail on him in the two weeks before.' Her face saddens. 'I blew it. Must have got too close. Know what the bastard did? Complained to his local station he was being followed, stalked by a woman, gave my description and my car's, said he was worried I might be a sacked member of staff, an obsessed admirer, the *Fatal Attraction* thing.' She smiles grimly.

Christ, that was a cheeky way of letting her know that she'd been rumbled. 'Did you pick up anything on the phone tap?'

She shakes her head. 'He must have some other way of communicating.'

'Did anything happen that Friday?'

'Not that we ever discovered. Kept working on it, though. Asked around his pubs and clubs for a week afterwards. Raided a couple. Nothing.'

She'd been making a big nuisance of herself, too much of a nuisance for Golden Balls so, I speculate privately, he got her off the case via that Voss Vision programme on Gabby Tring. 'Did you have Ball in and grill him?'

She looks surprised.

Should have known better than to ask. Know what else upsets me on TV? The interrogation scenes. Even *NYPD Blue*, a particular favourite, makes it look so easy – a few trick questions in that back room with the cage, a naked threat or two, a bit of plea-bargaining and out comes the confession.

'No point, was there, with a BTO?' she says.

True, I concede to myself. In real life, big time operators won't give you so much as a 'no comment' without their lawyer at their side and, when he arrives, not even that.

I once quizzed a crook who, when finally provoked into opening his mouth to speak, promptly found his solicitor's hand cupped over it to stop him.

I ask for details of Ball's lawyer and am a bit disappointed when she gives a name that is not McMichael, Voss's brief, but only for the second it takes her to add, 'The same mouthpiece is representing Tring, too.'

The lights are not only bright now. They are warm. I am getting warm. I can feel it. I inquire where Ball operates and I'm told he works from home, a revamped Tudor manor, near somewhere called Skipwith Common.

Mr Bigs have an Achilles' heel. Sex. A wife who suddenly wakes up one morning in an empty bed and overnight has decided she's had enough of his teenage bimbos, walks out and talks. Or maybe it's the bimbo who realises she's been used, abused and short-changed. 'Is he married?'

A headshake. 'Wife died just after their silver wedding. There's one child, a daughter, just finished at a drama college.'

'Does he play around?'

'Not that we ever discovered.'

Ah, well.

Let's see if I fare any better with the really big question, the one I've saved till last. Who tipped her off about Golden Balls and the drugs shipment? I could heavy her, I suppose, demand her note-books, examine the informants' payment accounts, get Cameron to serve her with a witness summons or something. Something else tells me she's the sort who'd stand firm, whatever was thrown at her; professional ethics, pride, and all that.

My approach is cautious. 'I know this is an unusual request but would you mind asking your September source if he or she will see me for a private chat?'

She bites her bottom lip, says nothing.

A subtle hint is needed. 'If your informant declines I'll make no further inquiries, but his or her co-operation to Sir Donald and our Commission would be tremendously helpful.'

'In what way?' she asks, very quietly.

I'm going to have to give her something. 'We've information that Golden Balls had money in Voss Vision.'

She goes quiet again, thinking, pretending to be following the action on the pitch which is whistled to a halt when a black player in all blue is clattered. He writhes on the grass, clutching an ankle. A tracksuited trainer trots on, carrying a big first aid box.

Idly, I look around me, giving her time.

Finally she says, 'I can only try. Put in a call. I can make no promises.'

I am hardly listening. Several empty rows behind us, way to our left, glancing in our direction, sits a black man, the only one in the small crowd that I can see.

He is not wearing a racy leather cap but a woolly blue hat that cheapens his expensive-looking, three-quarter length glossy black coat. He's, what – thirtyish, strong-jawed, rather handsome in profile, despite an unusually prominent nose.

Berk, I curse myself, whether it's politically correct or not, you should have taken closer note of that driver in the white Toyota. You didn't even memorise his index plate.

Am I being stalked? Or is this paranoia? Find out.

I pull out my pocket book, slipping free a blank postcard I always carry inside it. I write down the hotel and room numbers, and, underneath, add, 'Can you ID that black guy behind to our left?'

I hand it to her and fix my eyes on the pitch as play resumes.

Cleverly, a good operator, she takes her time before looking round. 'What guy?' she asks, quite loudly for her.

I look behind. He's gone.

6

A tap on my bedroom door ends a longish call home, not overly lovey-dovey, more a question and answer on our daughter's day. She's sixteen months old now, up to mischief all the time.

I smack kisses, put down the receiver, roll off the bed and amble over the dark pink carpet in stockinged feet.

Five years ago I'd have been hoping, rather than fearing, the caller might be Susan Herrick. Now I'm fearing, rather than hoping, so it's something of a relief to open it and find Cameron standing in the wide corridor.

He has changed into a dark blue three-piece suit. His face is slightly flushed. Through faint fumes of brandy, he asks how I've got on.

Gesturing with my head, I invite him in to sit on the spare bed. There is, in fact, a round table with two chairs in front of one of the curtained windows, but a dirty plate that had contained Whitby scampi and chips from Room Service is on it.

Back on the bottom of my bed, seated upright this time, I begin to give him the lot, apart from the black shadow. Not having seen him again on the walk back – or any white sports car – I've put him down to first night nerves that should affect any detective on a new, big case.

When I lament that Golden Balls doesn't appear to play around with ladies, his response is immediate.

'Ah,' he says, smiling. 'The Bertie Bigtimes of the underworld have a pair of Achilles' heels. Ego as well as sex.'

It did for the Krays, he continues nostalgically. 'They could have delegated much of what convicted them; did it personally because they wanted respect.'

He nods at a stack of videos, delivered in my absence, by a courier from Ridings TV which stand on their ends on the TV table. 'Had time to see him in that dreadful *Celebrities* thing?' he asks.

I shake my head.

'There's something of the Krays in Ball,' he goes on. 'Sponsoring sports events, mixing with showbiz types, the craving for public recognition.' A sly smile. 'Maybe he's not so untouchable after all.'

'Maybe,' I reply, unconvinced. I go on with the debriefing, dwelling for some time on the release of Gabby Tring, and venturing that he could be involved in the safe-blowing at the law office; a theory that can't possibly have been missed by the county's CID.

'Mmmm.' Cameron is thinking, deeply, frowning. Then he rummages in a waistcoat pocket, pulls out a visiting card I've seen before, nods at the phone. My head is used again to tell him to help himself.

He gets up and walks in the gap between the beds. Standing with his back to me, he fingers a number which a female voice answers. He apologises for bothering her, introduces himself and asks to speak to the chief constable.

While he waits, he turns and lowers the mouthpiece to his chest, smiling wickedly. 'Seems he watches telly after all, *Only Fools and Horses*, by the sounds of it.'

'Evening, sir' jerks out of the earpiece so loudly that it's perhaps as well that Cameron isn't holding it in place.

The receiver goes back to his ear as he turns away from me again. 'I take it, Mr Johns, that you are already looking for Edward Tring in connection with the incident at the solicitor's office.'

It's a long reply and Cameron murmurs 'Mmmm' and 'I see' here and there. Then he says, 'I'll check to see if that is acceptable to my colleague.'

He lowers the phone, turns again and looks at me. 'Phillip,' he says, in a ringing tone. Then he cups his right hand over the mouthpiece, so that Johns can't hear any more.

'It seems,' he reports, talking normally, 'that they have made a few discreet inquiries. In view of the pending retrial, they don't want to be accused of harassment.

'Thus far, they have established that Tring and his wife

37

went off for a few days by the sea after his release on bail from prison. She's returned home. He hasn't. They haven't questioned her, but they are putting out feelers. Is that agreeable?'

'Fine,' I say, honestly.

He puts the phone back to his mouth. 'Excellent tactics. Locate and observe only. Well done.'

It's more than acceptable. Cameron has just told the chief that I'm his boy, uses my first name. I'll get a free run, full co-operation, in this city now.

The music over the titles to *Celebs* is a brassy version of 'Who Wants To Be A Millionaire?'

Voss appears, in a lightweight suit. With a smarmy smile he introduces Ball, even more casually dressed in striped, short-sleeved shirt that exposes impressive muscles for someone who looks well into his fifties with a hairless head like an egg laid by some prehistoric hen.

A tour follows of a home that could correctly be described as luxury and large gardens filled with flowers. Interspersed is Ball's rags to riches story.

Golden Balls, prompted here and there by questions about old photos on antique furniture which are then screened in close-up, tells of his barefoot days, the beginnings and the burgeonings of his business empire, his love for his recently lost child-hood sweetheart, and for sport and dogs.

On cue, a black labrador bounds into view to lick his face; an encounter the dog enjoys more than his master. It's male and extremely well hung. I wonder if it's true that dogs acquire the characteristics of their owners; sincerely hope not when the next scene has them both at a dog track, because Ball will take some catching.

He is watching the star of his privately trained string racing against the clock. It must have done a good time, because, when it's led, panting and slavering, by a kennel hand towards him, he calls, rather mechanically, 'Well done, Dezzie.'

So, I think, Golden Balls had a winner at Doncaster after all – Desdemona in the 9.15.

The filming must have taken place last summer as both are dressed in shorts and sweatshirts in the next scene. They are sitting at a white table drinking what looks like fruit juice in the shade of a huge brolly by the side of an outdoor swimming pool.

They talk very briefly about the loss of his wife six months earlier, suddenly and tragically, at forty-six. Since they were childhood sweethearts that would make him about the same; something of a surprise.

Maybe I misread his age because his facial features, like his head, look like marble – so hard that he barely summoned up the briefest of smiles for either dog.

Though the boyhood photos showed him with a full head of hair, there's no explanation of his alopecia – whether it's cancer treatment, shaved or natural.

He's certainly not a TV natural, doesn't give the appearance of enjoying himself, changes his voice with the subject, soft Geordie for reminiscences, blunt about business, coy about charity work at which Voss hints.

Throughout, the questions are very soft, nothing of the Jeremy Paxman about Voss at all. There's no mention, naturally, not even a hint, of protection rackets, money-laundering and drug-running.

Still, I have to accept, Voss would hardly be likely to expose someone who, even then, was being lined up as a backer or benefactor.

'At least we were blessed with a daughter,' Ball says as the camera pans away to the pool out of which climbs a girl in a black swimsuit.

Long dark hair, straightened by wetness, sticks to her arched back, nowhere near reaching the rear plimsoll line of the costume which is just above the chink of her rounded backside. She turns at the top of the steps from the glinting water. Above a high bosom and a halter neck is a pensive face with classic cheekbones. Her eyes look down and away from the camera, Princess Di style.

Had she been blonde and wearing a red swimsuit, she'd have made *Baywatch*. Must take after her late mother, I decide.

Disappointingly, because she's something to behold, the next sight of Amanda Ball is in a white bathrobe, standing above and behind her father, drying her hair with a towel he hands her.

In a soft voice without any noticeable accent, she talks somewhat shyly of her hopes of keeping up the family traditions by going into show business.

'As an actress,' interjects Ball, dark eyes shining proudly. 'Just out of drama school. Twenty-two and never done a day's work.' He laughs briefly and affectionately.

Playfully, she hooks an arm round his neck. 'And what about my unpaid holiday job, cleaning out your kennels?' She tugs her elbow, gently tightening it around his throat. 'You notorious villain.'

Ball's smile now is more than genuine. It's loving, completely and utterly loving, like I know I must have looked when Laura said 'Dada' for the first time.

I can't be sure about this because for me one Shakespeare play sometimes merges with another, but I think I recognise a line from *Othello*. If I'm right, my guess is that his daughter picked the name of his winning greyhound.

What I am absolutely sure of is that if anyone else had called him a notorious villain they'd be floating face down in the pool now, as dead as William Holden in *Sunset Boulevard*.

Voss, who had wisely stayed out of this touching little family scene, reappears to ask Ball about future plans. 'More pleasure in leisure for everyone from the Tyne to the Humber,' he replies.

To 'No Business Like Show Business' in the background, lots of names are scrolled up. I recognise only one: 'Research by Con Clarence'.

The credits stop rolling at 'Produced and Directed by Clive Voss'. Underneath is: 'A Voss Vision Production for Ridings TV'.

I rewind, eject and replace it with *Cause for Concern*, zapping right through to the end. Again among the credits is: 'Research by Con Clarence'.

So, I think, lying naked under the bed sheets, Clarence was more closely associated with Voss than anyone let on during that chat with the team from Ridings TV.

And, since the *Evening Press* hasn't mentioned me and Inspector Herrick had never heard of me, who knows I'm in town? Who could have tipped off that black shadow to keep tabs on me, find out what I'm up to? Clarence? And is the shadow Pepper, the Yardie?

Voss was corrupt all right. Is Clarence? What's going on here? Blackmail? Bribery? Not charity, that's for sure.

I can feel my mind racing, faster than Dezzie in her time trial

or winning the 9.15. I know I must slow it down, think of
something else, or I'll never sleep.

My book for bedtime is a police thriller in hardback, a freebie,
a bribe, really, from its author, 'Jacko' Jackson. He's a great
pal, was with me, saved me, in fact, when I got shot. He's
retired now, writing crime novels based on his thirty years in
CID.

He's half-way through a series and is threatening follow-ups
featuring some of my cases, heavily disguised, names and locations all changed.

I've already briefed him on tapes on two or three and wonder
if this one will make a yarn for him. Only if I crack it, I decide.
That might seem like censorship to my wife. Chief Constable
Johns would call it professional PR.

On a blank page inside, Jacko has signed a jokey
inscription: 'Even money that a couple of pages will put you to
sleep.'

I turn to chapter one. Let's see if it works, I'm thinking,
yawning already.

7

SEVEN DAYS TO CHRISTMAS

Following the directions pinned to the green door of the
bank chambers, I am walking down Hall Street on a misty
Wednesday morning, wearing an off-white mac over my grey
suit, a precaution against the rain that low grey cloud threa-
tens.

My slow progress has more to do with a full house
breakfast than a gammy leg which, by the end of yesterday,
got its right balance of exercise and overnight rest, the latter
due in large measure to a single chapter of 'Jacko' Jackson's
latest.

Two left turns lead to a small, walled car-park in which no
vehicles stand; just a single-storey construction on wooden

41

blocks that looks like a mobile classroom, all glass windows and cream plastic panels.

Inside are half a dozen women at small desks, heads down over adding machines. At the far end, separated from the women with calculators by a hardboard partition, a man and a woman sit across a large paper-strewn desk. Despite the deep gloom no lights shine through any of the windows.

One wooden step up is a door. A knock produces a masculine 'Come in.'

I head for the man who doesn't rise. 'Mr McMichael?' I produce my card, identify myself and add, 'From the Cameron Commission.'

He sighs, motioning to an empty chair beside him. Across the desk a harassed-looking brunette, no more than twenty-five, has not even looked up from the mass of papers she is sorting through.

'Sorry to bother you when you're busy,' I add, taking off my raincoat before sitting.

'Total chaos.' McMichael, tubby, dark and fiftyish, looks and sounds exhausted at 9.30.

I listen patiently to legitimate grumbles – the late night call-out, the shock of hearing of the brutal death of his client, the shambles in the office, the inconvenience of not being able to get back in until yesterday when Forensics finally finished.

He begins to look on the up side – the speed with which his insurers provided this accommodation, despite temporary trouble with the electrical supply that makes the office cold as well as dark, the understanding of magistrates in adjourning some of his cases, the impending arrival of repair men and the hope of getting back to something like normal early next week.

Finally he stops and looks at me, inviting a question. For starters, I feed him a red herring. 'Since the raid virtually took place live on TV, we're naturally looking into the pros and cons of police co-operation on such programmes.' I pause. 'Were you in on the planning?'

A heavy headshake. 'Knew nothing about it. Clive never discussed it with me.' His tired eyes and mind drift away. 'No reason why he should, I suppose.'

He'd been Voss's solicitor for ten years, since he defended him on some minor motoring offence about which I don't seek details.

42

When Voss quit Ridings TV to set up his own production company, McMichael handled the paperwork and put him on to the empty shop further up the street.

Since he's gone back to where I want to start, I'll stay there. 'In that first series as an independent producer, that consumer affairs show, he was served with a writ by a plumbing –'

Huffily, McMichael breaks in. 'Nothing to do with me, that. Ridings' own legal staff vetted the whole series.' He smiles secretly. 'And picked up the bill for agreed damages and costs.'

I'll be a bit more blunt. 'How about the Tring exposure on *Cause for Concern*?'

No interruption now, no smile, just silence.

'Look.' My appealing expression and tone. 'I know this is putting you in ethical difficulties, client confidentiality and all that. But, surely, in these tragic circumstances, Clive would consent to your co-operation?'

He works his lips. 'He didn't consult me on that either, except –'

Annoyingly, a knock comes on the door which is opened without invitation. In walks a small, bespectacled blonde. 'Sorry.' She hesitates for a second, then comes further in so I get a better look at a figure that, for someone in her mid-twenties, is OK for a chunky green sweater but a bit too full for tight brown cords.

'Ah, Elaine,' sighs McMichael.

She complains that everyone next door is shivering their socks off and enquires when the electrician is coming. Within the hour, McMichael tells her.

She turns to his secretary and wants to know if tickets have been obtained for a girls' night out at the Riverside Shuffle on Friday. Yes, replies the secretary, looking up and speaking for the first time. She shoots an anxious look from her to me. 'You're interrupting,' she is all but telling her. 'It's OK,' I say, easily. Elaine departs with another 'Sorry', smiling at me.

McMichael shakes his head wearily in the direction of the now closed door, looks back at me, says nothing.

'So,' I prompt, 'Mr Voss went ahead and broadcast the Tring case without any legal vetting?'

He still says nothing.

I'm going to have to up the ante. 'If he'd survived and he'd lost that action, would that have finished the company?'

'Now look here.' He bridles. 'I can't possibly . . .'

I've placed a bum bet, must recoup. 'Or if the plaintiff, the policewoman, had lost, would that have ended her career?'

He goes silent again, but his annoyance is subsiding, recognising, I hope, a certain even-handedness in my approach.

I'm going to have to go as far as I dare at hinting that Inspector Herrick is under suspicion, not of carrying out the raid herself, but of somehow being implicated, to destroy evidence against her. Lots of lawyers like police conspiracy theories. 'You have to understand that I'm in the Complaints and Discipline Department from an outside force.'

He sits back, listening intently.

'You did, after all, write back to her solicitor on Mr Voss's behalf, stating that the company stood by the story,' I point out.

'Stood by his actions, actually,' McMichael corrects me. 'His instructions; a standard first response in threatened libel actions.' He pauses. 'I think I see what you're driving at.' He thinks some more. 'There was nothing in the safe pertaining to that case, no, if that's what you mean.'

In fact, he goes on, relaxing a little, he hadn't much in the file on it that hadn't already been aired on TV or in the appeal courts – the testimony of the scientist and sworn statements from the three witnesses who belatedly alibied Tring for the time of the gems raid.

He'd personally interviewed none of them. 'Didn't want to be accused of coaching them ahead of the retrial,' he explains. 'No rush. Everything hinges on that.'

I sit back now. 'Is Voss Vision, like Ridings TV, insured against libel?'

'No, but Clive had considerable support. There'd have been no financial problems, nor will there be, whatever the libel verdict.'

I arch an eyebrow. 'Financial backing from Golden Globe Entertainments, you mean?'

He stirs uncomfortably, troubled again.

I'm going to have to try some more flim-flam. 'You see, that's another aspect that worries our Commission from an ethical point of view.'

'Why so?' McMichael appears mildly surprised. 'Clive had plans for a fictional feature film, full-length, a sci-fi. He'd got an option, had been scouting locations. We're talking a major outlay here, ninety minutes to two hours, big cast and crew. Far beyond anything he'd ever done before. It's quite common for outside business to invest in a major movie production.'

'Ah yes,' I say pleasantly, then harden my tone, 'but it's not common for a TV company to devote half an hour to a big businessman who's got money in it.'

He is shaking his head.

I press on. 'That *Celebrities* programme, surely...' He is shaking his head, quite vigorously. I stop. 'No?'

'Wrong, quite wrong. Mr Ball invested after...' for emphasis he repeats, '...after that series. He had no money in Voss Vision at the time his profile programme was made.'

McMichael shrugs casually. 'I'm not saying for one minute that Clive didn't take the opportunity when he was filming Ball to interest him in the project for the future, but at the time of the screening there was no financial tie-up. All the contracts will prove that.' For good measure, he adds, 'Mr Ball did not sponsor his way on to that programme in the summer, if that's what you suspect.'

For sponsor, read bribe, I think. Time to fall back on the routine. 'What was in the safe? Money?'

Another short headshake then, 'That's what TV wanted to know.'

'Sorry?' I put on my puzzled expression.

He'd had a call late yesterday afternoon, he explains, from someone in the Ridings newsroom. They'd established that his safe, not the bank vaults, had been the safe-blower's target. McMichael had earlier had a call from the acting head of CID requesting him not to discuss details about the contents, so he'd fudged non-committal replies, including the misinformation that the remains were still being examined.

I ask for the reporter's name. The caller wasn't any of the Ridings trio, but the timing meant that one of them could have tipped off their newsroom after our meeting at the hotel.

Several papers I read over breakfast had also carried the line, but McMichael claims not to have spoken to any of them. The press had lifted it unchecked from TV, I suspect, the way that the media incestuously feed off each other.

I get back to my routine question. 'No cash then and nothing in the safe on the Herrick versus Voss Vision libel action? Nothing on the deal between Voss and Golden Globe Entertainments either?'

No answer.

I give up. 'What then?'

'Several Christmas presents, bottles of malt and brandy.' McMichael laughs lightly. Then his face goes very serious. 'The accelerant for the fire, the brigade boys suspect.' He pauses. 'Several wills, my own included.'

'Mr Voss's?'

'Fraid not. Badgered him, but he never got round to it.' Rather ominously, he adds, 'You have, I hope.'

I nod.

'Wise. Saves next-of-kin a lot of admin.' He smiles approvingly and continues to list the contents of the safe. 'Deeds of property. Client company seals. A few sensitive witness statements...'

I open my mouth to ask a question, but he's too fast for me. '...but nothing on the alleged libel or Golden Globe deal.' He pauses. 'And two or three videos.'

This time I won't attempt to speak.

'At least, I think they were videos. Felt like them, rattled a bit.' He dries up.

'Who lodged them with you?'

'Clive. Sealed. In a Jiffy bag. ''For safe-keeping'' was all he said.' He lets an amused expression flicker across his face. 'It wasn't labelled ''To be opened in the event of my death'' or anything dramatic like that.'

'What was on them?'

'Only he knew. Now we'll never know.'

'Destroyed?'

'Completely. Lucky we didn't lose a lot more. It was a severe fire.'

I need to get him away from his secretary, speak to him alone. 'Mind if I have a look for myself?'

Still no vehicles in the car-park when we walk through it in a light drizzle. Only one car is parked illegally round the corner in Hall Street, not a white sporty job, just a silvery-blue E-reg Cavalier. The figures that come next are easy to remember – 999 – but I don't make a mental note of the three letters that follow.

46

First night nerves always vanish the morning after when you get stuck into a big inquiry. Yep, I convince myself, it was paranoia. Forget it.

McMichael unlocks the green door and we climb a dim staircase. Deeper gloom descends down to my black shoes in the outer office on the first floor, darker than the grey light from the boarded windows.

The door from which we are surveying the room is scorched. The wallpaper, once lime green, is mainly smoky grey. A desk has blistered. A chair is in fragments. The smell, like an old bonfire, which greeted us coming up the stairs from the street door, is overpowering in here.

'A mess, eh?' says McMichael across his shoulder.

In more ways than one, I fret. Seen it all before, of course, the aftermaths of fires and explosions, but never at the scene of a safe-blowing carried out by an expert cracksman.

What's causing my deep depression is the knowledge that this can't have been the work of Gabby Tring.

A muffled bang, a puff of smoke is all it would have taken in the hands of a specialist.

It's the work of a bungling amateur lucky to escape from here with his life. The wonder is he wasn't found dead in the wreckage; an own goal, we call it.

A line of inquiry in which I've involved Cameron, Britain's top cop, has blown up in my face. And the chief constable will laugh in it when his CID track down Gabby, fully alibied for Friday night. Oh, shit.

I walk in, suddenly heavy-legged. The carpet has been swept clean; forensic routine. The lab staff will be sifting through every speck. It's damp underfoot from firemen's hoses and the carpet is so dark that it's hard to detect the original colour.

I stop in front of the safe, its interior built into the thick wall at chest height. Inside is not just empty, but vacuumed out. The ashes will be under the microscope, too, for all the good that it will do.

The door hangs open and off centre, one hinge gone, and almost touches the wall. A sharp tug is needed to peer on tiptoes over the top edge down at the front of it. The black paint has peeled here and there, but the maker's name is intact – Chubb.

A thrill runs through me, scattering all the gloom. 'Haven't I seen this before?'

'Er...' An embarrassed pause.

'On TV in that reconstruction of Tring's conviction?'

'Well. Er. Yes. Clive asked if he could film it.'

Voss, he goes on, wanted a bit of footage of a genuine wall safe for an item which he didn't fully explain. McMichael gave consent. He was, after all, a valued client.

McMichael knew nothing about the shots that followed – the door blowing off, the alarm clock being shattered. 'I can only assume they were mock-ups back at the studio.'

Voss...my mind is running away again and I'm happy to let it...cased the joint on film for whoever was hired as the cracksman. If not Tring, who? Why? To get at what? 'He'd made no will, you said, so who benefits?'

'Two sisters down south. The elder is next-of-kin. Both parents are dead.'

I nod. 'No lady in his life then?'

'Was.' He looks up at the smoke-logged ceiling towards the temporarily vacated offices of the calculating agency. His features are sad. 'Not seen her around for some time.'

I'm going to drop a name now, the reason why I wanted him on his own. 'Con Clarence.'

He gives me the strangest of looks – part startled, part old-fashioned.

I press on. 'Is he a partner in Voss Vision?'

A dumb headshake, lips clasped.

'What then?'

'An employee,' he says. 'Clive brought him with him when he left Ridings TV.'

'Will he benefit from the estate in any way?'

'Quite the reverse. He'll be out of work unless the company's taken over.'

'What's his role?'

'Research. Scriptwriting.' McMichael motions to the safe. 'He was with the cameraman when that was filmed.'

Interesting, I think. 'Voss wasn't insured for libel, you say, but for other eventualities, like life?'

'Double if he died on duty, but Con Clarence won't benefit, if that's what you're thinking. Everything's shared by his sisters.'

'Worth much?' I ask casually.

He doesn't bite.

'Depends on the outcome of that outstanding libel, I suppose,' I add, more or less to myself.

'Depends on whether his backer reneges now Clive's gone,' he finally replies. Like Inspector Herrick last night, he doesn't look very confident.

'Was Ball backing him in his libel case, too?'

'He's an investor in the company,' he answers obscurely. Abruptly, he changes tack. 'And the shop...' He flicks his head towards the boarded-up window and Hall Street beyond. '...that was insured. And equipment, of course, and accident or illness causing abandonment or delay on his sci-fi project. His backer insisted on it before he'd advance development money. In all other respects, he was fully covered.'

So, interestingly, is Golden Balls, I'm thinking.

Looking made to measure for the place in yet another elegant suit, navy blue with pin-stripes, Sir Donald Cameron is sitting in the hotel foyer, democratically drinking coffee with his clerk and chauffeur.

Satisfied that the inquiry is being properly conducted, our supervisor departed in my absence on a train to London with the promise of frequent progress reports, he recounts.

His morning, he goes on, will be taken up in receiving delegations from pressure groups like self-appointed viewers and listeners' associations arguing that there's enough violence on TV without the police providing the props for it.

I brief him, confessing that, judging from the inexpertly handled safe-blowing, Tring might be a bum lead, proposing that the net be widened. 'Whoever did do it could be injured,' I venture.

Assuming that the local CID would have already checked out the local hospital near the football ground, I urge, 'Will you request the chief constable to organise a ring round all hospitals in the county, seeking any burns or blast victims brought in since, say, 9 p.m. on Friday?'

'We can do better than that,' says Cameron immediately and confidently. 'Personal visits from experienced officers, sergeants or above. Details on any casualty, no matter under what name they are registered. If that doesn't produce by tonight, we go nationwide.' A slight pause. 'Anything else?'

I shake my head.

He ponders a little. 'Aren't there coalfields around here – down Selby way?'

I haven't a clue and hold my tongue and head.

'What about checks on all mines and quarries for missing or unaccounted-for dynamite in the last few months?' he suggests with obvious enthusiasm.

Good, I think, happily. He's very, very good.

He asks my plans. I tell him, promising to be back in time for the formal hearing with police witnesses.

He waves airily at his chauffeur. 'Take the car. Travel in the back. That should impress him.'

8

'Private Property. No Trespassers. No Hawkers' has been neatly branded into a tree log that's been cross-sectioned, varnished and fixed to a gate post. Or maybe it's black paint and the ringed wood is plastic, hard to tell in this gloomy light from the back of the Daimler.

The unwelcoming sign also announces my destination: 'Golden Leaves'.

A long, runway-flat lane is edged with vivid green mosses. On each side browned bracken merges with blackened nettles and runs into tall naked trees, the tips of which are shrouded in an ever-thickening mist.

Nothing looks plastic or mock about the Tudor-style house which Golden Balls rebuilt among vast tracts of native woodland a few miles short of Selby off the A19.

The timbers on the central arch aren't glossy black but naturally weathered. The plaster in between isn't gleaming white but a subdued sandy colour.

Well named, too, I have to concede, as fallen leaves stir on the damp front lawn at our approach and wheel away as we pass. No dog – guard, gun or racing – bounds up to us.

The frontage is long, three storeys. Below the overhanging eaves, the brickwork is part grey stone, part pale red. The only jarring note is a blue burglar alarm between attic windows, though I doubt any housebreaker ever calls – not if he wants to live, that is.

The car glides along a U-shaped drive at the end of a twenty-minute trip, dipped headlights, windscreen wiper working all the way, beyond police HQ through the southern suburbs and a couple of villages.

At right angles to the house, across the wide lawn, is a low building with a sloping slate roof; old stables converted into flats by the looks of the flower boxes on the sills of small, white-framed windows; all with lights shining out.

The problem with arriving unannounced at a big house, I sometimes find, is that you'll be told by the maid or the secretary that Mr Big is unavailable and to phone in for an appointment which will be kept days, even weeks hence, along with a solicitor. Don't want that. I'm some distance off the formal interview yet. This is just a recce, the start of the drip, drip, drip of something that could run as long as *The Fugitive*.

Half expecting the bum's rush, I climb out of the back of the car, leaving my raincoat behind, and walk just a couple of steps on to a square of York stone slabs in front of a studded, arched door. Beside it hangs one of those link chains you pull to ring, as if calling on the Addams family.

I turn round to wink at Tom, the driver. Over the roof of the car I see that a big man has emerged from the stable block to inspect his uninvited callers. Golden Balls, no doubt about that totally bald head and broad frame, clad today in a yellow sweater. I wave, climb back in and am delivered to him.

I step out again, as breezily as I can manage, holding out my hand, intent on jollying him along. 'Don't worry. I'm not hawking anything.'

Pale white skin tightens against a strong jaw-bone, an expression that's anything but jolly.

I switch off my smile. 'From the Home Office Cameron Commission inquiring into Friday night.'

He takes my hand, very reluctantly and rather weakly. 'You should have phoned.'

'On my way back from...' Out of thin air I clutch at '...the Selby coalfields. Thought I'd pop in on the off-chance.'

Suspicion darkens the tan-coloured bags under his ice blue eyes. 'Better come in then.'

Inside, four or five stables have been knocked into one to

51

create a tasteful, well-lit office. Matching, highly polished dark desks are in a T-shape, sturdy chairs each side of the stem, a massive brown leather chair at the top.

The plainness of the cream walls is broken by coloured photos, several of Ball with dogs and daughter, and corkboards with graphs, the coldness by a thick golden carpet and a double radiator along the window wall.

He walks ahead of me, slow of step in brown moccasins. His darker brown trousers are an expensive and perfect fit. He reaches the top of the T, the only desk with phones, three of them, and papers in grey-black boxes.

Also sitting on it, denimed legs dangling, is Amanda who looks up languidly from a magazine and down again.

Ball gestures me to the nearest chair on the stem of the T and sits himself. 'Now then, Mr Cameron...'

I shake my head, just slightly. 'I'm Phillip Todd, his senior assistant. Chief superintendent, East Mids Police.'

He looks irked, offended almost. 'Haven't got much time.'

I go through the spiel about the report we have to submit to the Home Secretary on future policy on police-media co-operation.

Amanda, in blue jeans and shirt, a white sweater tied round her neck, keeps her head down over the magazine, but doesn't turn any pages. She's listening, pretending not to.

She wears no make-up and her face is very pale with faint creases round her eyes that didn't show up on TV, making her look older than twenty-two.

Her father cuts a different figure, too, in the flesh. He seems tired and tense.

I end my longish intro. 'You were on the programme, of course.'

Ball forces a chuckle. 'Not in the crime scenes, thankfully.'

I smile. 'But at the dog track?' Through his slow nod, I add, 'How did that come about?'

Wayne Kirk, the controller of Ridings TV, phoned him a month ago to explain the concept, he begins, folding his hands together on the desk.

Concept? My, my. He has been spending time with telly types. 'Which was?' I ask with an innocent face.

A live police programme from nine to ten and ten forty to midnight or beyond, he explains, repeating what I already know.

A potential problem, he was told, was the first hour. Friday nights don't hot up until the pubs close and Kirk feared that he might be short of action. Ball was a great patron at the dog track, Kirk pointed out. What did he think about two or three races being televised from there as stand-bys? he'd asked.

Ball's Geordie accent is quite distinctive, but well toned down. I wonder if his broadness in that one-sentence presentation speech at the dog track was for public consumption, to protect his earthy 'howay the lads' image. That, the smartness of his dress, even in casuals, and his manicured fingernails suggest cultivated attempts to smooth out any rough edges remaining from his barefoot days.

'Jumped at the chance, of course,' he goes on. 'Our sport is poorly covered, only gets a few lines in the papers and only the annual BBC Trophy and the Greyhound Derby ever attract the cameras. There's satellite, of course, but not everybody takes that.'

'And you sponsored a race?' I ask, merely to move the story along.

'Wee not?' he snaps, proper Geordie. He controls himself. 'Wanted to show our sport at its best, didn't I? So I invited the best and put up a prize.'

'Of ten thou?'

A casual shrug. 'And the rest.'

I cock my head.

'Got to entertain the owners, haven't you? Took most of the restaurant. Well worthwhile for region-wide exposure, tax deductible, of course.' He realises he'd perhaps come across a touch flash, so, softer, 'Most of our business is based here, lots down the coast.' Then, almost coyly, 'Got to put something back into the community from whence it came, haven't you?'

He's in the habit of ending sentences with questions and I don't think he expects me to commend him. 'Why the 9.45?'

'Sorry?'

'Well, why invest that sort of money in that particular race, why not, say, the 9.15 or the...'

He sees what I mean. 'They couldn't guarantee coverage of the 9.15 in case an exciting incident had started before they came on air and they had to stick with it, following it through, sort of thing.'

'But nothing did?'

'There was a drugs raid, wasn't there, not a very thrilling one, so they did show the 9.15, as it turned out, but not the 9.30 because of that fire at that bank.'

He'd been watching it very closely, then. 'But the 9.45 was guaranteed a slot, come what may?' I ask.

'In the contract.' He nods at one of the boxes on his desk. 'Look at Littlewoods and the FA Cup and Carling and the Premiership, Cornhill with cricket. You've got to get value for money, haven't you?'

No arguing with that. They get plugged all the time, part of the deal with TV for exclusive rights, I suppose. 'Did Clive Voss play a part in these negotiations?'

Amanda stops pretending to read and looks at me with brown eyes that seem lifeless; nothing of the vivaciousness she displayed on screen.

It's a bit of a let-down, like meeting an old sporting hero – one of Derby County's championship side from the '70s, for instance, who dazzled you on the terraces – and finding him deadly dull.

'Sad about Clive, eh?' Ball is buying himself thinking time. 'Shocking.' He lowers his hairless head, not, I suspect, in remembrance, but to figure out his reply. He looks up suddenly, his mind made up. 'Not directly, no, but he may well have put up my name as a sponsor.'

'You knew him well, I gather.'

'Well...' His head dances left and right, wondering whether to confirm or dispute it, compromising on, 'Wellish, yes.'

He'd seen a lot of him on TV before he'd actually met him for lunch with his researcher when they were lining up subjects for his *Celebs* series.

'To which you agreed?' I prompt.

A nod.

A curved ball now. 'Was that value for money?'

He stonewalls. 'Howdaya mean?'

'I understand you are an investor in Voss Vision.'

He plays it back, very calmly. 'Not then. No. That came later. For a film. Quite separate. Nothing to do with that series.'

'So was it worthwhile?' I persist.

'If you discount having a crew here for two days...' He flicks his

54

head in the general direction of the house. ' ...tramping dirt all over the carpets, yes, I suppose so. Did no harm.' He looks to his daughter for support. 'Good PR, wouldn't you say?'

She merely nods, maintaining a non-speaking role.

'And...' I lean forward so that he'll catch the next word. '...subsequently you did invest in a feature film Voss had on the stocks?'

He shrugs, unconcerned. 'Natural diversification. Let's hope it goes as well as *Four Weddings and a Funeral*, eh?'

'Will it go at all now?'

A frown. 'Hadn't really considered that. Voss Vision still hold the rights. Suppose they could be sold on.'

'And, of course, you'll be insured against any abandonment or delay?'

There's a thin smile on his pale lips but his eyes are not amused. 'You're well informed.'

In reply, I strive for a much sweeter smile.

'Routine,' he has to continue. 'All film-makers do it. A normal precaution against delays, production costs escalating out of control.'

Time to drop that name. 'Spoken to his associate, Con Clarence, have you?'

'Whyshuda?' he shoots back so Geordie I'm surprised he didn't add, 'Yer bugger.'

'Won't he know the state of play...'

He's already shaking his head to which my eyes are constantly drawn. There's nothing, no nicks or anything, to suggest he shaves it like Kojak, so I still can't work out the reason for his complete baldness.

I concentrate and continue, '...about the prospects of going ahead or the insurance situation?'

A slight shrug. 'No rush. Early days.'

'Will he take on the company now?'

'Doubt it.' He looks up. 'Met him?'

'Briefly,' I reply, determined to give nothing away. 'What's he like?'

He considers his answer for some time, then uses only one word: 'Uninspired.'

I open a new front. 'Mr Voss was shot outside the Riverside Shuffle...'

He corrects me. 'Close to.'

'...which you own?'

A cautious nod. 'One of my companies does, yes.'

'Was Voss a regular there?'

'Wouldn't know. Don't go myself.' A playful smile. 'The clientele is too young for me.'

'Did he ever mention going – when he was here, filming, or over that first lunch?'

He thinks. 'Believe he did, matter of fact. Said he'd been a time or two.'

I look at Amanda. 'Do you know?'

Her father answers. 'Why not go yourself and ask?' He smiles again. 'You'll find it extremely well run.'

He's protecting her, I realise, feeling thwarted, unable to do much about it here and now. 'We're also going to have to ask around about the anonymous emergency call that sent the police and Mr Voss and his crew there.'

A sullen expression. 'Malicious call, you mean. A drunk who's been ejected and turns out the fire brigade. A rival nightspot trying to stir it for us with you lot' – the police, he means. 'We get our share.'

I sit back a second in thought; a mistake. He makes a show of looking at a gold watch on his wrist. 'Afraid we're running a bit short of –'

I lean forward. 'How did you rate Mr Voss?'

He gives me a glare, not used to being interrupted.

'I mean,' I speed on, 'trustworthy, ambitious...'

He nods.

'...malleable.'

A puzzled frown. 'How do you mean?'

'Well, was he the type who could be manipulated or was he his own man?'

'Why do you ask?'

'He was lured to his death, wasn't he, by a phoney call? Was he that naïve?'

'Anything but. A sharp mind, wouldn't you say?' He turns to his daughter again; his mistake.

'Yes.' The first word she's spoken to me is flat and dull.

I address her. 'You know him, too?'

'Of course.' Her tone and face are impatient. 'He filmed here. I knew him anyway from the club.'

'The Shuffle?' I ask.

56

She nods slowly and continues, 'And we'd discussed other possible projects.'

'Such as?'

Ball's turn to break in, the protective father again. 'We're getting a bit removed, aren't we, from the stated purpose of your visit?' He looks from me to Amanda. 'Best get ready,' he tells her quite sharply.

Without demur, she slips gracefully off the desk and walks, no sway today, out of the office without a goodbye.

'Oh, I don't know,' I drawl, keeping my eyes on Ball. 'As a matter of policy, we have to go into the credentials of journalists we grant access to, even retrospectively.' I pause, then add, 'And their business associations.'

His steely eyes lock on mine, finally full of fight.

I rise, job done here for the time being. 'Or, indeed, whether we should provide co-operation for these sort of programmes at all.'

I look down at him, a steady look. 'There's a view being expressed among MPs that, instead of nursemaiding the media and providing them with free entertainment, we should be out on the streets, catching drug-smugglers, protection racketeers and money-launderers.'

I smile, politely thank him for his time, tell him I may want to see him again, turn, don't look back, but I can sense, almost feel, those cold eyes boring like ice picks into my back.

9

A supposedly short break for lunch at an out-of-the-way village pub with a log fire roaring in an open grate lasts longer than planned, Tom, the driver, talking me out of York ham sandwiches and into beef and beer stew.

He's a dark, diminutive man, no more than eight stone, with a sit-down job that burns nothing off, yet he eats with great gusto, leaving a clean plate and me wondering where he puts it all.

Like Golden Balls, his accent seems to change according to the company he is keeping. In Cameron's absence, it's native East End as he complains bitterly about being held up for a minute or two on a narrow lane by a herd of cows moving fields. 'Shittin' all over the place,' he grumbles. 'Should have their soddin' road fund licences revoked.'

Back on the A19, traffic builds up and slows to a crawl in steady rain. He seems more at home. 'Civilisation,' he sighs contentedly.

Beginning to run short of time, it's my turn to moan when we come to a stop at temporary traffic lights which restrict traffic to one way for roadworks.

For something to do, to take my eyes off the dashboard clock, I look each side of me, not seeing anything of note, then, out of habit, behind me.

My God, I think, craning my neck still further round, a silvery Cavalier, E-registered. Surely not? 999 comes after the E.

It is.

It's right behind in a line of stationary vehicles that's lengthening all the time. It's not a black face behind the windscreen. The driver is late middle-age, too old to be either of Tring's white alibi witnesses. Even so, I muse, deeply troubled.

The lights on a metal tripod turn to green. Tom moves away, driving carefully alongside red-and-white striped barriers behind which pipes are being laid in a long, deep trench.

They've changed shadowers and vehicles because both were too distinctive yesterday, I suspect. (No, stronger, I'm damned sure of it.)

So what are you going to do about it, fret for another twenty-four hours, sharing your suspicions, your fear with no one?

Check him out. Ask him who he's working for. Hold him till he talks. Never mind about being late for Cameron and his Commission. Leave the routine to him. You're here to solve a murder and someone is going to a lot of time and trouble to find out how you're getting on, who you're seeing.

You'll never have a better opportunity. Now. Right now. He's trapped, us ahead of him, a dozen vehicles behind. Come on. Do it. 'Stop,' I say to Tom.

'What?' Momentarily, he takes his eyes off the road to shoot me a puzzled glance.

'Now.'

'Here, guv?'

'I have to talk to the driver behind.'

'But –'

58

'Now. Tom.'

He pulls to a smooth stop. Not bothering with my mac, I get out, heart pounding, feeling for and finding my warrant card in an inside pocket of my jacket, wondering whether I should be doing this without a gun.

The driver of the Cavalier is watching me, nonplussed, as I walk between the Daimler boot and his bonnet. He's wound down his window by the time I reach him.

I hold up my card, steeling myself to bully him. 'What's your game, mate?'

'Eh?' He's clearly unnerved, as if about to be confronted by a motorist in the grip of road rage; the wrong reaction.

I soften my tone. 'Were you parked in Hall Street between nine and half-past this morning?'

'Er.' He gulps, 'Why, er, yeah.' Then, tentatively: 'Why?'

I pull out my pocket notebook. 'Name?' Rain drips on an open page. Belatedly, no longer sure of myself, I add, 'Please.'

'Why?' He's over his shock, more demanding.

'Documents, please. Now.'

He fumbles in an inside pocket.

The driver of the car behind pokes his head out of his window and shouts, 'What's going on?'

'Police business,' I call.

Horns to the south begin to toot. Dipped headlights flash to full beam and off again.

The driver hands me a card which gives the name of a security consultancy. 'Work for myself,' he grunts.

My eyes go to the back seat where brochures for burglar alarms are scattered.

Horns blare north and south.

From a creased brown wallet, he produces credit cards in the same name. Yes, he'd been in Hall Street, he says. Two businesses wanted quotes. 'Always the same after a break-in in the neighbourhood,' he adds as I note their names.

Voices to the south are shouting. 'Move it.' 'Get on with it.'

He's on his way back from a pre-arranged appointment in Selby, he goes on. Another address is noted in ballpoint that quickly becomes smudged. 'What's it all about?' His confidence rises as mine ebbs.

The lead car in the queue on the opposite side of the road held up by a red light that now must be on green flashes his lights repeatedly. Pipe-layers in yellow capes in the trench stop working and lean on their shovels.

'A routine check,' I say, beginning to feel wet in more ways than one.

'Well, when you've bloody well checked...' He raises his voice, angry now. '...I hope I'll get a bloody apology.'

I smile down at him, disguising my embarrassment. 'Along with a summons for illegal parking in Hall Street.'

Resuming my place alongside Tom, I say, 'False alarm.'

'Seem to get a few in this place,' he replies, still baffled.

Outside the conference room, backs to the corridor wall, sit a line of police employees, both regular and civilian. They look like nervous job applicants, as well they might be if Cameron, having reached a formal stage in his inquiry, doesn't like their answers.

Susan Herrick isn't among them. The acting CID chief is. I stop in front of him. He looks up, but seems too tired to stand. I ask him to cross-check the details the Cavalier driver gave. I read them out. He notes them down.

'Know a black guy with Yardie connections, name of Pepper?' I ask.

'Of him,' he tells his notebook.

'Find out his address and what transport he's currently using.'

Inside the conference room, the lights are on, the net curtains are drawn and the titles of *Friday the 13th Blues* are on hold on a TV set that wasn't here yesterday.

Cameron sits at the oblong table facing the screen, his clerk to his right, two empty chairs to his left.

In front of the clerk are two remote controls, a tape machine, witness statements and high piles of still photos taken from the film, frame by frame.

Cameron gestures me to sit beside him, doesn't inquire how I've got on or why I'm five minutes late. He picks up one of the controls, points it at the screen. From it – yet again – come those jumpy shots of blue lights flashing and the voice of doom intoning, 'Twelve days to Christmas...'

I know it so well that I turn off mentally before Cameron does with his thumb. 'Right,' he says, looking at the clerk. 'The drugs squad inspector, please.'

Inspector Herrick's successor as head of the drugs squad is a fair, heavy man, a veteran of twenty-five years' service. He wears a shiny blue suit that looks as if it joined up with him. The fact that he hasn't dressed to impress even Britain's top cop impresses me.

Like Ball this morning, he cuts a different figure to the man we're watching on the screen – in a blue boilersuit, leaping out of a white van, loudly banging on the door of a terraced inner-city house, calling forward his men with the battering ram, standing wrong-footed as the door opens before it can be broken down, racing up the stairs, issuing orders, ransacking the bed, triumphantly holding a small plastic bag of white powder, leading out his captive, face obscured by dancing dots.

The video is switched off. 'When and how did you first get involved in this?' asks Cameron rather disdainfully.

A week before the programme, the inspector begins quietly, he and other heads of departments were called to a conference to be briefed by Chief Constable Johns. Wayne Kirk, the controller of Ridings TV, was there, but not Clive Voss.

It had already been decided that the show would start with a live drugs raid, unless anything better turned up in the natural course of the evening. He was deputed to liaise with Clarence of Voss Vision to work out the details. Three meetings, just the two of them, followed, several phone calls in between.

'He was hoping for something dramatic. "Sexy" he said. Kept harping on about it.'

'Such as?' asks Cameron.

'A joint op with Customs at one of the harbours...' He flicks his head eastwards in the direction of the coast. '...or a shake-down at a nightspot.'

The inspector couldn't promise anything that sexy. 'I told him you don't hit clubs looking for drugs at just past nine and we'd no intelligence about anything spicy coming ashore.'

He pauses, a bit puzzled. 'He already knew that Customs at Whitby had a watch on, but I told him it was long term, not likely to produce results until the New Year. The chief had

61

agreed to organise a raid, any raid, up to me, and hold it back to 9.03. That job....' He nods at the still screen. '...was all I could offer Clarence for sure.'

He looks down, muttering, embarrassed. 'Mr Johns wanted a bit of a show putting on for them. "Make it heavy," he said.' He shrugs unhappily. 'We had tips about that bedsit...' He nods again. '...had it under surveillance.'

Cameron breaks in, smiling mischievously. 'So the information was genuine, though the timing and some of the acting wasn't?'

'We could have done it days before,' the inspector replies laconically.

'Was Clarence disappointed it was so low key?'

'Not really.' The inspector stops to think. 'Except that he kept asking right up until the last minute if anything else, anything better was breaking, was Whitby likely to produce, but seemed to accept it.'

Cameron isn't smiling now. 'How did he know about the Customs surveillance at Whitby?'

'Mr Johns told Kirk at the original briefing, as I understand it, and Kirk must have told Voss and Clarence.'

Cameron doesn't comment, wince or let his eyes go heavenwards; too much of a diplomat for that, but he's so professional that he's bound to have noted that Johns was totally out of order to discuss another authority's operation with anyone, let alone with the media. Instead, he asks, 'What did Clarence do, where did he go afterwards?'

The inspector takes a detour before answering. Clarence was in the A team out of a dozen TV crews, he explains, all being driven around in vehicles with either satellite dishes or aerials on the roofs, either following police patrols or on standby at strategic spots.

'We parted outside the house after the arrest. He didn't expect to get another assignment till after the *News at Ten*, if at all, with so many of them out and about. I had to process the paperwork. Never saw him again.'

Cameron sums it up. 'So you don't know?'

'No,' he finally concedes.

There's something I'd not really noticed about this segment of film before and now only because I'm married into the media.

Normally, TV reporters can't keep their faces off the screen. Even when the film has been bought from abroad, and all they're really doing is reading other people's words, they'll pop up, mike in hand in, say, Whitehall, putting a thin national spin on to a foreign story merely to get themselves on camera. Yet Clarence had not appeared. I point this out.

'Yes,' agrees the inspector. 'He did the commentary over his cameraman's shoulder. He was unobtrusive, no trouble at all. I'll give him that.'

'Did the drugs pusher you arrested object to the presence of TV cameras?' Cameron asks.

He shakes his head.

The dealer couldn't have stopped the police entering with a warrant, of course, I realise, but why targets in these fly-on-the-wall documentaries let TV invade, trespass and trample all over their own homes defeats me.

For his few minutes of fame, I suspect. Everyone sees themselves as a star these days.

Cameron fast forwards while his clerk calls in the head of traffic.

Reading between the lines of his evidence, the arrest of the joyrider was just as stage-managed as the drugs raid; stunts for the media, really.

His patrolmen had known the car had been missing all evening, the inspector says. One crew had spotted it soon after eight, recognised the schoolboy driver, a persistent offender, knew his regular route and his habits, but didn't intercept immediately.

All they had to do for an hour or so was cruise up and down the northern end of the ring road with the B team from Ridings TV in tow.

Their reporter, a young eager-beaver, was more pushy than Clarence, padding out his piece to camera with loads of prepared statistics about road deaths caused by drink-driving and in police pursuits.

According to the traffic chief, he grumbled mildly off camera that the patrol crew had pulled the joyrider over so quickly that viewers had been denied a ninety mile an hour chase, or, better still, a grinding crash.

I groan inwardly as Cameron rewinds to the beginning. The

operations room sergeant, a forty-year-old woman with the calm, efficient air of a headmistress, talks us right through it.

She'd handled the messages from both the drugs squad and the motor patrol. At her side was Wayne Kirk, the controller, equipped with portable TV, mobile phones and two-way radios.

He thought the first item, the drugs bust, was a bit flat, but no real complaints, she relates. With nothing else breaking he told his studio-based director to go to the greyhound stadium for the 9.15.

After watching Desdemona, the even money favourite, flash by the winning post in a streak of white, we have to sit yet again through the joyrider's arrest.

Kirk, she recounts, was getting bored with it and was about to order a return to the dog track for the 9.30 when three 999 calls were received variously reporting an explosion, fire and 'a bloody big bang' at the bank chambers in Hall Street.

The video is stopped. The 999 recordings are played. All three callers gave their names and addresses, two males, one female. All had been checked out as genuine passers-by, she reports.

In a statement given later when the initial panic died down, the woman witness recalled seeing two men. One was a six-footer, mid-twenties, the other six inches shorter and older. Both were black, in dark hooded tracksuits. They were stumbling, rather than running, towards a car-park some distance away.

Both black, I repeat to myself, closing my eyes momentarily in frustration. We can definitely rule out Tring as the safe-blower now.

The sergeant dispatched the nearest patrol. Kirk dispatched the H crew.

'The C crew, surely?' Cameron queries. 'Since A and B had been used.'

'No,' she corrects him. Kirk had designated A and B to the first teams to be engaged, but only because both their jobs had been pre-arranged.

The rest had been scattered about various locations in the city and county. It was never part of the planning that he should call them out in strict alphabetical order. H was at the Minster, nearest to Hall Street. Police, fire, ambulance and the H crew arrived more or less at the same time.

The sergeant continues, 'You could tell from the pictures Kirk was getting back on his portable that the fire was centred on the floor above the bank. It didn't seem to bother him.'

The bigger the fire got, the more engines turned up, the more excited he became. 'Spontaneous, he called it.'

The reporter on the fire, a seasoned performer, appeared in shot, hinting that the bank, rather than the office above, had been the target. A bank job is sexier, I suppose.

'There was no mention on TV of the two fleeing men seen by the passers-by,' Cameron observes.

'We didn't know about them until the officers at the scene had interviewed all the 999 callers in more detail.'

'Did you subsequently act upon that info?' Cameron asks.

'We hadn't got a make or number for any getaway car, but, yes, we did alert all patrols to watch out for two black men on the move.'

'Any result?'

'Two were stopped on the A1. A heavyweight boxer and his trainer. They were alibied.'

'You were nice to them, I hope,' responds Cameron with an engaging smile.

The only incident that happened during the blaze, the sergeant continues, was a report that a Whitby-bound fishing smack was being towed into Scarborough after a minor fire on board. She offered it to Kirk.

'No waterborne crews, too samey, small fry anyway,' he decided.

The flames above the bank under control, the commentary becoming repetitive, Kirk opted to return to the dog track in good time for the build-up to the 9.45, the Golden Globe Invitational.

We watch the parade, crowd scenes, tic-tac men signalling in indecipherable semaphore, the bookies taking bets, and listen to the commentator urgently reporting a sudden surge of money for Jaffa Cake which brought its odds spiralling down to even. The former evens favourite, High Society, drifted out to five-to-two against, but won anyway. A betting coup gone wrong, I suspect.

Once more I see Golden Balls, hear his not so modulated tones – 'For your collection' – as he hands over the trophy to the winning owner.

It was while the winner, High Society, was on the home straight that the call that took Voss to his death came through to the control room, the sergeant resumes.

The video is turned off. The tape machine is switched on again. 'Trouble at the Shuffle.' A man's voice, almost as southern as Tom's, the driver, but more muffled. 'Spilling out into the street. Looks close to a riot to me.' The line goes dead.

The sergeant activitated a button that called up the number of the public phone box from which the 999 call was made. The location surprised her. It wasn't round the corner from the Riverboat Shuffle, from which a genuine call might have come, but a box outside the car-park near Hall Street, a good distance away.

Cameron looks at me, frowning, then turns back to the sergeant. 'What did you make of that?'

'I didn't come to an immediate conclusion,' she wisely replies. 'It could have been a hoax or a genuine call from someone who had driven past the Shuffle, saw trouble and drove on before making up his mind to report it.'

Cameron nods approval. 'It happens. So what did you do?'

'Dispatched the nearest patrol . . .' She flicks her head towards the railway station. '. . . based in the forecourt . . .'

'Whose shadow was Voss's crew?' Cameron puts in.

She nods. ' . . . and detached an officer from the fire in Hall Street to check the phone box.' She shakes her head. 'He found nothing.'

Off with the tape and on with the video to watch Voss being jerked violently against the passenger door as his Land Rover van takes a corner sharply. Or, at least, he appears to be thrown about. I'm no longer sure how much of this show is play-acting, hamming it up.

'We are on our way to . . .' he gabbles. I know the script so well now that I'm only having to half listen, other things on my mind, notably: Did one of those two black men fleeing the scene of the fire stop and make that 999 call? Is this the missing connection between the safe-blowing and the shooting?

I concentrate again. From the angle of the shot, the cameraman must be behind the driver. He trains through the windscreen to home in on the police car ahead sceeching to a halt, brake lights bright.

Brighter still in the background are the flashing, multicoloured lights in their tubes on the letters which spell out Riverside Shuffle.

Voss opens his door but doesn't pull back his seat to permit a quick exit for his colleague with his cumbersome equipment.

The cameraman trails a long way behind, Voss out of sight now. In vision are two officers talking loudly to two broad-shouldered young men in dinner jackets. 'Not tonight, no. Not out front,' protests one doorman. 'That's what the caller said,' insists a PC. Then, turning to his fellow officer, 'Let's try round the side.'

They run, shaky camera following, into the alley, almost tripping over Voss, who lies on his side, blood running between cobblestones around his head.

One officer kneels. The other is overheard summoning an ambulance through a radio attached to his collar.

The voice of doom comes in. 'We're not quite sure what's happening, but we'll be back after the news.'

Cameron switches off. He begins to question the control room sergeant in fine detail about the complaints he's getting from MPs over the non-availability of patrols to accompany the ambulances with the mother in premature labour and the woman in trauma after watching the death scene I've now witnessed for the umpteenth time.

Nothing to do with me, this. Mentally, I switch off too and stay that way through the evidence of the two patrolmen who found Voss, my mind churning.

An examination now, a very slow one, of the scenes of crime material, police photos, forensic reports, witness statements, detectives and experts coming in one at a time to explain and theorise.

No noise on the film hinted at gunfire but the enhancement of the soundtrack is not yet complete, says the last specialist we hear.

Nobody could explain why Voss headed for the side door, says the acting CID chief, the final witness.

'If he'd been there before,' I venture, 'he may have known that's where he might find any trouble.'

'Our background inquiries have established that he was a Friday night regular,' says the superintendent.

Cameron thanks him politely, but before the superintendent stands, he slips me a folded piece of paper.

I open it up, reading two neat handwritten paragraphs, formally prefixed (A) and (B). (A) tells me that the Cavalier driver's story checks out. (B) tells me that Pepper lives in the same block of flats as Clive Voss and his current car is a white Toyota MR2.

Alone in my room, I view the *Cause for Concern* item again to study Pepper and his two fellow witnesses who helped free Tring and libel Inspector Herrick.

All have wide bodies built either in the gym or on steroids. All have the same slow swagger. All have not much more than five o'clock shadow for hair.

Bouncers run a cutter over their hair daily, so that in a rough-house there's nothing to pull and hang on to.

Surprisingly, Pepper has no thin lines shaved down to the skin in what little hair is left, signs by which a Yardie signifies to which posse he belongs back home.

He'd a right to be here in this hotel and at the soccer match yesterday, I conclude, and an unquestionable excuse for being at the flats since he lives there. No point, then, in pulling him in and quizzing him; not yet.

Aching head on pillow, sore eyes closed, I go through it again and again in my mind. Nothing new forces its way in because it's too full already with the knowledge that I've been studying the wrong bloody videos.

The answer to all of this had been in McMichael's safe in his law office and, blast it, no one will ever see what was in that Jiffy bag now.

The bedside phone rings. 'Hi. It's me.' My Em. Just the sound of her voice brings a smile to my face. 'What you up to?'

'Resting,' I reply, not lifting my head from the pillow.

'That busy, huh?'

She tells me of her day and our daughter's, seeks reassurance that I'll be home, if not for the weekend, in good time for Christmas.

Two days away and I miss them already, just can't get into a seasonal mood without them around. I always used to moan about the crowds, the traffic and all the hassle, but these days I love it – love meeting up with old pals, seeing the joyful anticipation on the faces of kids, hearing the carols, the general buzz. Suddenly, I feel out of it, a stranger.

'Yes,' I promise and immediately I feel better.

She wants to know what I'm doing tonight. A boring dinner, I reply, as if I hadn't eaten enough today, with Cameron and a county MP determined to put in his twopennyworth; an excuse for an early start to his holiday from the Commons and to get his name in the papers.

'How goes the case?' she asks.

'An afternoon before the TV set watching videos.'

'Not blue, I hope.' A low laugh.

'Only in the title,' I sigh.

'Bored?' She always senses my mood. 'You'd have been better off watching one of those interminable detective series that drive me to bed early.'

'Why?'

'Well, whenever the action flags, they just toss in another corpse, don't they?'

'Not in real life,' I say, cheering up.

The phone goes down after smacked kisses and rings again almost immediately.

Operations Room have a message from the chief constable for Mr Cameron, who is not in his room, I hear.

I offer to take it.

It's so startling that I automatically pull myself up on the bed while I listen.

10

On the A64 to the coast, Tom has the Daimler at a constant twenty miles an hour above the national speed limit; too fast in rain that's now very heavy; not fast enough for the frail, care-worn woman at my side in the back.

'Please,' she mutters, 'just get me there.'

Mrs Tring had accepted my offer of a lift and ran upstairs in her semi to pack a bag after I broke the news that her husband was in hospital and might be there for some time.

She left me waiting in the hallway, not for long, so I could only gain an impression of their two-up, two-down. The carpet that ran through the small hall and up the stairs was plain mid-green, not new, but clean. The leafy patterned wallpaper was fading, the paint on the cream door chipped here and there.

The tiny front garden had a saturated, shaggy square lawn and roses that hadn't been dead-headed, let alone autumn-pruned. The impression gained was of a house that had been bought on the cheap from the council and of a woman struggling with no man about it.

'When was he taken in?' she'd wanted to know as she locked and tried the front door. 'Friday, about half-ten,' I'd replied.

'Why wasn't I told before?' she'd demanded hurrying down the short concrete path, small bag in one hand, pulling up the collar of a thick, well-used herringbone coat with the other.

'Because he was registered under the name of a Dutch seaman,' I'd answered, almost trotting at her side, 'and we didn't find out until this evening. I came straight away.'

The most difficult question of all – 'What state's he in?' – came as Tom clocked sixty driving through the outlying estate where we collected her.

'Serious, I'm afraid.' More than that, in truth. He's dying from seventy per cent burns. His kidneys are certain to fail – and soon. The doctors can break that news.

She's about Gabby's age, fifty, her mousy brown hair flecked with grey. Like him, she's small, looks all the more so huddled in the corner in her oversized coat that she'd declined to remove, despite the heat in here.

At journey's end, when the truth is told, she will be unfit for questioning. The way Tom's driving isn't leaving me much time, so I'd better make a start. 'When were you last in touch with him?'

'He phoned every day since he came out on bail,' she replies. 'Thursday was the last time. Then nothing, not a word since. Been worried sick.'

'When did you last see him?'

'Had a long weekend together down in Brighton after he was released.' A sad smile. 'Smashing time. Lovely hotel. Never been there before.'

70

They travelled back to London together. He put her on a train home from King's Cross. 'He had to stay in the Smoke, he said, to sort things out with his barrister for the new trial. Promised he'd be home well before Christmas.'

Like me, I think, with a sudden, heart-tugging pang of homesickness.

No point in asking who funded the stay in London and the hotel in Brighton. Whoever hired him to blow McMichael's safe and get at those bloody videos. He wouldn't have given her his name or told her he was lying low, preparing for the raid.

I move her back to his conviction for the gems job at the stately home fifteen months ago. 'Did he ever complain that Inspector Herrick, sergeant as she was then, manufactured the evidence against him?'

A firm headshake. 'Not to me. Not in all the time I was visiting him and I trailed all over, once a month.' She lists the jails he'd been in, some a twelve-hour return journey away.

'Why did he appeal then?'

'Somebody inside put him up to it,' she says bitterly. 'You know what they're like, some of them. Nothing better to do than read law books all day. "If he's that clever, why's he in here?" I asked him.'

'What did he say to that?'

'Just shrugged, as always, and said, "May as well give it a go. Nothing to lose." '

Only his life, I brood.

Yes, she says, she'd seen the *Cause for Concern* programme, but had never met Clive Voss or heard of Con Clarence. She knew of Golden Globe Entertainments and Alex Ball, but only because she had seen the *Celebs* show; not much else to do on her own every night than watch telly.

'I had no idea about those three blokes who said they were drinking with him at the time of the job,' she adds.

She recounts another chat with her husband – again verbatim. 'Why didn't they come forward at your first trial?' she'd asked him. 'You might have got off.' 'I was badly defended,' he'd replied. 'I'm getting a better brief for the appeal.'

She'd attended the hearing at the appeal court in the Strand. 'I was able to see him in the cells twice a day,' she adds, pitifully grateful.

71

'Do you believe the new evidence?' I ask.

'Never know what to believe, what to make of what he gets up to,' she replies with a look of resignation. 'Thirty years we've been married, half of them apart, bringing up two bairns. The next job was always going to be the big one, the last one, to set us up for life.'

'Did he send money from London?'

'A few quid, that's all. Said that when he wins the retrial there'll be lots in compensation for wrongful arrest and detention and things. A new home, a place by the sea, perhaps, a second honeymoon. He promised.'

A thoughtful moment. 'Oh, Lord,' she groans.

I wait for some important revelation, but all that's happened is that the thought has jumped into her jumbled mind that she hasn't informed her bairns – a boy and a girl, now man and woman, both married, parents themselves, and living away. She starts to weep softly.

All I can do is to promise to make contact and then stay silent, too, as the Daimler, windscreen wipers on overtime, sprays like a speedboat down dual carriageway that's as black as liquorice.

They'd cleaned away the smoke grime from his face and hands that had made the woman witness outside the bank chambers think he was black.

All I can see beneath crepe and gauze are dark eyes, nostrils to which a drip is attached, cracked lips and fingernails. In a shiny cream smock, he lies, very tiny, on a huge white air-bed.

He doesn't raise his head or a hand when she stands over him. She can't kiss his cracked lips or hold hands that are curled in tight balls.

'How are you, love?' she asks with a brave smile.

A gleam shines in his dark eyes.

'Don't you worry. The bairns will be here soon,' she says softly. She wiggles a thumb towards me, standing at her shoulder. 'He'll tell 'em. Promised. Straight away.'

His eyes move from her to me as she goes on, 'He brought me over in no time at all, as soon as we heard, in a real posh car. He's a detective. He's been ever so kind. He wants to know what happened.'

The gleam in his eyes becomes a glint. His cracked lips tighten together.

Not telling, Gabby is telling me.

'This black fella...'

No doubts in my mind that the fella being spoken about now is black because an experienced nurse is doing the talking and she's black herself.

'...well, he came running into Casualty and said he'd got a seaman in the back of his car who'd been in an accident, a boiler burst. Two orderlies took a trolley out and wheeled him in.'

A hospital administrator, young, dark and intense, breaks in, reading from notes. 'Admission logged at 10.25 p.m., Friday.'

Almost an hour after the blast at the bank chambers, I calculate; a fast drive, but not equal to Tom's time in our Daimler from York to here.

'Massive burns about an hour old,' adds the Asian junior doctor who'd examined him on admission. 'All consistent with the story we were getting from his supposed Samaritan.'

'The timing ties in, don't you see?' asks the administrator, a touch pleadingly.

Anxious to prove no cock-up on his part, he is getting ahead of the story that's been told around his desk at the hospital, a smart, modern building, half-way up a dark hill on the outskirts of town. His small office is overcrowded with the five of us, two sitting, three standing, including me.

'He told me they were from a Dutch vessel that had had a boiler burst just outside the harbour and had been towed in,' the nurse explains.

I've caught up now. 'So when you checked with the police and the coastguards they confirmed they'd had a report of that accident about 9.30?'

Ties up, too, with what that woman sergeant in the operations room told us this afternoon. A Whitby-bound boat with a minor fire. She'd offered the incident to Kirk for possible inclusion in *Friday, the 13th Blues*. He'd shown no interest.

'Correct.' The administrator is nodding. 'And it would take about that length of time to sail into the harbour, moor and bring him here.'

'Did he say, this black guy, why he hadn't called an ambulance to the harbour?' I ask.

'He was meeting the boat, an agent or something, had a car on the quayside and thought it would be quicker,' the nurse replies. 'The orderly got the car number.'

I look at the detective sergeant, a woman of about thirty, a sharp-featured brunette called Howard, in a sharp grey suit. Her cross-checking cracked this end for us.

'A bronze-coloured Rover reported stolen from a city centre car-park late Friday, found near the racecourse back in York next day,' she states crisply.

The nurse and administrator start to read from notes. The black man gave his own name as Aron Veltman, the patient's name as Johan Mulder and a care-of address and phone number of a company in Rotterdam which leased the boat *Goud Wereld*.

The sergeant pats her green notebook, informing me: Got that, too.

'He spoke English...' says the nurse.

'So does Mr Mu...er, Tring, when he's conscious,' interrupts the doctor whose eyelids are so heavy that he may well have been on duty since Friday, the lot of junior doctors in the NHS.

'They all do in Holland,' interjects the adminstrator, 'so we didn't suspect anything was amiss.'

'He spoke with a Jamaican accent, I'd say,' the nurse finally gets to say. With a flashing smile, she chuckles, 'We Caribs are all over.'

'Got the description, sir,' says the sergeant respectfully with another touch of her book.

'We'd no idea the patient was English with a wife forty miles away, or that the car was stolen,' says the administrator with a bit of a whine. 'His boss, at least he said he was his boss, phoned up twice for progress reports and we phoned that Rotterdam number once when his condition deteriorated. "Single, no family to travel over," he told me. Everything appeared to be in order.'

'No one's blaming anybody,' I say, to break up the meeting.

'I asked for the stolen Rover to be held at the pound and not returned to the owner without your say-so,' says Sergeant Howard when we're alone. 'Too late, I'm afraid.'

Looking worried, she goes on, 'The boat left for Holland on Saturday, sorry to say.' She opens her book. 'I'll give you those Rotterdam details.'

'You stick with it.' I give her a grateful smile, well deserved. 'Why change a winning team?'

Don't phone the number direct, I instruct her. Give it to the Dutch police and let them check it out on the QT.

'Do you think you are winning?' she asks, returning my smile, relaxing, feeling, I hope, part of the team.

All I tell her is: 'At least we're in the race.'

The winning post is a long way off yet, I tell myself, and it was a slow start but we're finally out of the trap and running.

Voss, I'm convinced, plotted with Golden Balls to get Tring out of jail with the aim of blowing McMichael's safe to get at those videos.

What's on them, or at least one of them, must be dynamite.

Tring somehow bungled it and blew himself up. Strange, that, for an expert.

His look-out, the black guy, pulls him from the debris, carries him out, steals a car to get him to hospital. Not the local district hospital on the doorstep, the first place the CID would have looked.

But why here? And how did he know about the explosion aboard the *Goud Wereld*? He can't have driven to the harbour on the off-chance, picked up the news there, used it as cover. No, he must have known the *Goud Wereld* would be here. Maybe that boiler blast was a put-up job so the boat could come in here and not Whitby. Maybe he wanted the skipper to take Tring out of the country, dump him overboard when finally he died.

Instead, he used the blast story as a reason to get rid of Tring at the hospital, a good story that's held up – and held us up – for five days and nights. Then he fled back to York.

I ask for the black man's description. Six foot, thickset, wearing a black tracksuit, Jamaican accent, thirtyish and handsome face.

It all points to Pepper. I ponder whether to send Tom back for the *Cause for Concern* film, play it through for everyone who saw the man who brought Tring into hospital. Or whether to go back myself, collar Pepper and bring him here for an ID parade.

I'm on the verge of solving the safe-blowing. I know that. But solving the shooting is my brief. Solve one, I've already decided, and you solve the other. But, then again, if I nick Pepper and he says nothing, I'm stymied on the murder. I need something else, some leverage, to get him to talk.

Sergeant Howard is slipping down an elastic band that keeps her page place in her notebook, freeing a white fax message. 'There's something else I've been asked to pass on.' She hands it to me.

It's a message from HQ who, as Cameron had ordered, have been back into the records of thefts at pits and quarries.

'Useful?' she asks.

I nod, thinking: Dynamite.

Don't ask me what I'm doing here, standing in the wind and the rain in an elegant clifftop square, listening to the waves rolling on to the sands far below, looking down on the harbour with its white lighthouse.

Tom didn't, as he parked and I got out. I couldn't have answered anyway, because I don't really know myself. Only that I need this private minute, this memory, that's all.

At my back is the hotel in its smart terrace where we stayed, my grandparents and me, for a week's holiday every summer for seven years; same week, same crowd.

Not as grand as the massive Grand Hotel opposite, with marble pillars, white veranda railings and leaded domes, but clean and comfortable with good cooking.

Across the square, next to the Grand, is the lift down to South Bay where I'd dig in the sands, oblivious to the wind that came off the sea; sometimes so cold, even in August, that grandma wore a coat as thick as Mrs Tring as she sat in a deckchair and watched over me.

It was on that beach that grandad taught me cricket, the love of his life, even more so than Derby County; how to play a straight bat and spin a wet tennis ball on the flat, hard sand after the tide had gone out.

They raised me, the result of a fling their daughter had in her college days. She's thrice married, lives on the other side of the world. We're good pals, penpals mostly, these days, but I never call her 'Mother' and she has no part in moments like these.

Hope Mrs Tring and her bairns have some good memories, too. Not that they'll be much use in the numbed, muddled weeks to come; too painful. But soon, though, in time, memories can help.

My grandad died suddenly when I was fourteen. Gran and I never went on holiday that year and the following year it was North Wales. After that, I went off to new places with my best mate while she toured the likes of Southern Ireland and the Alps on a coach with a close friend. We never came back here, ever.

My grandma passed away almost three years ago, peacefully in hospital, after a long illness, so I've no comparable experience of what Mrs Tring will be going through now, watching him go – too young, too soon, but, in his agony, not soon enough.

I hope that in a few months happy recollections will return for her, as mine are now. I think of graduating from playing beach cricket to watching a first-class game with Test players down at that cosy, friendly ground on the other bay, sitting in a deckchair, eating dressed crab from its shell. I remember as if it were this evening walking over that long bridge to my right over the valley to the Floral Hall to listen to music, the love of grandma's life, being played by Max Jaffa and ...

Jaffa, I repeat with a start.

Jaffa. Jaffa Cake. Scarborough. Code? Was that dog's name some kind of coded message?

All thoughts of Mrs Tring, all warm memories of my grandfolks vanish as, cold-hearted bastard that I am, I feel myself rounding the first bend, gaining on the field all the time.

11

SIX DAYS TO CHRISTMAS

'!'

That's a bloody good start to a new and dreadful day, I brood, passing a road sign displaying just a single exclamation mark at the foot of a deeply rutted hill down which rainwater rushes in dark torrents.

'Danger!' warns the next notice fifty yards further up the hill which becomes so steep and muddy that a four-wheel truck is making protesting work of it, travelling at nowhere near the twenty mile an hour limit imposed throughout the colliery.

An extra slice of black pudding from the serve yourself counter in the hotel breakfast room repeats on me.

'Keep Out. Quicksands and Slurry!' says a third sign, black words on yellow triangles, on top of black-and-white striped poles.

The brow of the hill is slowly breasted and ! ! !

It's as though we have landed on another planet. Acre upon never-ending acre of waste from the bowels of the earth stretch out before us.

The Land Rover, streaked with grime, scrunches to a stop on a surface that's more grey than black.

Ahead, as far as the eye can see in this downpour, is a rough shale roadway, fifty yards wide. Each side is a series of still lagoons, banks so black it seems the tide has just gone out after a disastrous oil spill.

Four hundred yards away dumper trucks with giant wheels are filling their backs from a constant stream of ash-like spoil that pours from a high, filthy hopper, itself supplied via an enclosed conveyor belt that runs downhill towards the pit yard. Further on, a massive bulldozer is sculpturing hillocks from the loads they deliver.

I adjust my safety hat, wishing it had a nose mask as well as unused ear muffs. A foul smell is so strong that I pull a face and sniff loudly.

'Nowt to do with waste,' says my driver, not Tom this trip. 'We manured the outer hills of all tips before seeding 'em. Come spring sheep will be grazing on 'em and no one will know what's here.' He switches off the idling engine.

I wrap a borrowed yellow cape around me and get out, good leg first. The surface crunches and crumbles beneath green wellington boots. A wind from the east cuts at my face.

The colliery's assistant manager, just as colourfully attired, joins me at the back of the vehicle. He's fair-haired, blue eyes alert, young for such a senior position, slightly built for such a tough job, in which he obviously takes great pride.

Down below, in his warm office, going through the story for the first time, he paid meticulous attention to detail, as they have to in the mining industry where lives depend upon it.

Wind at our backs, we gaze down on the pit yard, very small

from here. Only the railway lines look Toytown. The headstocks aren't the Meccano type I've grown used to in the coalfield on my patch, but are clad in smart brickwork.

He points to a single-storey building, surrounded by rusting scrap metal. The magazine, he'd called it, where explosives are locked away and stored in cool darkness. 'Got your bearings?'

I manage a frozen nod.

He starts to reprise the story, raising his voice to be heard over the rapid drumming of the rain on our capes.

It was a Sunday, six weeks ago, about dawn. The pit wasn't coaling that day because of essential maintenance work. Few workers were about.

He drove into the yard and saw a big, dark figure fleeing from the direction of the pile of rusting metal. 'We sometimes have trouble with gypos, coming in, nicking scrap.'

He gave chase, through the yard, over the railway line, by the huge wash box and up the hill in front of us.

'Like I said, he was big, but fit and fast and I didn't get that close, but close enough to see he was no gypo, him being black, like, at the neck of his tracksuit.'

'Sure he wasn't an underground worker on his way to the baths?' I grin, thinking of Pepper again.

He grins back at what's admittedly a racist joke, but no worse than the one about the white worker in the flour mill in darkest Africa, which ends, 'He was in the crust on the pie you just ate, bwana.'

My witness describes how he gave up the chase at about the spot where we're standing, watching his quarry lengthen his strides down the shale roadway.

Turning, he points into the wind. 'Up there.' It's 9.30 in the morning, but darker than dusk. In this visibility, I have to concentrate to make out a line of trees at the far end of the tip, well beyond where the heavy vehicles are working.

He returned to the pit yard and found that the locks on the magazine's outer door and to a temperature-controlled locker where explosives are kept had both been snapped. 'Three sticks were missing; new stock, much more powerful than the explosives they used to use,' he goes on.

He called the police who sent out Special Branch, my old department. They took the view that it wasn't a terrorist raid because the thief would have taken off with every stick and shot him for good measure. They bounced it back to CID who did the routine, found a bolt-cutter among the scrap, but no trace of a waiting getaway vehicle. No arrest had yet been made.

'So,' he says, swivelling round, surveying the utterly desolate scene rather fondly. 'Whatya think?'

'Very useful, thanks,' I reply honestly, turning, too, hearing the made-up ground give beneath my feet, feeling as though I'm on egg shells.

'No. No.' One flap of his cape rises as he motions with a hand inside it round the bleak, sodden landscape. 'Wouldn't know it was here, would you?'

I voice the thought that came when I first set eyes on it. 'Like an alien planet.'

'Yes,' he says, with a pleasurable smile, 'that's what TV thought.'

I hold my breath.

'That bloke – Voss, the one who was shot – and his mate.'

Almost breathless, I can only mumble, 'Run through that for me, too, will you?'

'Let's get back in the cab,' he pleads.

Behind the driving wheel, not restarting the engine, he moves his story on.

Towards the end of September, his boss called him in. The public relations department had been on from head office. They'd been approached by TV producers scouting locations for a science fiction film. They wanted to visit for a preliminary recce. He was deputed to escort them.

A white Land Rover van with a satellite dish on top and 'Voss Vision' on the side turned up. Voss, whom he recognised from seeing him so often on screen, introduced himself and his companion whose name he couldn't remember. Con Clarence, I'm pretty sure, when he runs through a description.

He showed them round the yard, the full VIP tour, then accompanied them up here in their van.

I take him back a bit. 'Did they see the lot? I mean...' A cover question now. 'The hopper and the wash box, for instance?'

80

'Everything, more or less.'

I break cover now. 'And the magazine?'

A brief nod. 'The story calls for some explosives to be on hand, they said.'

I lapse into a contented silence, almost preening. When I drew back the bedroom curtains this morning and looked out, I almost decided to do this interview on the telephone, save a bit of time or keep dry. Why not? Every other cop seems to do it these days.

'You learn so much, much more by taking the trouble of turning out and just chatting,' my old grandad used to say in his days on the rural beat. He was a better cop than most.

'Very impressed, they were,' the assistant manager chatters on. 'Thought the whole set-up was ideal. A moonscape, Voss's mate called it. Took loads of pictures. With an ordinary camera, not cine, to show to their associates, they said. Thought it was just the job.'

Holy Moses, I'm almost singin' in the rain.

Voss got a pictorial record of the colliery's whole set-up, the magazine, this escape route if disturbed, so Pepper (no, let's not jump to conclusions), so this black accomplice could get away with the dynamite.

Then Voss organised the filming of the safe, the actual target, for Tring to study before he blew it.

A brilliant operation, fatally marred by the fact that Tring, just out of jail and out of touch with advanced explosives, used much more than was needed.

A brilliant theory, I acknowledge, no longer so thrilled, flawed by the fact that Voss wouldn't have gone to all this trouble to get something out of his own lawyer's safe. All he had to do was ask McMichael for it. Unless, of course, there was something else in there, other than videos, something that didn't belong to him which McMichael wouldn't have handed over.

What? I can't think. Stick to facts, I urge myself, not theories.

Carefully, I recheck the dates, confirming that both the dynamite theft and Voss's visit here came after the *Celebs* programme featuring Ball, but before the *Cause for Concern* about Tring.

That, I conclude, means Golden Balls could have funded Voss for Tring's release and the safe-blowing operation under the guise of backing the sci-fi film.

81

Through the windscreen my eyes range a wilderness too barren for wildlife or weeds. 'How did Voss know it was here?'

'Sorry?' He turns towards me, looking perplexed, his cape rustling.

'Well, you can't see it from the road and you said yourself...'

'Ah.' He sees what I mean. He nods towards the long, shale roadway and the trees in the distance. 'One of their partners has a shoot down there.'

My turn to look lost.

'This film idea of theirs, right?'

He begins to talk to me as though I am a dim apprentice, so I oblige him with an uncertain nod.

'There's a scene, see, where a spacecraft or some UFO or something lands by mistake and causes a toxic fallout. They'd been searching all over for a suitable location. One of their partners, a sleeping partner, they said, knew about this place 'cos he shoots next door and he put them on to it.'

Heart in my mouth, I can't bear to ask the real question in case his answer comes as a bitter disappointment, so I skirt round it. 'Do you know him too?'

'Course. Patrols his bloody land every Sunday teatime, in or out of the shooting season, regular as clockwork. Complains every time a lagoon overflows a few drops on to it that we're killing his game chicks or toxics in the air are killing his trees. I'm the weekend duty manager, so it's always down to me. I'm often late away 'cos of him. Pound to a pinch of shit, he'll be on moaning this Sunday, if this rain keeps up.' He grits his teeth. 'Bald-headed bastard.'

Before it's asked, he answers the real question. 'Name of Ball, that big entertainments bloke. Know him?'

I shake my head, smiling, can't stop myself, seeing myself so close behind the leader of the race now that I'm sniffing at his golden balls.

12

No answer comes to repeated knocks on the outer door. I try the handle. It's unlocked. I step out of the still pouring rain on to brown carpet tiles in a porch, no warmer inside than out, and finger a bell on the white frame of an inner door with fluted glass.

Another long wait, anxiety mounting. Knew it was too easy, I fret. You expect to meet an informant, certainly another officer's informant, in a car or a park or, ever since Robert Redford and Deep Throat in *All the President's Men*, a car-park, not be invited into his home.

He's changed his mind, done a runner or someone may have got here before me. Knew it was too bloody good to be true. What did my Em say about police thrillers on TV? Throw in another body. I ring again, longer.

Finally a shadow approaches, a broken blue figure, pixilated by the fluted glass.

The door opens. Such is my relief that the beam on my face is genuine and the matey introduction honed in the car sitting beside Tom comes easily. 'Hi. Thanks for seeing me. Sorry I was so rude on Tuesday.'

'All right.' Con Clarence smiles rather ruefully. 'Doubt if I'd have agreed to this if you'd been more forthcoming. Can't be too careful, can we?'

'No,' I concur as he looks beyond me and the unkempt front garden towards a dank road of semis with dripping trees. The only vehicle he'll see outside is his company's own white 'Voss Vision' truck, Tom and the Daimler out of sight round the corner.

He opens the door wider and waves me into a hall with rust-coloured carpeting that hasn't been vacuumed for some days. He shuts it, then guides me into a kitchen where a yellow plastic laundry basket sits empty on a cluttered breakfast bar. 'Sorry if you had to wait.' He nods towards a washing machine with a misted porthole. 'The final rinse makes such a din.'

He should have laundered his stained, ill-fitting denim trousers while he was at it. His matching shirt, though clean, is unpressed.

He finally notices that I am trailing drops of water from my off-white mac, beneath which a brown suit is having its first Yorkshire airing. Now that I am standing still, the drops are joining each other into a spreading pool on the tiled floor. He tells me to take off my coat and hang it on the back of a stool at the breakfast bar.

Then, with a fussy little flourish, he gestures towards a transparent jug standing on a wide ledge beside a full sink. Above it, the kitchen window runs with condensation inside and rain outside, totally obscuring any view of the back garden. 'Coffee?'

'Love one,' I say sincerely.

While he transfers a load of twisted washing, mixed colours, from the machine to a spin-drier, he apologises for the mess – 'a hectic week'. He asks me to plunge the cafetière and get milk out of the fridge. I do as I'm told.

The waxed carton is on its sell-by date and there's little else inside the fridge apart from a jar of Marmite, lard, margarine and some hard-looking cheese. His task completed, he takes over the job of pouring the coffee and milk into two unmatched mugs.

He leads me, each of us carrying a mug, into a quite cold lounge with a dull dining-table and six chairs at the kitchen end and bronze-coloured three-, two- and one-seaters towards the front window. There's no Christmas tree or seasonal decorations.

Passing a dark teak unit along the wall I catch glimpses of a not very big pile of Christmas cards that haven't been put on display and of framed photos. One features a brunette in a white wedding gown with a morning-suited Clarence at her side.

She no longer shares this place, I deduce. No woman does, judging from the almost empty fridge, the undisplayed cards and a cactus on the windowsill that is dying instead of flowering.

Like Voss, his boss, he lives alone. Now, it's no more politically correct to speculate about two closely associated singles of the same sex than it is about blacks driving flash cars, but that's not going to stop me thinking about it in passing.

He takes the three-seater and motions me to the two-seater at right angles to him and facing a TV set in the corner. He sips his coffee politely. 'What did Inspector Herrick tell you?'

'Only where and when you'd see me,' I reply, accurately.

'No notes?' he says anxiously.

I put my mug on a slate place mat on a small table next to the wall, spread my hands, then pat the front of my jacket. 'Or tapes.'

A curious smile. 'Where shall I begin?'

'Well,' I reply, reclaiming my drink and inching myself back to be comfortable for what could be a longish chat, 'you're the journalist. Tell it in your own way and time.'

'At the beginning then?'

He's twenty-five, a surprise. At our first meeting at the hotel on that first afternoon, I'd mentally made him at least five years older.

He came to York as a student at an arts college. Instead of going home for the long vacs, he took menial part-time work for menial pay at Ridings TV; more or less the messenger boy. 'To be near Liz,' he adds, not explaining who she is.

With graduation came a full-time job at Ridings, not in the drama department on which he'd set his heart, but as an editorial assistant in the newsroom, fixing up interviews, often suggesting the question-line to presenters like Voss.

Clarence himself was judged not to have the presence for on-screen appearances. In an industry that often puts presentation before content, this is certainly no surprise.

His small face has a twitchy left eye. His complexion is too flaked for pancake make-up to do much about. He mumbles in a West Country burr that's difficult to cut through with the drier spinning behind the closed kitchen door.

He'll never get to earn the astronomical fees charged by TV personalities, even weather girls these days, for opening shops and galas.

'Liz...' No explanation still. '...wanted a nice wedding, you know, with all the trimmings, and a honeymoon and a place of our own, so we didn't get married till two years ago.'

He gets up stiffly and walks to the wall unit, talking as he does so. 'Lived together before, of course. She comes from a big family, not very well off.'

He returns with the wedding photo which I take, looking through cracked glass down on Liz's exceptionally attractive face – black hair, bright brown eyes, high cheekbones, wide mouth.

The crack in the glass makes me wonder if things were thrown in the final bust-up, not really listening as he returns to his seat, talking about her parents having a small cottage in the middle of nowhere, difficult to get back and forth to the calculating agency where she worked.

I'm listening now, intently.

He was head-hunted by Voss to be his right-hand man in his newly formed private production company, he continues. 'Lots more money, but lots more work, irregular hours, missed meals, weekend duties.'

About eight months ago, the marriage hit a bad patch. 'She blamed the hours I was keeping, seeing so little of me. I had to stick with it because Clive had long-term plans to get into drama, what I've always wanted. I told her to get out more, with her friends from the office.'

Six months ago he began to notice her mood swings, violent headaches, days missed from work, forgetfulness with shopping, neglecting the home. In August, he found her unconscious on the sofa where he sits. 'Thought I was going to lose her. Ecstasy, doctors diagnosed.'

He pulls a grim face. 'Suddenly everything made sense. Her spaced-out expressions, the general malaise. She's been on a variety of drugs for some time.'

In hospital, she confided to him that she'd been buying them at the Riverside Shuffle, a regular haunt on girls' nights out from the office.

At that time he and Voss were working on the *Celebs* series. They spent two days filming Alex Ball at his home near Skipwith Common.

During one break for lunch, a camera with built-in microphone was inadvertently left running in the stable block office while they all ate outside in the sunshine.

Back in the offices of Voss Vision in Hall Street he played over the day's work. Ball could be heard, but not seen, discussing – on the phone, he presumed – the impending arrival on Friday, September 13, at an unspecified destination of a consignment of drugs.

'Well...' Clarence sighs and gathers himself. '...I had Liz in hospital, dangerously ill, knew where she'd got the stuff, knew who owned the place, and now I knew how it was getting in so...' He shrugs heavily and stares into his drink.

He phoned the drugs squad, arranged to meet Inspector Herrick and told her what he'd heard.

'Did you actually play her the recording?' I ask after draining my mug and putting it on the table again.

A headshake. 'I just told her what I'd overheard Ball saying in conversation, one-sided, I admit, but I gave it to her word for word.'

'Why didn't you provide the taped evidence?'

'Because I couldn't get it out of the office without Clive know-

86

ing. He heard it, too. He'd have realised where the tip to the police came from.'

'So he wasn't in on the arrangement to inform Inspector Herrick?'

A harsh laugh. 'He'd have sacked me...' Pause. '...worse, shopped me. After we'd played it through at the office, he swore me to secrecy.'

'Why?'

A sly smile. 'You work it out.'

I shake my head to tell him I can't.

'Within a month, Golden Globe Entertainments had put up a hundred thousand for the development costs of *Fallen Angel*.'

A tingle runs down to my cold toes as he enthusiastically explains that *Fallen Angel* is a story on which Voss Vision had bought an option and which he was scripting for the screen.

I'm hardly listening again. Instead, I'm thinking: Golden Balls wasn't a showbiz angel. He was the victim of blackmail. 'What happened to the recording?'

Clarence bends forward to put his empty mug at his feet and doesn't look at me as he replies. 'Clive lodged it in his solicitor's safe.'

The connection, I realised, as more than a tingle, a charge shoots through me now. At long last, the link. Ball, aided by Voss, sprang Tring to blow the safe at McMichael's law firm and get that evidence. Then he ordered the hit on his blackmailer.

'Were you involved...' I've hit the wrong word. 'Did you work on, I mean, research the Tring case for *Cause for Concern*?'

His head comes up. 'Some of the legwork, yes.'

'Tell me about that, too, will you?'

The *Celebs* series over, they began to put together the *Cause for Concern* programmes. 'Voss brought in the Tring case. Never knew his source, still don't. I read up the back issues of the *Evening Press* for his trial, and organised signed affidavits from the three new alibi witnesses.'

'Where did you get their names and whereabouts?'

'From Voss.'

'What about the safe?'

'Sorry?' His look is slightly startled.

'The Chubb safe at the law firm which featured in the TV item. You filmed it.'

'Ah.' A sheepish expression. 'I went with the cameraman, but Clive fixed for us to do it with his solicitor.'

Odd, I'm thinking, that he should admit to routine legwork but hold back on that. I'll not press him, not yet. Instead, 'Having tried to help Inspector Herrick with the tip about the September drugs shipment, did it occur to you to forewarn her in confidence that she was about to feature on TV in an unfavourable light?'

'No.' Firm, final.

'Why?'

'Well, I ran a terrible risk, still am. She didn't catch Ball, did she, or find any drugs? All she did was drop me in it, left me high and dry in a very big way.'

I'll get back to this later, too, I decide. 'Weren't you, as an experienced researcher, worried about libelling Inspector Herrick, if you got it wrong?'

'I did point out the risk, yes, but, equally, Clive pointed out he knew the law better than me, had been in the business longer. Besides, he was convinced of Tring's innocence. Or he seemed to be.'

'So he wasn't worried about a big bill for damages?'

Clarence smiles. 'The business had never been so flush.'

So Golden Balls was going to pick up the legal bill, too. I muse. Another hundred grand, at a conservative estimate, in damages and costs. Still, money well spent to destroy evidence that would not only put him in jail for years, but also result in a court order for the confiscation of his drugs-funded fortune.

What's more, *Cause for Concern* served the dual purpose of getting persistent Herrick out of the drugs squad and off the case.

I'm going to firm up my questioning. 'Did Alex Ball play any part whatsoever, funding, laying on contacts, anything, in the preparation of the Tring item?'

'Not that I know of, not directly with me, certainly.'

'But, indirectly, pulling Voss's strings?'

He begins to shrug a don't know, changes his mind. 'One of the witnesses who alibied Tring works for Ball.'

'Who?'

'Pepper.'

'The black guy?'

A nod.

'How do you know that?'

'He was at Ball's place when we were shooting *Celebs*, just hanging around, a sort of minder, I suppose. Behind his back Ball calls him Black Pepper.'

He pauses, eye twitching. 'And I had a visit from him. Pepper, I mean. Here at my home. Terrified the life out of me.' He shakes his head.

'Tell me more,' I say with an encouraging smile.

A knock came on the porch door. Pepper barged his way in when he opened it. 'He's a big bugger, you know, all muscle. He talks in a patois, hard to understand.'

It wasn't difficult to get his message. Clarence had been rumbled as a police informer. Inspector Herrick's nosying had resulted in the shipment being postponed.

'He waved a black gun with one hand. He grabbed me by the throat with the other, pushed me back there.' He flicks his head towards the two-seater where I'm sitting forward, engrossed.

'He went into the corner, by the TV and just peed up the wall on the socket. He'd shot men for less back home in Jamaica, he boasted, and would be happy to kill me. He picked up that from the shelf...' He points to the cushion where the wedding photo sits beside me. '...just dropped it on the floor and trod on it. One more word, he said, and she'd never be coming out of hospital.'

He got off lightly, I'm thinking. Why didn't Ball have him killed, or, at least, have his legs broken?

In a roundabout way, he'd partly answered the question on hold. 'So you blame Inspector Herrick for that nasty experience, do you?'

'Well, it all happened after I'd spoken to her and she started her inquiries. Pepper reckoned Ball was being tailed and suspected his line was permanently tapped. It's possible, I suppose, that she was too thorough.' He stops. 'Or careless.' He shrugs. 'I don't know. All I know is that I thought I was a dead man.'

Even more likely is that Voss discovered that Clarence had shopped Ball to the police and he shopped Clarence to Ball. Since the idea has not occurred to him, I'll not float it here and now.

'Having tried to help Inspector Herrick originally with your information, why not seek her help when you were subsequently subjected to death threats from Pepper?' I ask.

'I wanted nothing more to do with it.' He wrings his hands. 'Nothing.'

'Yet,' I continue, 'despite the terror of that experience, Pepper's threats, everything, when Inspector Herrick contacted you again, you still agreed to see me.'

I'm expecting something modest like, 'The only public-spirited thing to do now that Clive Voss has been shot dead.' Instead he becomes very agitated. 'You will protect me, won't you?'

I nod gravely.

It's not enough for him. 'Promise?'

I offer him surveillance everywhere he goes, a panic button here in his home, even a video link-up to the nearest police station.

He shakes his head. 'Just promise you'll put none of this in writing.'

He clearly knows more about the law than he was earlier letting on. These days, before a trial, there has to be full disclosure of all documents we've collected. It's an open invitation to defence lawyers to comb through our files, seeking out our tipster. Commit this to writing for them to see and pass on to Ball and I'm committing Clarence to an early grave.

'Promise,' I say.

I take him back to last Friday. With such a big area to cover and not enough staff to do it, he explains, relaxing a little, Ridings TV had asked Voss and, unusually, Clarence to be out and about in live transmission vehicles.

Clarence was assigned to the pre-planned drugs raid, freeing the more experienced Voss to respond to any impromptu, more dramatic incident.

I seek what the drugs inspector couldn't tell us – his movements after the raid.

Back to the railway station car-park with his two-man crew to await their next assignment, he replies. He remained there until about ten when news filtered through that Voss had been hurt and taken to hospital.

'All the time?' I enquire casually.

'Apart from slipping into the station refreshment bar to get us all a coffee.'

'About what time?'

'Around quarter to,' he replies, unconcerned.

About 9.45 – no alibi then at the precise time that the call was made that took his boss to his death, I think with the familiar charge of excitement.

To disguise it, I ask why he didn't appear on screen, just commentated over the drug inspector's shoulder.

'The camera should do the talking, in my view,' he replies rather primly.

This leads to a freewheeling chat about TV style and about Voss's in particular. Clarence is so lukewarm about his late boss that I wonder if his reservations are personal as well as professional.

'He made lots of enemies, you know,' he says darkly.

I recall what McMichael hinted at about the lady in Voss's life from the office above and wonder if Clarence is among those enemies.

I approach the question very carefully. 'Going back a bit, in the reconstruction of the Tring conviction, you used that Chubb safe.'

He nods, untroubled.

'At Clive's solicitor's office.'

Another nod.

'The same one that...' I just save myself from saying 'held'. '...holds the incriminating recording against Ball?'

'Yes.'

'Are you a regular visitor there?'

'Not to McMichael's, no. Clive handled all the legal stuff. But to the bank chambers, yes. Liz works...' He corrects himself. '...worked there and I used to pick her up from the calculating agency one floor up.'

A turn of the screws now, just a slight one. 'Did Voss and Liz know each other...?'

A cautious nod. 'We all had drinks together, farewell parties, barbecues, social events like that. Not lately, of course. She's still in hospital; a complete breakdown, I'm afraid.'

'Did they know each other well?' I persist.

He knows what I'm driving at, eye tic-ing. 'Not that well. Not as well as Mandy Ball, if that's what you're thinking.'

'Ball's daughter?' I blurt, can't help myself. 'What's between them?'

'Search me.' A heavy shrug. 'She comes with her daddy's hundred thou investment. She wants to be a TV actress. There has to be a part for her in *Fallen Angel*, part of the deal. I've had to write one in.'

'Were Voss and Ball's daughter an item?' I ask, making my tone more demanding.

'I don't know.' He thinks. 'Dangerous, I'd have thought.'

'Why?'

'Well, they say – it's only a rumour, mind – that she runs around with Pepper.'

I'm shocked, stumped for words. Is he saying that he suspects Pepper of killing Voss? I ask myself. If so, Pepper can't have been in on the safe-blowing and I've read this completely wrong. Go on, ask. Out with it. 'Are you saying that Pepper killed Voss?'

'No.' It jerks out. In more of a waver than a burr, he adds, 'All I'm saying is that he has a gun.'

To give myself time to think, I ask a few easy questions about the film project. Enthusiastically, back in control of himself, he trots out a not-too-quick synopsis on what strikes me as an old theme about the cover-up of a UFO landing.

I need to test if Clarence is holding anything back. Only Cameron knows that we have the source of the explosive used by Tring with self-destructive effect on the safe. I want it to stay that way, so I back into it again. 'How far advanced is the project?'

'We have a script, tested a few potential cast.'

The test question now. 'Difficult to locate, though, I'd have thought?'

His answer is immediate. 'Found the perfect spot – a pit tip down on the Selby coalfields.'

'Really!' I feign enthusiasm. 'How did you find that?'

'Alex Ball put us on to it. It's right next to some of his land. He showed us it one Sunday afternoon and we got the official OK for a full recce. Ideal.'

'So it will still go ahead?'

'Oh, yes.' He nods energetically. 'The money, the script, the location. Most things are in place.'

'Won't Clive's death alter things?'

He shakes his head firmly. 'We had a one-off partnership agreement on the film, quite separate from Voss Vision. We're insured, anyway, against any delay.'

The spin-drier finishes its final run, noisier than ever. He pleads he must start the ironing.

I must iron out my scrambling thoughts, too, the first one of which occurs as he shows me out after collecting my coat from the kitchen; the same one that first came to mind when I stepped into the porch.

His story is just too bloody good to be true.

13

To clear our heads, Cameron suggested an evening stroll while I brief him. The rain has stopped. The wind has dropped. It's unseasonably mild.

I do all the talking, rattling through it, gabbling almost, as we walk beside flower-filled, tree-dotted verges, under an arch and over a river bridge.

He puts in his only word as we pass the black gates of a park. 'Look.' He points towards a notice-board with a peeling poster for 'The York Mystery Plays'. We both laugh briefly.

Just before the floodlit Minster, one of its towers encased in scaffolding, he hesitates. With so many gates and ancient arches, he observes, it's an easy place in which to get lost.

He leads me right, somewhat uncertainly, into streets packed with late night shoppers laden with plastic bags.

From one crowded shop blares canned music, a boy soprano singing 'Walking in the Air'.

'Statistically,' he comments with a dry smile, 'Christmas is a peak period for murder; small wonder having to listen to that dreadful dirge on top of all the usual hassle and expense.'

I laugh again, feel quite calm now, confident in his company. Just as calming are the illuminations, small white lights strung among the bare branches of trees; understated and tasteful.

'Ah.' Somehow he's found what he was looking for – The Shambles, so narrow that the eaves of Tudor buildings almost touch each other across the street.

Here we dawdle, browsing in the bowed bay windows of art, book and jewellery shops, me spotting an antique brooch, a ruby surrounded by tiny pearls on a rose gold pin, that Em would love.

'So what are your thoughts?' he asks, turning, walking leisurely again.

Lost and in a shambles, to tell the truth, but you can't admit that to Britain's top cop. Nor can you close other options by saying 'My theory is...' or 'The scenario has to be...'

My eyes are straight ahead, ignoring the bustle all around me, firmly fixed on my future and the next word, the shortest in the dictionary. 'A.' I pause and reprise it. 'A possible theory has to be that Ball and Voss or Clarence or all three were in the conspiracy.'

'You don't trust Clarence, do you?' he asks, looking across his shoulder.

What he'd said about the 13 September tip checks out with Inspector Herrick, I answer. I'd caught her at her station behind the ornate courthouse as she signed on for another six-to-two shift.

'But what I can't understand, if his story's true, is why Ball didn't take revenge, have Pepper kill him or maim him.'

'Yet he stumps up a hundred thou for a project that sounds more Clarence's baby than Voss's,' says Cameron, displaying his complete grasp on my long briefing.

We walk several paces in thoughtful silence. Then, very businesslike, he says. 'Let's recap.' He pauses. 'Confirmed fact. Clarence overheard Ball arranging a drugs consignment and told Inspector Herrick. She tapped Ball's phone and trailed him. That – or something else – alerted Ball who, we presume, called off his operation.'

'That something else,' I point out, 'could have been Voss shopping Clarence to Ball.'

'Motive?' asks Cameron brusquely.

'Money. Clarence is dispensable. Researchers, scriptwriters, call him what you will, are two a penny. Millionaire angels aren't.'

He repeats the question that nags at me. 'Why didn't Ball have Clarence eliminated there and then?'

I shrug, still unsure. 'Because, by then, Voss was blackmailing him with the incriminating tape locked away in his solicitor's safe. He didn't want either of them killed and the big murder inquiry that was bound to follow.'

Cameron again, catching on. 'Not until the tape was destroyed.' Several more steps in silence. 'Put yourself in Ball's place. You're Mr Big, untouchable. A bad stroke of luck has leaked evidence of a drugs shipment to Clarence and/or Voss. You buy off Voss Vision with a hundred thousand. What's the price of Clarence's silence?'

'Haven't a clue,' I answer honestly.

He repeats that same question. 'Why wasn't he silenced for good then?'

'I don't know,' I sigh, becoming bored with it.

Cameron ponders. 'Perhaps he is telling the truth. Maybe his assistance to Inspector Herrick three months ago and to you this afternoon is a public-spirited act. Which means he's at risk.'

'Or,' I conjecture, 'it's an act of revenge for his wife's addiction. He was anxious to dump the entire Tring case on Voss and Voss's murder on Pepper. I don't think his hands are completely clean.'

Cameron looks down at the wet pavement. 'Assume, for a moment, Clarence is telling the whole truth. Take it from there.'

Easier that, and I rattle it off. Voss blackmails Ball with that recording. Ball plans to destroy it and his blackmailer. His contacts come up with Tring as the expert for the safe job.

'He's got to get him out of jail,' I go on. 'Never mind the cost or Inspector Herrick's reputation. Behind the scenes he pulls all the strings on the *Cause for Concern* item. It works, Tring is freed.

'Voss organises film of the Chubb safe and photographs of the explosives magazine, never realising he's plotting a course to his own death.

'Last Friday, Ball is well out of it at the dog track, a million or so viewers as alibi witnesses. The safe is blown. So, accidentally, is Tring. His look-out – Pepper's the favourite – takes him to Scarborough.'

I pause, expecting 'Why Scarborough?' I have an answer to 'Why not a local hospital?' Just that – local, too close. But not 'Why Scarborough?' – not a good one anyway.

Instead he says, 'Which means, of course, should you be right about Pepper, he can't have shot Voss. He was otherwise engaged, first as the look-out for Tring and then driving forty miles to take him to hospital.'

I take up the thread. 'Which means, in turn, that Ball has a hit man we haven't come across yet.'

'Yet,' repeats Cameron, ominously. Now he asks, 'Why Scarborough? Why not Leeds? Hull?'

All I can do is put into words the notion that came to me at the seaside last night. Pepper, I theorise, knew the *Goud Wereld* was coming in there, wanted rid of the dying Tring out of the country, found there was a hold-up because of the boiler burst, dropped him at the hospital instead, came back to York.

Feeling foolish, I add those other thoughts about Jaffa Cake, the greyhound that ran second in the 9.45 Golden Globe Invitation, and Max Jaffa, the violinist at the Floral Hall.

Cameron's expression is not at all incredulous. 'Heard his Palm Court orchestra on the radio many a Sunday night. A name synonymous with Scarborough, of course. So what do you make of that?'

'Well...' That foolish feeling still. '...I just wonder if Ball somehow – don't ask me how, a tame tic-tac man perhaps – put the message out to his collectors that a load of drugs was definitely coming into Scarborough. He did, after all, say "For your collection."'

'Live? On TV?' He's astonished now.

'Well,' I answer, looking down, 'Ball suspected, correctly, that his phone was tapped in September when Sue Herrick was on to him. He may assume we're still tapping into his lines as a matter of routine. That being so, he'll have worked out other means of communicating any sensitive info.'

Cameron gasps. 'Brilliant. Breathtaking.' He all but slaps his thigh. A spurt of pride shoots through me.

'Having been thwarted by Inspector Herrick on 13 September,' he continues, 'he brings in the shipment on 13 December.'

I realise, somewhat humbled, he is praising Ball's brilliance, not mine.

By another bridge, where the Ouse runs very high, he stops suddenly and says with great enthusiasm, 'Let's try the local brew.'

We go down a long wide flight of stone steps into a packed pub, white stucco on the outside, low beams, slabbed floor on the inside and, mercifully, no music.

While he squeezes his way to the crowded bar, I study a black panel on the wall with golden lines which indicate the levels floods have reached over the years. Another twenty-four hours of rain and I suspect the regulars will be paddling.

He returns with two pints of Old Brewery Bitter. It's so busy and noisy, even without music, that we continue our conversation only obliquely, not naming current names.

He reminisces about his days as a young detective in Scotland Yard, working on the Kray twins case under the fabled 'Nipper' Read.

He tells a fascinating story I'd never heard before about how, long before they were household names, one twin visited the other in a mental hospital, took off his street coat, made himself comfortable while his brother went to fetch tea, claimed he'd dozed off, awaking hours later to find, to his great shock, naturally, patient and coat missing.

'His brother had just walked out, posing as him, and stayed free long enough to force a rehearing of his mental health order.'

He shakes his head, rather admiringly. 'They loved taking the mickey. The public might never know all the scams they pulled, but their close mates did and rejoiced. The legends of their invincibility and the fear of them grew.'

He looks at me intently. 'Maybe your main man is the same.'

Outside again, on the cobbled towpath, he doesn't head for the steps. 'Let's eat out for a change.'

For a change? I think, amused. I've not yet dined in since we arrived.

He leads the way next door, up more steps and into an Indian restaurant where he picks a table by a shuttered window.

He doesn't study the menu by the light of a table lamp made out of a brass kettle. Instead, he ask the waiter, 'What's the hottest?'

'Phall,' he's told. I glance down the menu. It's not even listed.

He looks across for my approval. I nod, wondering what I'm letting myself in for, and, as a precaution, add a cooling raita to his order for Phalls with white boiled rice, nans on the side and two pints of lager.

While we drink and wait, I gently probe his past. It comes as a surprise to learn that he's never been further east than Suez where he dropped, as a red beret National Serviceman, on the canal.

The table next to us is vacated and, with no one within ear-shot, he gets back to the case, talking softly to the accompanying drone of a slow-moving fan on the ceiling. 'Clarence is entitled to presumption of innocence, and to be protected as an inform-ant at risk.'

That, I point out, rules out bringing in Ball and grilling him on any lead Clarence has given me without revealing its source.

Cameron concurs. 'Will he give evidence against Ball if –'

'No way,' I break in, shaking my head vigorously. 'He's terri-fied. He wouldn't even let me make notes in case, in the event of Ball being charged, we have to disclose them to defence law-yers.'

'...if –' he goes on.

He stops as the dishes are served and the waiter leaves.

'...if,' he resumes, 'we give him protection?'

I take my first mouthful of chicken, so hot that I almost have to splutter that he'd been offered and refused surveillance, a panic button and a video link.

I ladle on cucumber in cold yoghurt as he smiles pleasurably. 'Just because he's turned it down doesn't mean we can't give it to him. And if Ball thinks his calls are being intercepted, why disappoint him?'

He looks directly at me. 'Any objections?'

To calling in MI5, the security service, he means. Since the Iron Curtain rose, they've been diverted into the fight against organised crime and have the manpower for surveillance and the eavesdropping equipment to do a better job than the police.

Frankly, I like working on my own, always have since this bum leg took me out of Special Ops, like a crippled footballer no longer fit to play in a team. But then, I'm muscling in on the local CID, so I can hardly object.

Besides, Pepper, if I'm right about him, was otherwise en-gaged when Voss was shot which means there's another armed heavy on the loose. 'I could use more bodies,' I reply easily.

I tell him between hot mouthfuls about the black shadower on Tuesday, but not about the innocent Cavalier driver yesterday, hoping that Tom hasn't either.

He wants to know my schedule for tomorrow. I request a look at everything the local CID has compiled. 'Personally, I can't go into too much detail with witnesses about movements and timings without blowing my cover of being the assistant on your Commission.'

He eats without apparent pain and says nothing.

'For instance,' I go on, 'I need to see the statements of Clarence's crew to work out if he had time to make that 999 call that took his boss into murder alley.'

Eventually he nods. 'I'll fix that. And I'll tell Mr Johns that you are to have whatever assistance you need whenever you request it.' He will, too. No one will dare to argue with his right to inspect anything on any force's files and demand back-up.

At some time, I tell him, feeling hotter all the time, wishing the ceiling fan would speed up, I'll go to the dog track, see the bookies and tic-tac men, and maybe drop in on the Riverside Shuffle tomorrow night.

'Before that, I want to concentrate on the paperwork on Pepper,' I continue. 'According to both Inspector Herrick and Clarence, he's a Yardie.'

I don't have to tell him that Yardies, ruthless though some can be, have a reputation for being stool pigeons. Once you've got a cast-iron case against them, they'll name names, act as informants, go undercover, sell their twin brother, anything for a deal to keep them out of jail.

He promises records and intelligence on Pepper and the two white alibi witnesses in the Tring TV item. 'You know how "Nipper" Read cracked the Krays?' he says, reminiscing again.

Vaguely, because Read later became an assistant chief constable in my own force, part of its folklore. To humour him I shake my head.

'Got just enough against them to charge them, remand them, take them off the streets. Once they were out of harm's way, all manner of witnesses lost their fear and came forward. His case was formidable in the end.'

We finish our meal, me sweating now, my tongue feeling so scalded that I'd love an ice-cream to follow, just to dangle it in.

He doesn't order a sweet. Early start tomorrow, he announces, seeing more police witnesses at HQ. 'I'll tell them all that, in my absence, you speak and act with my full authority.'

'You're off then?' I say regretfully.

To London, he replies, for a meeting with the Association of Chief Police Officers to outline his proposed guidelines.

'Will Chief Constable Johns be there?' I ask, not an idle question, seeking a bit of gossip.

'I think we can take it that he's attended his last meeting of ACPO,' he says grimly.

Quite right, too. When an army is not performing, fire the general, I say. The ground troops I've met have impressed me. Low in spirit they may understandably be, but all have been efficient.

The police authority won't officially sack Johns, of course. Someone in Whitehall will have a quiet word with a nationwide security firm. He'll be offered a directorship, and depart, talking publicly about putting his expertise to wider use in another, but associated, field; the usual tripe.

In a few months the company that hires him will win a government contract worth hundreds of times what they are paying him. That's the way it works at the top.

I just wish I was an assistant chief, one rank higher than I am, and I'd apply for the vacancy. Em, I'm sure, would soon settle here, come to love the place, and I reckon I could soon lick this force into shape.

In a couple of years or so, perhaps, I think wistfully.

'You know . . . ' Rather theatrically, Cameron wipes his mouth on his maroon napkin that matches the tablecloth. ' . . . I've a good feeling about this case.' Nonchalantly he tosses it on to the table. 'I think you're going to crack it.'

You, I note, thrilled and apprehensive at the same time. Overnight, an MI5 convoy will be heading north up the A1, and soon more and more local CID officers will have to be drafted in.

Still my case, though.

14

FIVE DAYS TO CHRISTMAS

A long bath instead of a quick shower this morning, imagining the water sizzling as, gingerly, I lower myself in, sheer bliss. Hot curry always has that effect.

A close shave in a mirror flanked by two lights in shades

shaped like oyster shells above the brown marble handbasin in a grey and cream tiled bathroom that's bigger than most hotel bedrooms.

Such luxury. With the big boss away, I'm going to enjoy it today, take my time, chill out a bit after all this rushing around.

Casual dress, I decide, brown suit trousers, but a grey sweat shirt instead of shirt and tie.

I walk down the two flights of stairs, the last beside the giant Christmas tree, and cross the foyer. Next to the porter's lodge I browse through newspapers on a stand, about to take the *Telegraph* for its cricket coverage from Zimbabwe.

My eyes light on a massive headline, can't miss it, really, in a tabloid: 'Shot TV Star Filmed Me Naked'. Above is: 'World Exclusive'.

After six days every other paper has finally cleared Voss off its front page. The exception has my stomach churning already, nothing to do with last night's Phall.

I pay 28p for it and £1.25 for a street map and head back across the foyer down a corridor to the breakfast room. A small wall table is booked with the paper, no need for a window table. The room is on the same corner as mine two floors up, same view, different angles. In any case, I'll be engrossed in reading.

There's no point in staying at a four-star hotel on the taxpayer, in my view, unless you're going to have a big breakfast, the full fry-up. This morning, I give my stomach a break and return from the self-service counter with scrambled eggs and fruit juice.

I can't claim to be enjoying them much as I read that an ex-page three girl is recounting that she posed for a porn video filmed by Voss at his luxury flat.

Over three pages, no detail is spared: water bed, handcuffs, the whole kinky lot. There are several topless photos of her, but no still clips from the video itself.

I appreciate ex-page three girls need their photos in the papers in the hope of reviving careers that sag with their busts. They may need the charge of reappearing in the limelight and, unless they've got lucky and married well, they need the money. To achieve these aims, they will exaggerate a story, especially one that can't be denied because the dead can't sue, but usually it has some small basis of truth.

I have love-hate feelings for the media.

I hate TV programmes like *Cause for Concern* and liberal broadsheets when they question convictions. Sure, the police and juries get it wrong now and then, but the media never point out that the blame for miscarriages of justice usually rests with defence lawyers. To say a prisoner was badly defended, however, would result in a writ, so they always blame us; safer that way.

They set themselves up as great investigators seeking the truth when they're really seeking commercial success. In real life, journalists (and, indeed, private eyes, élitist dons, little old ladies in picture postcard villages so beloved of novelists) don't solve murders. Only we do.

But I love 'em to bits when they splash out money, far more than we could afford from the informants' fund, and turn up angles like I've just read. They provide some good leads which a detective ignores at his peril.

The local CID, I trust, will be seeing her, routine background. Undoubtedly, she'll stick to her story, like Voss did, via his lawyer, over the Tring libel.

What's still unsettling my gut is this question: Was Voss in the habit of shooting such movies and, if so, who else starred? Liz Clarence? Amanda Ball?

It's got to be checked, thoroughly checked. One decision is already made; disco dancing for me tonight.

Tom, the driver, joins me over a second cup of tea, helping himself to what's left of the toast and marmalade.

He brings me another sealed parcel, a thick dossier inside, from force headquarters where he'd left Cameron and his clerk, their packed suitcases in the boot of the Daimler for a quick getaway before the Friday rush.

'The Old Man's seen that.' He nods at the paper. 'He's getting the local boys to have a good sniff round it. You stick to the game plan, he says.'

At the foot of the red carpet, we shake hands, wish each other a merry Christmas, and I watch him drive away, sorrier to see him go than Cameron in a way, because it leaves me without transport on tap.

Back in my room the street map is spread out on the bed, not me. As acting top cop (on this job anyway), I take up a workmanlike position at the table with a view of the city walls.

Going through the statements takes all morning, checking and double-checking. Now and then I pad in stockinged feet to the bed to take rough measurements off the map or gaze, deeply troubled, out of the other window through the gloom down on the railway station.

At the end of the morning, two facts are firmly implanted in my mind:

One, the block of phones in front of the car-park towards which the two men, one black, one blackened, were heading is on the east side of the city centre, some distance from the Riverside Shuffle.

Two, Clarence may have no alibi for the precise moment that his boss was shot. The statements confirm he'd driven back with his crew to the collecting point at the railway station after the drugs raid, and, yes, he had wandered off for coffee, as he'd told me, when he realised that there was no chance of a fresh assignment before the end of *News at Ten*.

But his two colleagues, questioned independently, had put the time that he was away from them at no more than three and five minutes. What's more, when he returned, he wasn't out of breath, his hand didn't shake when he handed over their plastic mugs and the drinks were piping hot.

No time, then, to get to the block of phones to call 999, not even if he'd rehired that speedway star who featured in *Cause for Concern*.

But the alleyway where Voss was shot is closer. What, I ask myself, if Voss did make a habit of filming good-lookers in the buff? What if the lady upstairs from his solicitor's office in the calculating agency is Clarence's wife? What if, zonked out on drugs, she, too, starred on the video that Fleet Street's finest have failed to dig up? What if Clarence found out?

And, if this line of inquiry is right, who made the phone call to set Voss up?

Pepper? He would have had to pass the phone box on his way from the safe-blowing to steal the getaway car. But, surely, he would have been in too much of a hurry with the mortally wounded Tring at his side?

Anyway, Pepper's Golden Balls' heavy and Clarence's enemy. It doesn't make sense, none of it.

The ringing phone disturbs a long bout of self-questioning. Distractedly, I pick up the receiver, certain no answers will come from the other end, only more problems.

'Sergeant Howard, sir,' says a warm, female voice. In case I'd forgotten, she adds, 'Scarborough.'

'How's Gabby Tring?' I ask.

'Hanging on.' She goes down a note. 'Just.'

Good, I think. It's not that I want his or his wife's agonies prolonged, only that I don't want even a line to appear in print anywhere about anyone, under whatever name, dying in hospital from burns and blast injuries.

The longer Golden Balls and his mob think they're getting away with it, the better. 'When he does go, report to me, not the coroner. We'll want a news black-out on it.'

'Sir.' She pauses, then: 'Rotterdam.' Another pause. 'The police there have traced that number the black suspect left at the hospital when he brought Tring in. Belongs to an importer-exporter, lots of international connections. Just an office and a phone. No warehouse.'

'How's he operate then?'

'As a middleman, a supplier meeting demand. They suspect he could also deal in drugs.'

'Why?'

'Well, *Goud Wereld* is Dutch for Golden World.'

I gulp. 'Ball owns the boat?'

'It's Rotterdam-registered, leased for last week's trip to the dealer, but Ball could have an interest in it.'

He could indeed have money in it, I think, if it does a regular drugs run for him. He's showing off by giving it a name that's close to his company's, good for a bit of a giggle from people in the know.

Answers, I privately rejoice. I'm not sure to what questions, but answers at last. Decisions now.

'Get over there,' I tell her. 'Ask the police to prepare warrants or whatever they need to carry out a search of those premises and that boat and question the crew.'

Somehow Christian Pepper doesn't sound half as menacing as Black Pepper, but that's his real first name. His place of birth is Wimbledon, close to Kingston-on-Thames, not Kingston, Jamaica.

You've got to laugh, haven't you? I think, smiling to myself as

I read the intelligence files over a lunchtime ham sandwich from Room Service.

In the way that some Met officers based in outlying London suburbs boast to their country cousins that they are 'at the Yard', Pepper is going around claiming to be 'from da Yard'. Gives him street cred, I suppose, instils that bit of extra fear.

It's not an untypical CV: hard-working, God-fearing family; introduced to soft drugs while truanting from school, hard stuff hanging around with the gang, purse-snatching, then muggings to finance his increasing purchases; probation with a rehab programme, community service, youth detention and finally four years for armed robbery.

It was in a northern prison that he cleaned himself up, spurred on by the grisly drugs death of an old school chum at the age of eighteen that made big headlines at the time.

You know the type of item. Parents weeping before the lingering cameras: 'Our lovely child was never made aware of the dangers.'

In my college days, a student was found dead in bed after a day-long binge. He'd suffocated on his own vomit. I don't recall his parents going on TV and weeping, 'No one told him fifteen rum and cokes might be bad for him.'

I long for one of the pundits or counsellors or police chiefs who are invariably wheeled out on these occasions as follow-up interviewees to say, just once, 'If you're old enough to vote, you're old enough to know that drink and drugs can kill and the rest is up to you.'

They don't because it's bad PR and so the tedious treadmill of the same news bites and the same shots of tearful flower-laying go on and on and round and round.

It was in prison – at weight-training classes, so popular in jails – that he teamed up with a thug called King who gave him a bed in York when they came out. King's mate, Nelson, fixed him up with a job as a bouncer at one of Golden Globe's rowdiest pubs.

'Staying out of trouble and making good progress,' recorded his after-care visitor in his last report.

You've got to laugh at that, too, haven't you?

All that means is that he's not been caught while rising within the organisation, never front of house, because you don't get a pub or club licence with his sort of record, but high enough to run a racy car and rent a place in a so-called luxury riverside block of flats.

He won't be taking drugs these days. He'll be escorting consignments, organising their sale, collecting debts; making lots of money instead of stealing and spending it.

He's making good progress all right, I think glumly.

Nelson works in security, often at Golden Globe establishments. King is temporarily away from his current sinecure post as assistant manager of a health club. He'd been arrested on Thursday, the 12th, charged and remanded over the sale of steroids. At least he's got an unbreakable alibi.

The *Cause for Concern* video is played yet again. Listening to their glib lies, I suspect that some heavy debts over the supply of steroids were repaid when they gave their perjured evidence against Inspector Herrick.

Both white witnesses talk with strong northern accents. Now that I know his history, Pepper's sounds more Eddie Murphy than Yardie.

I go back, start the section again, repeatedly pressing hold.

The more I study Pepper the more convinced I become that his nose isn't prominent enough to be the man who so unnerved me at the soccer match. Maybe the spectator was a relative of one of the black players on the field, as blameless as that Cavalier driver.

I press the video on. Excluding accents and skin, they could come from the same mould. Even the uniforms are uniform – grey sweat shirts, more slobby than mine, tight faded blue jeans, thick-soled trainers.

Their facial expressions fluctuate between forced smiles and practised scowls with nothing in between. They have the same bull necks with shoulders broad and sloping, strong arms hanging, ape-like, nipped waists, shot putter's legs.

I wonder mischievously if it's true that steroids make your nob go small. There'll be a chance to ask them pretty soon when they're all safely inside.

I'm wet, in a sweat, hotter than last night at the curry house.

Not from the rain, no more than a drizzle leaking from low black clouds. Not from the brisk walk, almost a trot, from the railway station.

Just from watching the second hand on my wrist-watch. Six minutes, sixty seconds beyond the outer limit of Clarence's alibi, have already ticked by and the Riverside Shuffle is not in sight yet.

I push my aching leg as fast as it will go. Maybe there's a shorter route. Don't kid yourself. You pored over the street map, measured distances out with pen and paper against the scale.

From some distance away I can smell the composty ripeness of the fading flowers that have lain in the alleyway for almost a week now and curl up my nose when I reach the corner before the Shuffle.

Almost seven minutes, my watch tells me.

I turn back, limping heavily. OK. OK. Get a fit young cadet to run it tomorrow, I half decide, trying to cheer myself up. Stand in the station forecourt and time him. He could knock two minutes off.

What? Without breaking sweat? And then go to the refreshment bar, buy three hot coffees and hand you one without his hand shaking? And he's not just committed a cold-blooded murder.

Come on, face it. Clarence is in the clear for both the shooting and the 999 call. He's not part of any conspiracy at all. You were wrong, never had the slightest evidence, to suspect him in the first place. It's a bum theory, always was, and I feel as depressed as the dismal weather.

Half a day you've been on your own, the top cop, in charge, and the inquiry going backwards.

Clarence is innocent. Ball is alibied before half the nation. Pepper can't be the gunman if he was with Tring at the law firm. The 999 caller maybe, but not the killer.

All of it comes back to the possibility you and Cameron discussed last night.

It has to be someone else, a hired hit man, and you haven't a clue who.

No, this sweat has nothing to do with the rain or the walk. It's the inner panic of someone who is losing the plot.

15

To quiz a bookie or a tic-tac man just before the off would be like interrupting my novelist mate 'Jacko' Jackson in mid-sentence when he's on a hot streak. You'd be inviting a mouthful of abuse. So, after a short, fast train trip and a shorter, not so fast taxi ride through Doncaster's rush hour, I arrive at the stadium before the turnstile operators and all the punters.

In a wired compound, a greyhound in a muzzle empties both tanks on a sandy surface. More bark and yelp behind the green doors of kennels, stacked one on top of the other, in a smart, tiled building.

I seek out the manager in the busy staff room beneath a grandstand which is clad in grey metal. Producing my warrant card, I ask for a private word.

A tubby, jovial man, he leads me through a side entrance up two flights of steep staris to a deserted bar/restaurant that covers the whole of the first floor.

One wall is entirely glass with a bird's-eye view of an oval track, as well illuminated as the soccer ground. Lights overhang the railed circuit every ten yards and a battery of lamps stretch out on a gantry above the mirrored winning post.

One black dog streaks alone after a white rag, noisily being towed on the outer rail, a monorail, I assume, only catching up when the noise and the rag stop, pouncing on it gleefully. 'Individual time trials,' the manager explains.

The bar is unmanned. All the tables have crisp white paper covers, but are not yet set with cutlery. 'Quiet enough for you?' he asks.

I take off my raincoat, put my briefcase, black leather, no match for my brown suit, on a table and sit before it. He takes a chair at my side, both of us facing the track, backs to an empty bar the size of a barn.

The Cameron Commission is used again as cover for my inquiries. 'Some Methodist MPs are questioning whether a public service like the police should provide the in-filling for a race meeting at which there's gambling,' I begin, putting on a distasteful expression.

'It was the other way round,' he protests, not unnaturally.

108

'They already had the chief constable on board when they approached me.'

Wayne Kirk, the controller of Ridings TV, phoned to outline the idea. The manager was enthusiastic. 'Great publicity and a good facility fee.'

A supper was arranged here in the restaurant when a Friday night meeting was in progress to go into details. Clive Voss and Con Clarence were among Ridings TV's large party. So was Alex Ball. 'A big owner, several dogs in training.'

'Yes, but who introduced him?' I ask.

'Know him well.' An in-the-know smile, a local accent, not quite eee-by-gum. 'Good patron.'

'No.' I shake my head, at myself mainly, for a misunderstood question. 'I mean, who brought him in on the supper, who suggested him as a sponsor?'

He ponders for a second. 'Voss, I expect. He had him on that *Celebrities* series. Very pally, they were, all four of them.'

'Four?' I query.

'Alex had his daughter, that actress, with him.' He raises his eyelids, widening his eyes, to tell me. 'Some looker. Enjoyed herself thoroughly. Backed a few winners. Knows a winner when she sees one. Chip off the old block. Good fun.'

I'm going to have to be careful here. 'Did they bring a chauffeur, a big, young guy...' He's already shaking his head. '...black with –'

He cuts me short. 'Not in here, no.' He supposes they could have left him with Ball's BMW in the car-park.

It emerged over supper that Ball had already agreed in principle with Ridings TV to sponsor a race for ten thousand and provide a trophy.

The only condition was that the event would publicise Golden Globe Entertainments plc and the six dogs would be restricted to his personal invitations to ensure a top quality field. The only real debate over the meal was what time the race should be staged.

'They had loads of bumph, schedules and things, all over the tables.' He spreads his hands. 'Kirk ruled out the 9.15 because they had something lined up – a drugs raid to be covered by Con Clarence.'

'How do you know that?'

'They kept geeing him up, pressing on him that, unless something better turned up, he'd have to kick the show off, get it started with a bang. Kirk seemed to think it could overrun 9.15.'

'Did you watch the programme?'

He looks up at a closed circuit TV set, one of many hanging from a high ceiling that's festooned with colourful paper streamers. 'We fixed a few monitors to take it.'

In the event, he resumes, the drugs raid didn't last long and they did cover the 9.15, briefly anyway.

'Big debate over the 9.30, though. Even the Balls couldn't agree. He was keen. She wasn't.'

'Why?'

'Very clued up, she is, what with being in showbiz and all. She argued that millions of people watch the nine o'clock BBC news all the way through to the weather forecast and they wouldn't turn over in time.'

'What was the outcome?'

'Got her own way.' A smile, difficult to detect whether admiring or puzzled. 'The rest backed her after hearing from Kirk that the traffic department hoped to provide a bit of action around that time. From then on, though, till ten o'clock, he made it clear they'd have to take pot luck on what turned up from 999 calls.'

He looks at me, definitely puzzled now. 'Didn't realise you lot laid on arrests to order like that.'

'Er...' A valid point has me floundering for a moment. 'Contingency planning in case of a slow night.' I hurry on, 'Did they discuss how they would respond to genuine 999 calls?'

'Oh, aye. Like a bloody war room in here, it was. Maps. Coloured markers. Lists. That caused a bit of a row, too.'

'In what way?'

'Voss wanted to be first out of the traps, as it were, when anything big broke, claimed he knew his way around the city better than anyone. But some older guy...' He thinks. 'Their star reporter, always does the big stories for them.' He shakes his head, can't remember his name. 'He wanted the first job.'

'Who won?'

'Kirk ruled the other bloke was newsroom staff and had to bat first.'

I grab at a cricketing term myself, 'And when each city-based crew had completed an innings they returned to the station yard to wait for the next job to break.'

He nods.

Go back a bit, I tell myself. 'So what was the final decision about the race?'

'Kirk guaranteed coverage of the 9.45 and said he was prepared to put it in the contract. He'd also screen the two races before that, if the outside broadcasts weren't working out.'

'Were you happy with that?'

'Absolutely.' He looks it.

'And Mr Ball?'

'He didn't seem to mind as long as he got the written promise of a plug for his company.'

I move him on to a week ago tonight.

'Alex booked several tables...' He waves an arm airily around the restaurant. '...for his guests, invited owners and their partners and so on. Quite a party. A long meal with lots of champagne.'

'Was his daughter here?'

His reply is a disappointed headshake.

'Did they watch the show?'

'As they were eating.'

'Was Mr Ball interrupted while eating?'

'How do you mean?'

'By a message, either handed to him personally, or by a phone call?'

'He wasn't called away, if that's what you mean.'

'Sure?'

'I should know,' he replies, a touch testily. 'I was with the party all the time.'

'Did he have a mobile phone?'

'No.' His expression has become distrustful.

Behind us the bar is staffed and slowly beginning to fill with customers, small groups, widely scattered. The floodlights around the track are dimmed, signalling the end of the time trials.

Time's running out for me, too. 'Another question being raised is...' I flick open my briefcase, lift out a stack of photos and place them on the white table-cloth. 'What do these signals mean?'

'Why?' he asks sullenly, shuffling through stills from the *Friday the 13th* video of the tic-tac man in operation.

'There's this awkward MP, see. Is it right, he wants to know, for TV to be used to send messages that only a few professionals can read?'

111

He pulls a face, not coming round.

'Would it be possible to put out some sort of subliminal messages? he's asking.'

'Tripe,' he snaps.

I put on an appeasing face, desperate to win him over again. 'He's the type of interfering old sod who'd ban sign language, if he could, 'cos he can't read it.'

A slight smile and I'm getting through.

One final push. 'I have to come up with some answer. We don't want to queer John McCririck's pitch on Channel Four racing, now do we?'

He gives in, sighing. 'Don't know it myself.' He hooks one arm across the back of his chair and looks into the bar in the direction of three burly men, standing, drinking shorts.

Two are dressed for outdoors in waxed coats and scarves. The other, dark suit under a white raincoat, looks like a well-heeled punter who's going to spend the evening in the restaurant.

The manager calls out two first names. The two warmly attired men detach themselves from their drinking companion and walk slowly towards us. As they get closer, I recognise the tic-tac man and a bookmaker from the oft-seen video. Each is carrying a glass of whisky to keep out the chill of the night's work on the rails that's ahead of them.

They look vague as the query is explained, leaning forward as I slip the photos off the pile one at a time. Between them they obligingly demystify their secret craft.

As last-minute money was piled on Jaffa Cake its price came down from five-to-two, the bookie begins. The tic-tac man touches either side of his nose with index fingers.

Together they demonstrate seven-to-four, with two fingers to shoulder, six-to-four with fingers to elbow, five-to-four with fingers to wrist.

'It went off at evens,' says the bookie, while the tic-tac man wags two fingers up and down in front of him, like scales balancing.

To make sure I've got it, they go through it all again to explain how the price of High Society went in reverse – from evens out to five-to-two.

'Is it possible,' I venture slowly, 'to signal to someone sitting at home, oh, I don't know, "Abort bet" or "Proceed as planned"?'

They snort, very dismissively. 'It's a standard system, not as many signs as horse-racing, but any expert watching would spot any deviation.'

Shit, I think, a bum theory, I look ahead of me, thinking frantically.

The scene in the bar behind me is reflected in the blackness of the long glass window. There's a sizeable crowd now. Standing apart from it, the well-heeled punter pretends to be studying his racecard, but, now and then, glances over the top of it – at me.

If he had a companion he'd be nudging him by now and whispering, nodding or pointing.

Since she started reading the regional TV news my Em has had to get used to strangers' sneaked glances when she walks into a pub or a shop, but they unsettled her at first; the way I feel right now.

He has taken off his raincoat and holds it in one hand. The sharp cut of his dark suit is marred by a bulge at the left armpit. I'm more than unsettled now. I'm unnerved.

I look away from the window and up at the bookmaker. 'Why was there a sudden shift in the betting?'

'Lots of money, piles of it, not petty Tote stuff...' His face shows disapproval of the bookies' big rival. '... for Jaffa Cake, all from up here down to the rails.' His head circles the restaurant. 'Ball's party. Since he was the race sponsor, we thought they had an inside track.'

'But they lost?'

'Yeah.' A broad grin. 'Made the night for us.'

Yeah, I think, alone again, eating roast beef and Yorkshire pudding, looking down on the first race. Golden Balls had a good night, too.

He'd used his guests' money to manipulate the prices, make Jaffa Cake favourite, not to skin the bookies, but send a message to his waiting team that the drugs consignment was coming into Scarborough. And when he handed over his trophy to the winner, on that square green platform in front of the winning post, he'd underlined it with, 'For your collection.'

Rather than risk interception of phone calls, he'd confirmed live on TV where the collection was to take place.

Breathtaking. Brilliant. Cameron's right about him.

His gang, watching TV for his final instructions, would be

briefed that if Jaffa Cake started favourite, never mind where it finished in the race, Scarborough was the landing spot.

And they would have thought what I'm thinking now. Three months later than originally planned, but he's pulled it off right under the cops' noses on their own crime show.

What a coup. What a star. Brilliant. Breathtaking.

Modest Tote stakes are collected by a cheerful girl attendant in a paper hat from my lonely table.

Every race is reprised immediately on the closed circuit monitors. Excited shouts, groans, oaths, even the drone from the hare's monorail, can be heard accompanying the commentary.

The announcer gives a minute-by-minute countdown to the next race to the background of happy chatter of several Christmas outings. To add to the bubbling noise, they are singing 'Happy Birthday' at one full table. To my intense relief, the well-heeled punter has joined them and the singing. Another false alarm, I rebuke myself.

Time to go, I decide, after four losers on the trot, not reclaimable on expenses.

I pick up a taxi that's just deposited a tipsy trio at the main gates and am at the station five minutes before the express north.

Settling into a second class window seat, my train of thought sets off before the 20.16 for York.

Ideally, I conjecture, Ball would have liked the shipment to come in at Whitby. Not sure why. Nearer Teesside and Tyneside where he'd have lots of addicted clients, perhaps.

But the fact that TV ran the drugs raid in inner-city York meant that the Customs watch was still on at Whitby and its harbour wasn't clear of Customs.

What a crazy thing for the chief constable to do, leaking that surveillance to Ridings TV. Who tipped Ball off that Whitby was to be avoided? Voss? Clarence? How, if Ball was incommunicado down here?

As if searching for an answer, I look out of the window and along deserted Platform Four. The well-heeled punter from the dog track is sprinting, raincoat flapping in his slipstream, towards the next coach, first class.

Bloody hell, I think, tensing, more than unnerved now; nervous.

16

Stalked. Yet again I'm being stalked.

Not by a bouncer built like a warrior out of *Zulu* tonight; by a sharp operator who's armed, a real pro.

What's he after? a thin inner voice demands. To find out where you're going, who you're seeing? Or the contents of your briefcase? Or you?

I feel the comfort of having so many passengers around me in the well-filled carriage.

Looking down at the case on the table before me, I run through what's inside – a video of a programme that a million or so viewers were just about to settle down to watch this time a week ago, stills from it and a few statements about it, all easily replaceable.

My stalker doesn't know that, though, so... A pause to ponder... why not let him have a peek, let him try to pinch it? Then pinch him and ask him.

Easy.

I leave the case on the table, walk with some difficulty, both legs feeling weak, down the swaying centre aisle to the lavatory, don't use it and don't quite lock the door, either, peering through a tiny gap. No one walks through from the first class coach.

Too easy, I think, swaying back. He's too smart to take the bait. Judging by the way he melted into that party at the dog track he's probably already in a card school biding his time in first class. And that's another thing. First bloody class. Golden Balls' substitute shadower is on more liberal expenses than Britain's acting top cop.

I smile to myself and feel better for it.

Resettled in my seat, my mind sways on, back and forth, then back again all the way to the beginning three months ago.

Right then. Think this through.

Clarence learns about Ball's drugs deal – by accident, he says. He tells Inspector Herrick he heard it with his own ears. He tells me he got it on tape. That's a major conflict that makes him a questionable witness.

He says Voss heard the tape, too, and used it to extort a

hundred grand out of Ball. Why didn't Ball demand the tape in return? Perhaps he did, and what Voss lodged in his solicitor's safe was a copy. Maybe my stalker thinks what's in here – absent-mindedly I strum my fingers on the lid of the briefcase – is another duplicate.

Hmmmm. Nothing.

If there was an original, of course, that inner voice pipes, jolting me.

Why think that?

Because we've only Clarence's belated word that it ever existed. Three months ago, when he was talking to Inspector Herrick, he never mentioned a tape. The solicitor doesn't know what was in the Jiffy bag. Voss can't be asked.

Hmmmm.

A blank mind.

Use the Cameron technique. Put yourself in Clarence's position. Your wife becomes a junkie on girls' nights out at the Shuffle.

Confirmed fact, I tell myself.

No, it's not. All we know is that she isn't living at home. She's in hospital, he says. Make a mental note to check.

Start again. Your wife is a junkie and you blame Golden Balls. While making *Celebrities*, you hear (put it no higher than that) a drugs deal being set up.

Out of revenge or public-spiritedness – never mind the motive – you tell Inspector Herrick. Confirmed fact. Right? Right.

Ball discovers Herrick is on to him. He sends Pepper after you. You're in fear of your life. What do you say?

Well? Something like, 'There's a tape in my company's solicitor's office that's to be opened in the event of my death.'

In other words, you make it up to save your skin.

So far, not bad, I compliment myself.

Pepper has to spare you. He tells Ball who puts a plan into operation to retrieve or destroy what, in truth, may well be non-existent evidence.

But why have Voss killed immediately after the evidence is destroyed, and not Clarence, not so far anyway?

Not so good after all, I silently sigh.

Christ, it's complicated, is this. Yet there must be a simple answer.

Think. Think.

116

The video. There were videos in the safe. Not quite a con-firmed fact, but the solicitor was almost sure of it.

What's on them, if not evidence of the drugs deal? Porn like that ex-page three girl claims? Featuring Amanda? Or Liz Clarence?

Clarence. Clarence. Clarence.

Just because he was being helpful to Inspector Herrick three months ago, doesn't mean that he was telling you the whole truth yesterday.

He's been bought off, you mean; changed sides?

Well, he worked behind the scenes on the *Cause for Concern* programme, the filming of the safe, the recce for the dynamite at the colliery. He, not Voss, could have helped to plot Tring's release.

Last Friday he established from the drugs inspector that the coast at Whitby wasn't clear. Did he signal to Ball that the boat should come into Scarborough? How? Something said on TV in the commentary on the drugs raid?

It can't have been Voss tipping off Ball via TV because he didn't appear on the screen until after the race and then not for very long.

Have you ruled out Clarence too early? Blast, I've pored over every word, every bet, every bloody tic-tac on that video, and ignored Clarence.

Interesting, too, come to think of it, how Pepper turned up at the hotel so soon after I'd first met up there with Clarence.

Clarence. Clarence. Clarence.

Christ, it's complicated.

My mind empties again.

So – slowly it's refilling – let's simplify this:

Crime No. 1: Safe-blowing. I think I know how Tring was sprung and why he's finished up dying where he is. If the hospital staff ID Pepper in a line-up, I can prove it.

Crime No. 2: Drug-smuggling. I think I know how and where Ball got the consignment ashore. If the breaks come in Rotter-dam and the small fry in the plot deem it safe to talk, I can prove it.

Crime No. 3. The murder of Voss, your personal assignment, down entirely to you.

That's what the public want – the killer brought to justice. Solve the safe-blowing and all they get is a sad, dead safe-blower. Crack the drugs and you take one mob off the streets. A fair collar, true, but not the big collar.

Think. Think. Well, there's not a hint anywhere that Ball said anything on TV to order Voss's execution to go ahead. The drugs operation, yes. Murder, no.

Clarence is not precisely alibied, but he disappeared for five minutes at the outside. He had no time to get from the railway station to the alleyway beside the Shuffle and shoot Voss or to make the 999 call that took Voss there.

Then how the devil can I rule him back in?

Pepper does Ball's dirtiest work, present company on this train probably excepted. He can't have shot Voss. He was otherwise engaged with the dying Tring.

He could have found time to make that 999 call using his native Wimbledon voice instead of his acquired Jamaican.

Lining Voss up for who? The gunman in the next coach?

The train begins to slow in the expanding light of the southern suburbs.

Rather groggily, I stand and head for the door before it comes to a stop.

Don't run away from him, says that inner voice, stronger now. Force him into the open.

See how good he is, I urge myself, stepping off the train with a crowd of passengers. I dawdle along Platform Five. Coat over his arm, he overtakes me on a footbridge with see-through sides without a glance over his shoulder.

Bait another trap, I order myself.

I turn away from the revolving doors that would take me into the back of the hotel, following signs on Platform Three to 'Left Luggage' beyond a waiting-room.

A pound and a fifty pence coin rents space for my briefcase in the cheapest and smallest locker in a stainless steel stack of them.

I amble back to a wall telephone outside the waiting-room.

Eyes on the locker all the time, I am listening to Em's justifiable complaints about facing a weekend of minding Laura, doing the shopping, the tree-trimming, the gift-wrapping, all on her own. Here and there I mumble a sorry.

'Where are you?' she wants to know, moodily.

'On sodding observations' is all I tell her.

She softens her tone. 'You sound as fed up as me.'

Needing an excuse to stay where I am, wanting to talk to her anyway, I summarise some of the complications, the questions that are piling up in my mind.

'Maybe it's a bit like your beloved *NYPD Blue*,' she says.

I ask what she means.

'Do you just sit there every Saturday night with your mouth hanging open in admiration? Don't you ever discuss them with "Jacko" Jackson?' She sounds quite cross. 'Don't you ever study the construction?'

I still don't know what she's driving at.

'Often,' she says, patient again, 'they have two stories, don't they, running in tandem? Sometimes they're inter-linked. Sometimes they're quite separate. Maybe this case is like that.'

'Maybe,' I agree.

17

So many flowers have now been placed at the spot where Clive Voss was shot that they have spread round the corner from the dark alley as if their roots run under the cobbles.

'Lovely, aren't they?' says a young blonde to no one in particular in a longish queue standing in shadow.

My mind goes back a quarter of a century, to queues outside the Ritz at Matlock, feeling conspicuously young and solitary as I tried to sneak into 18-rated films.

Tonight I feel too noticeably old and solitary in a crowd that's youthful and seems to buzz with suppressed excitement.

It's cold without a top coat. Even so I'm overdressed in the grey suit with an open-collared yellow shirt after a quick change at the hotel that followed my abortive observation at the railway station.

The attempt to look trendy and cool has failed. Some males around me are in shirt-sleeves. Many females wear skirts so short that there's lots of naked leg to study. I'm trying not to.

I do, however, need to strike up a conversation. 'Gorgeous,' I agree.

Useful, at least, I acknowledge, as the blonde keeps on talking, wanting to know why I'm on my own, me explaining I've got parted from mates already inside. Her friends join in, discussing Voss, me telling them I saw the show.

Slowly the queue approaches the canopy. Lights from the front entrance bathe the street in pale yellow. Above it rainbows dance round the tubes that form the letters of 'Riverside Shuffle'.

By the time we step under the canopy I've virtually been adopted as one of their party.

Two dinner-jacketed skinheads stand on the top of three tiled steps in the regulation pose – feet apart, hands folded over groins, waiting to single out and bar anyone they don't like the look of.

Both are white. One is Nelson, ex-jailmate of Pepper's, who is scowling in my direction.

'What beautiful biceps,' coos the blonde to a friend.

The scowl turns to a tight smile which I manage to match as I wonder about the size of his cupped willie.

I reach the pay desk without being bounced.

Beyond a set of glass doors is a long lounge with subdued lighting. Balloons hang in massive bunches among security cameras from the low ceiling. Groups of people sit around scores of littered tables. More stand at a long bar to my right. Some are perched on high stools.

On the left is a wide set of stairs. Down it, like an electric thunderstorm, rolls almost deafening noise and flashing lights.

Upstairs the heat matches the hellish noise. Gone is the glittering globe that revolved in the ceiling, highlighting the dandruff on your shoulders, in *Saturday Night Fever* days. Gone is the floor of glass squares of ever-changing colours.

To a driving drum beat they are dancing in frenzies, singly or in circles in blackness through which strobe lights cut like lasers.

In the hotel foyer, on the walk here and in the queue outside, I'd been on constant look-out for the well-heeled punter from the dog track and the train.

Automatically but pointlessly, my eyes scan the twisting, heaving mass of bodies, the flashing lights not resting anywhere long enough for me to pick out faces.

I try to listen for a moment. The music has none of the Bee Gee's melody and the words make no sense. I descend from hell,

120

join the crowd at the bar, wait some time for a half of lager, time spent surveying the tables; no fresh sighting.

Now my eyes start a second round. On this tour they do find who they are seeking heading across the brown carpet towards twin doors over which a notice says 'Rest Rooms'.

I park my glass on a narrow shelf bracketed to a mustard-coloured wall and follow into a chilly, dimly lit corridor with a concrete floor. Handrails run each side along black walls to double doors at the end locked by a steel horizontal bar.

She turns right. I turn left with, as on the train, no intention of using the facilities.

'Evening,' I say, with a friendly smile.

Elaine, the calculating woman, gives me a fierce look as I fall in limping step alongside her as she clip-clops on her way back from the Ladies.

She's all in black. Her velvet dress has lace over shoulders, arms and above her cleavage. Her shoes are mid-high court. A bag hangs from one shoulder by a gold chain. She looks much slimmer than in her office outfit.

I talk as I walk. 'Saw you on Wednesday morning. Remember? I was talking to Mr McMichael and your friend.'

Her step and that get-lost expression lessen. 'Oh, hi.' Her face, glistening from dancing, smiles faint recognition.

I push open a door into the bar, stand aside for her. Catching up, I say, 'Look, this is not a chat-up line.' I hold out my left hand, tucking my thumb under third finger to make my gold ring more prominent. 'I'm happily married, with child.'

A few paces inside, she stops and eyes the scene. 'Wicked, isn't it?'

I'm clued up enough to know that to her generation wicked means terrific, not terrible.

'Yes,' I agree, not sure what's wicked – the vibrancy of the place or my marriage. I give my name and rank and tell her I'm with the Cameron Commission. 'I don't want to drag you away from your party, but have you time for a quick talk?'

An undecided look, head slightly on one side.

'Over a drink,' I offer.

She thinks, just for a second or two. 'Diet coke,' she says. 'Let

121

me tell 'em where I am.' Over her shoulder, she adds, 'But not who you are.'

She goes to a corner where several tables have been pushed together and dumps her shoulder bag. In this light I can't be sure if McMichael's secretary is with her crowd.

I return to the bar, deciding: Be open, as honest as you can, or she'll blow you out.

She waits for me close to the doors to the corridor, as far away as possible from the stairs and the worst of the noise, so we can hear each other speak.

I hand her the cold glass. 'Did you know Clive Voss?'

'Yes.' She sips. 'Sleazebag.'

I'll try a quip. 'You haven't laid a floral tribute outside then?'

She laughs quite joyfully.

A serious expression as I go on, 'We have to build up a profile of him, background, associates and so on, try to establish a motive.'

She holds the glass to her lacy bosom. 'Plenty of people in here would have liked to have put a bullet in his big head.'

My eyes follow hers round the bar, resting on Amanda Ball at the far end, sitting on a stool, surrounded by a small group that includes Pepper.

He looks tropical in a white dinner jacket, she sensational in a red Lycra dress that clings to every bit of her. A scooped neck displays a lot of chest. She appears to be enjoying herself more than him.

'Why?' I'm so distracted that I'm not looking at Elaine.

'He was creepy. "Look who I am" sort of thing, right up his own backside, on the make all the time.'

I turn my attention fully back to her. 'You didn't fall for his chat...?'

'Do me a favour.' That fierce look returns.

'...like that page three girl in the *Sun*?'

'I believe her, though, don't you?'

'Yes,' I say positively.

'I reckon it's true,' she says, frowning.

I'm not going to push her on that just yet. Instead, I ask her if she was here a week ago. On a regular Friday night out, she says. 'No TV here, so I missed all the fun and games.' She's making it sound like a quiz show in which Voss lost.

She knew him not just from the Shuffle, but also the pub near her office. 'When he came to see old man McMichael downstairs, he'd sometimes drop in for a quick drink after work.'

'How about his sidekick Con Clarence? Know him?'

She seems surprised I've asked. 'Much better. His wife worked with us. He often dropped in.'

Careful now, I caution myself, don't get over-excited. 'What's he like?'

A pensive pause. 'This between us two?'

Be honest, I command myself inwardly. 'Well, I can't promise I won't make follow-up inquiries, but I can promise you won't be mentioned.'

She sips again, then lowers the glass to her chin. 'He's a creep, too.'

'And his wife?'

'Liz? A lovely lass, warm, but, well...' She strives for a phrase. '...emotionally troubled.'

'Drugs?'

'Good God.' She groans it. 'You're like my mum. You think the younger generation does nothing but drugs. No.' Firm. Then, softening, 'Well, not recreational.' A tiny shrug. 'But medicinal, yes, from a doctor.'

'What's the trouble?'

'Depression. Panic attacks. Headaches. Took too many pills one night and finished up in hospital.'

'Still there, I hear.'

'Just gone in again.'

'Again?'

'She'd been out for, what, a month, more. Went back again last weekend. All this bloody trauma.'

'So she was allowed home?' I ask.

She nods.

'Home to Con?'

'All finished, that.'

'Why?'

'Voss.' She puts on a disgusted expression. 'Fancy fooling around with a workmate's wife, eh?'

Steady now. 'Did she tell you that?'

A cautious nod. 'Is Con a suspect?'

'He's well alibied.'

'Pity.' She gives me an appealing look. 'Couldn't he have hired someone like they do on TV?'

123

'You know...' I'm going to be dangerously honest here. '...I'm beginning to ask myself that same question.'

She laughs without mirth. 'It would serve him right.'

I ask if she keeps in touch with Liz. Visits every week, she replies, either at hospital or her family's home, a longish drive.

Alarm spreads across her face. 'You're not thinking of going yourself, are you?' There's no time to respond. ''Cos don't. She's in a hell of a state.'

'I don't plan to,' I finally get out. 'If it can be avoided.' Pause. 'You're obviously close to her. Is it possible, I mean, without bothering her...' Difficult this, but I have to take the plunge. 'Do you think she'd mind if you tried to help me understand the situation?'

She'd known Liz for five years, she resumes over a second drink, since joining the agency. Liz was already there, unmarried then.

'She's...was...' She takes time to think. 'When she's well, she's very placid. But she has these...well, emotional problems, lots of hang-ups, very naïve. Her mum and stepfather are deep country, a brother and a half-sister a bit slow.'

I can tell that for 'emotional' problems I should read 'psychiatric'. She's going as close as friendship will allow to hinting at incest somewhere in the family.

'Her hubby's a bit...well...' She's lost for words.

'Unsupportive?' I prompt.

'Yes,' she accepts without enthusiasm; still not really the right word. 'She needs tenderness. Instead, he was always out. Busy. Busy. So we...' She nods in the direction of her workmates. '...took her under our wings.' A sad face. 'A mistake that. Voss started sniffing around.' Her face is angry now. 'In here.'

'How did she react?'

'Well, he made a big fuss of her.' She responded to his advances, she means. 'I reckon he was giving Con jobs on a Friday to get a clear run.'

'So romance bloomed?'

A stern look at what's a wrong phrase. 'Besotted, she was.' A deep sigh. 'Then he dumped her.'

'When?'

She thinks. 'Late summer.' A deep sigh. 'Then she OD-ed.'

124

'On prescription pills?' I ask, double-checking.

She nods.

'How did Con react?'

'Stopped visiting her in hospital, told her not to go home when she got out.'

She'd told him, or he'd learned, the truth about her fling with Voss, I speculate privately.

Elaine's party mood has completely gone and I think I've ruined her night. 'She still carries, carried, oh, I don't know, carries, I suppose, a torch for the slimy sod.'

'Her hubby or Voss?'

'Voss.' She has difficulty speaking his name.

'Was she hoping for a reconciliation with him?'

'No chance. He'd found a new plaything.' She nods to the far corner of the bar. 'The big boss's daughter.'

My eyes must be staying on Amanda Ball for too long because Elaine says, 'Deserting me for her now, are you?'

I look back at her. 'I've got a job to do.' I want to say thanks in a way that just might cheer her up. 'But if I hadn't and I was a few years younger, before marriage and fatherhood, I'd have been happy to dance the night away with you.'

'Smooth bastard,' she chuckles. And she walks away.

Amanda Ball slips off her high bar stool and walks towards me, slowly, a sort of animal prowl, in red shoes with stiletto heels. Her slender legs look tanned, but I can't tell if that's because she's wearing tights or not. Since the eyes of her hangers-on are travelling the same way, I'll not dwell on the question.

She's not bringing any bag, hand or shoulder, so I guess she's not planning to stop long.

She reaches me. 'What are you doing here?' she asks, not at all politely.

'It's police routine to revisit the vicinity of a major incident a week after the event.' I shrug. 'You never know. Someone might remember something useful.'

'And did she?' She twists her head sideways, just slightly, towards Elaine's table.

I'm going to have to duck this. 'She works in the bank chambers where the fire was, that's all.'

Now Amanda tilts her head inquisitively, all but demanding 'And?'

'Wrong office.' I need to change the topic. 'Been to the greyhound stadium, too.'

A surprised face. 'What on earth for?'

'We're trying to answer MPs' queries about how the local force got involved in the whole dog's breakfast of a project in the first place.' I pull a loser's face. 'No winners there, either.'

A winning smile. 'You should have taken me along. I got both televised races last Friday in a double.' She laughs lightly. 'Tripled my stake.'

'Inside info?' I ask.

She arches an eyebrow.

I go on, 'You worked in your dad's kennels for a while, didn't you?'

'Been checking up on me?' Her expression is more intrigued than petulant.

I suspect she's really checking up on me, either showboating in front of her friends or keen to establish if I'm making progress. 'I saw the *Celebs* series.'

'Ah.' A satisfied smile. 'The home movie.'

She relaxes, placing her feet wider apart, one knee forward bringing her other hip up. Her dress tightens.

'All I learned in the short time I was there is to ignore form and tipsters. One was ours and the other, well, it's named after a rather good musical.' A sugary smile, far sweeter than her perfume which smells faint and expensive. 'Just a lucky girl, I guess.'

I put on a disappointed tone. 'I didn't see you with your father at the track on the video of last Friday's programme.'

'My, my. Seen that, too, have you? Busy boy.'

'I've seen everything that Voss appeared in. Every video he ever made, I think.'

Her brown eyes are giving nothing away. 'Didn't go. Saw it up there.' She's turned off her smile and is nodding upstairs where, I presume, there must be an office with a TV that isn't available to the paying public like Elaine.

'Must have been a helluva shock,' I say, 'seeing Clive Voss lying there in the alley...'

A sharp look. 'Didn't go out rubber-necking.'

'...on the telly, I mean.'

She shudders slightly. 'Thankfully, I'd come down here after I'd seen dad making his little speech. I wasn't watching.'

'Even so,' I persist, 'it must have been a shock when the word went round in here what had happened outside.'

She wears an amused smile, says nothing.

'He was a well-known regular, after all,' I go on.

'So you've discovered that much, have you, from your little chum in black?' Elaine, she means.

'Your father did invite me to ask around,' I point out bluntly, deciding that I've got all I need from acting smooth so I'll try a touch of the rough. 'Was Clive a big chum of yours?'

Her face sets. 'That's what people have been saying, is it?'

She's got Elaine on the brain, so more cover is required. 'Quite apart from both you and he frequenting this place, you did have a deal going, correct?'

'What deal?' she asks edgily.

'*Fallen Angel*, the film your father's backing.'

She tries to pass it off with an airy little hand gesture. 'Oh, dad dabbles in things like that.'

'Yes, but you were due to star...'

'Were?' she replies, with a querulous expression. 'It's still on, I hope, just delayed, that's all.'

'Good,' I pronounce. 'Still starring in it? The title role?'

There's no smile for what I rate a merry little quip. 'Not exactly starring, no. A smallish part, for experience. It will look good on my CV.' A worried little frown. 'I just hope it isn't going to clash with other engagements.'

'Busy?' I ask.

'Reading for a part in rep, spring Shakespeare series, you know,' she replies, rather regally.

I'll try humour again. 'One of the witches in *Macbeth*?'

A flicker of a smile at last. 'Not quite. The mistress of Cassio.'

'Lucky Cassio,' I say, deadpan.

She looks rather pleased again.

'Did he...' I stop. '...Clive, I mean, audition you?'

Not at all pleased now. 'How do you mean?'

'Screen test you?'

She answers in a flat tone. 'It's not got that far yet. The script's still being worked on.'

'Yes, but he was rather fond...' Wanting to get it right I plunder her phrase. '...of home movies.'

'Blue movies, you mean.' Her expression is becoming hostile. 'I read the papers, too. What are you suggesting?'

'Did he ever approach you with an invitation like that?' I pause. 'To pose, I mean. Take part.'

'You've got a dirty mind,' she says, very aggressively.

'It's a dirty job. Did he ever ask you to take part in home-produced –'

'No,' she snaps.

I press on. 'With your training and experience...' Deliberately I give her a quick once-over. '...and looks...'

'No, I said.'

'Look.' I glance at her partly exposed bosom. 'We know – and the public knows from the *Sun* – that he made skin flicks on the side.'

She brings her red shoes together and pulls herself up, almost standing at attention. 'You're suggesting that I'm some sort of slag, that I won the part on the casting couch.'

'I'm asking –'

'You've already said you've seen every video he ever made...'

Did I? I ask myself urgently. 'I said most.'

'...yet you make this most damaging allegation in a public place.' She all but stamps a foot. 'I'll sue.'

I'm none too sure of civil law, but I'll chance this: 'It isn't slander to ask a direct question in a private conversation with no third party present.'

'Who says it's private?' She glances up at the ceiling and smiles sourly.

'They haven't got mikes.' Unlike Voss Vision's camera, I comfort myself.

'Really?' she says mysteriously.

Or have they? I ask myself. Are they like the closed circuit at the dog track? What did I say? Anything actionable? Have they earwigged on Elaine and me?

'Who says the security staff aren't listening?' she asks, her chin up.

'They won't have heard much of interest,' I reply calmly.

'They'll have heard you imply that I've appeared in porn. Highly damaging to my professional reputation, I'd say.'

Christ, she's set me up for a writ. She'll be funded by her father's fortune, me fighting her claim for damages with no financial backing from legal aid. And another cop who's getting too close will be off the case.

I think of Voss's solicitor McMichael and what he called 'the standard holding response' and order myself into a smile. 'I shall stand by my actions.'

'We'll see, then, Mr Todd,' she says, turning away from me, with one last, long glare across her shoulder.

18

Anxiety runs through me. Not fear. Shame. It was stupid, stupid, stupid to let her set you up like that, running off at the mouth, too clever by half.

What the hell did I say? I can't remember, not word for word. Are those security cameras movable, fitted to a track or anything, to monitor conversations as well as movements? I look up but can't really see among the balloons.

Amanda has returned to her crowd at the bar, talking urgently, head close to Pepper, who keeps looking my way.

Standing apart from their group among a crowd at the foot of the stairs is the well-heeled punter, glancing at me too.

Fear grips me. Get out, I order myself. Get Elaine out, too.

I walk as briskly as I can to her table. Her chair is empty. 'Where is she?' I ask her friends.

'Dancing.' They motion to the stairs. I head towards them.

An arm hooks mine and I'm propelled away, not to the front door, but towards the ill-lit corridor to the toilets and emergency exit.

'A word, please' is hissed along the broad shoulder of a dinner jacket. The sweating face of Nelson is set in the standard scowl.

'I'm looking for a friend.' I try to pull my arm away.

'Let's not make a scene.' He grips it tighter, shouldering open the swing door, pulling me in front of him into the corridor. I go with the flow; no option.

In the corridor he lets go of my arm and pushes me with his other hand against the wall, the rail to the small of my back.

Both arms drop to his side, hands clasped together at his groin, the classic position of bouncers to defend against a knee in the balls. 'You've been propositioning respectable ladies –'

'You're misinf –'

He's not listening. 'Making obscene suggestions.'

All I can think of is Harrison Ford's line in *Witness*. 'You're making a mistake.' Hurriedly, I add, 'I'm police and –'

He leans forward, face so close that I can smell rum on his breath. 'Pestering the boss's daughter.'

I start to crook my left arm, elbow rising from the rail slowly up against the wall, fist lightly clenched, the classic first strike position. 'If you want the facts, check your security videos.'

'Pervo.' He stands back a pace, to give himself room to knee me. 'We don't like pervos.'

There'll be no meeting of minds here, I decide.

My elbow isn't quite shoulder high, the recommended height, but I let my fist go anyway, up slightly and then straight out like a piston, just a short distance.

There's a crack from my over-clenched knuckles. Pain jangles all the way to my elbow.

He stumbles back in stunned disbelief, but stays upright. 'Bastard.' Blood drips from his chin on to his white shirt front.

There's a frightening bang as the door swings open against the wall. Someone else in a dinner jacket is pinioning my right arm.

The door stays open just long enough to catch a glimpse of the white-coated Pepper striding out towards us. Behind him, the well-heeled punter is elbowing his way through a knot around the bar.

Escape, my brain screams.

You're outnumbered four to one. A rending tear as I wrench my arm free and I side step, back to the wall, towards the exit. 'Hold him,' snarls Nelson, cupping his nose. 'I want him. He's mine.'

'Outside. Outside,' calls Pepper from the reopened door to the bar.

My right kidney explodes. Both knees buckle. Don't go down, my brain pleads. Keep on your feet.

I lock my disjointed knees and slide, crouching, backside to wall, further along towards the door. I'm throwing lots of jabs and crosses, missing more often than I'm scoring.

My head is jolted sideways by a punch I failed to see. A metallic sound disorientates me. So fast and so often are blows landing, stomach, side, small of back, I'm only vaguely aware of being pushed and pulled, almost bent double. Gravy and two lagers swirl together in my stomach and I feel sick, about to vomit. Drums beat in my head. Strobe lighting flashes.

Don't fall, my brain commands. It's fatal to fall.

My head drops to my chest. The doors to the bar swing back again. Through them steps the well-heeled punter. There's time for just a muzzy view of a hand reaching inside his dark jacket.

Pepper holds the emergency door ajar with one hand and hooks the other under my right armpit. 'Get him out first,' he calls.

Someone else has my left arm up my back so far that it's a merciful release when I'm pitched forward.

Ice cold air rushes over my face. The surprise of a softer than anticipated landing is swept away by the knowledge that I'm down, prone, finished.

All I can do is hug the back of my head with both hands to partially protect my lower skull and neck and hope unconsciousness comes quickly when the baseball bats rain down; quicker still with a bullet.

'CID.'

A muffled shout comes from above and behind me.

'CID. Back off.'

'Fuck off.' An angry mumble. 'He did this. He started it. He's mine.'

'CID – and he's mine.' That same muffled tone.

I lift my arms from my ears and my face off something soggy and foul-smelling. Shit, I think, disgusted. I'm face first in my own vomit. I turn my head upwards.

The well-heeled punter has his back towards me. His feet are set well apart. He is holding something up in his right hand.

Facing him, shoulder to shoulder, are Pepper, Nelson and another heavy in evening dress.

'Importuning, mon, he was, interfering with lady customers. I'm tellin' ya,' drawls Pepper.

'I'll sort it,' says the punter firmly.

'We'll sort it.' Nelson takes a step forward.

My saviour holds up his other hand, like a traffic cop. 'You are using more force than necessary to effect an eviction.'

'He fucken asked for it, the shithead,' Pepper sings out.

'You are committing an offence of bodily harm, all of you,' comes the matter-of-fact reply. 'Now go back inside. Uniformed reinforcements are on the way. They'll take statements.'

'Yer,' slurs the second doorman. 'One of yours, ain't he?. You'll do f –'

'So,' says the punter slowly, 'you admit you are aware that he is a police officer acting in the execution –'

'Executing?' snarls Nelson, taking another threatening step forward. 'He was importuning, I tell yer.'

'Come on, mon,' says Pepper, reaching forward, pulling him back. 'Another time.'

'. . . acting in the execution of his duty,' the punter finally gets to finish as they turn their backs on him.

'You ain't heard the last of this,' says Pepper, turning to pull the door shut on us with a clang.

The punter kneels at my side. 'OK?'

I blow out. 'Thanks' is all I can manage.

'The flowers saved you from nastier injuries.'

On my stomach, I look around me, head still spinning. I am almost up to my watering eyes in bouquets. 'So did you,' I add gratefully.

'Hope you didn't mind me posing as CID,' he says apologetically. 'It was all I could think of to defuse the situation.'

'Then who are you?'

He leans closer and says, almost in a whisper, 'Haywood.

Security Service. Cameron detailed me to keep an eye on you. Lie still.'

I lie here for quite a while, eyes closed, fighting pain, shock, and shame that's not lessened by the realisation that I haven't been sick, but buried my face in a wreath that's gone rotten.

Police sirens are sounding, closer and louder all the time. Soon I hear a female voice issuing orders and footsteps that don't echo in the alley soundproofed by flowers.

I roll on my side. Inspector Herrick is looking down on me. 'Good Lord.' She puts her hand on Haywood's shoulder and crouches, nipping her knees together, ladylike. 'Want an ambulance?'

I move my head just slightly, making it hurt all the more. 'Just a bath, then bed.'

I introduce Haywood as a colleague, no more. They nod at each other. 'What happened?' she asks.

'Like you, I got too close to Golden Balls,' I reply through gritted teeth.

Haywood jerks his thumb at the closed door. 'They evicted him with unreasonable force. They'll say he was importuning women. He wasn't. I had him in view all the time.'

'Want them arrested?' asks Herrick.

With lots of grunts and groans, I pull myself into a sitting position. 'Just take their statements and have tabs kept on them for the next twenty-four to thirty-six hours.'

Haywood butts in. 'That can be arranged, sir.'

Since he's so keen, I also ask for a protective eye to be kept on Elaine, explaining that I don't know her last name or address. 'I'm worried they might put the frighteners on her.'

'The woman in black you were first talking to?' he asks.

I nod.

'Leave her to me.'

Christ, I think admiringly, he's some operator, a real pro.

The mist is beginning to clear. 'Take their security video, as well as their statements,' I tell Herrick. 'In fact, take the last week's films, all of them.' Unless it's been deliberately fogged, I brood.

They pull me to my feet. I look down at the flowers that saved me a stoved-in face. Thank God for floral tributes, I think.

19

FOUR DAYS TO CHRISTMAS

A long bath this morning, much longer than yesterday's, repeatedly topping up on hot water, double-dosing the foam, trying to soak away the aches and stings from scattered bruises and abrasions. Some pain fades, but not nearly enough for comfort.

I hate waking up in a bed that's not my own, at the weekends especially. Should have stayed on that train south and gone home last night to Em and Laura, I brood, wallowing in self-pity.

Drying myself tenderly, I inspect the main damage – purple rib cage, blackening hip, skinned shoulder, swollen left hand.

I wipe steam away from the mirror above the handbasin. The sort of lop-sided face you get with an infected wisdom tooth looks back at me. No shave today, I tell my battered reflection. Straight back between the sheets for you.

But, back in bed, sleep won't come. I call Room Service for hot croissants, black coffee and three papers against my bill.

The *Sun*, I read, has tracked down the video that starred their ex-page three girl. 'For hire at several shops,' it reports.

Photos from it appear under the headline 'Secret Shame of Shot TV Star'. They're so raunchy that even they have blacked out bits with a square 'Censored' stamp.

The *Daily Mail* has its own exclusive, much more sedate, much more interesting. Amanda Ball is pictured, fully clothed but looking more seductive than any page three girl, under a head-line: 'TV Shooting: Sad Actress Speaks'.

It's an extremely yucky story in which she talks of her distress over the death of her 'close professional colleague', her admira-tion for his untapped creative ability, her hopes that *Fallen Angel* will go ahead as a sort of lasting memorial, making Voss sound on a par with Dennis Potter leaving *Cold Lazarus* behind.

It was obviously planted before our confrontation at the Shuf-fle last night by, I wager, her publicist. In view of what the *Sun* are doing posthumously to the reputation of her close colleague, she'd have been wise to have kept shtum, but publicists on piecework don't always see it that way.

Any plug is a bonus in showbiz – it doesn't really have to be new or true – and middlebrow papers like the *Mail*, and, indeed, quality papers like the *Telegraph*, will happily run photos of tasty crumpet when there's half an excuse.

For the second time, I climb out of bed to examine last night's other damage. My grey suit and yellow shirt are beyond repair; won't even qualify as cast-offs for a charity collection.

I'm OK for shirts because I've used the hotel laundry, but I'm down to my last three pairs of underpants and socks, including those lucky black-and-white socks; Derby County's colours.

My grandad used to take me to watch them at the Baseball Ground and my grandma bought me a pair, black-and-white, the Rams' colours, to wear when they played in a championship decider. 'To bring you luck,' she'd said. We'd won.

My sock drawer has never been without a similarly patterned pair in the twenty-five years since. I wore some on my wedding day and every Saturday last spring when they were pushing for promotion back to the big league; worked both times.

In Special Ops, I used to pull them on whenever we went out on an armed job; never failed. We weren't armed on the railway line three and a half years ago so I didn't have them on and I got this leg. And, if I'd had them on yesterday, I wouldn't be feeling like this today.

Who are the Rams playing today? I go back to the bed and turn to the *Telegraph*'s sport pages. Southampton down at the Dell. Easy. Won't need 'em. Anyway, there are too many loose ends to get lucky today.

I take out plain tan-coloured, fresh underpants, put on my brown suit trousers and I'm buttoning up a beautifully pressed white shirt when, dead on ten, the bedside phone rings.

'Two people to see you,' announces the receptionist.

I know they will be Haywood and Herrick keeping a date made when they dropped off the remains of me last night. 'Send them up,' I say, sitting down on the bed.

The phone rings again and the door is knocked almost simultaneously. 'Hallo' is spoken into the mouthpiece and 'Come in' called loudly.

Herrick comes in first. For someone who would have signed off at gone two this morning, she looks remarkably bright in navy blue, trousers slim-fitting, blazer with brass buttons, and a cream shirt.

'Switchboard, Scarborough,' says the voice at the other end of the line. 'Duty inspector for you.'

There's just time for a thumbs-up for a raincoated Haywood as a different voice starts explaining that there's a note in daily orders on what to do in the event of Edward Tring dying in the local hospital.

Knowing the answer, I ask, 'And has he?'

At 6 a.m. I hear, his wife at his bedside. He'd said nothing that was of any help to us in the week he'd been in intensive care.

Under no circumstances, I order, is the news to be released to any media. Even the coroner is not to be informed until Monday. I thank him, replace the receiver.

Still sitting on the side of my unmade bed, I break the news, eyes on Herrick.

Suddenly she's wearing an up-all-night look. Tring was someone who was part of a conspiracy to ruin her professional reputation. Had he survived for a retrial and won, she'd have been ruined financially, too. Yet, in this brief moment, she seems to be thinking of his widow's pain. I like this woman.

My own wounds are so slight in comparison that neither asks how I'm feeling.

I stand and invite both of them to sit. Haywood takes off his white mac and tosses it on the spare bed. He's wearing another sharp suit, pale grey.

Herrick goes ahead of him to the table by the window. She draws the curtains back on to a day with clear skies and, at last, some sunshine. She folds up the newspapers and carries the breakfast tray to the dresser top.

When she sits, so does Haywood, opposite her across the cleared table.

I pace in stockinged feet and begin to sketch in the whole background, including my musings on the train last night.

Interpreting the significance of Tring's death, I explain, 'The retrial on the gems job is as dead as him and Voss. Pepper and the other two phoney alibi witnesses can be pulled in and turned over without running the risk of allegations of harassment. Nothing we do from now on can be viewed as contempt of any court.'

In a soft, southern voice, Haywood recounts the overnight activities of his sizeable squad of watchers and listeners. Elaine was seen safely home. Pepper is in bed at his luxury pad. Amanda went home by taxi to daddy.

Golden Balls and Clarence are making few phone calls. 'And when they do, they're so monosyllabic they clearly take no notice of BT's slogan, "It's good to talk." '

Herrick laughs for the first time and reports that she impounded eight days of security videos from the Riverside Shuf-

136

fle and was setting up a viewing at her station behind the court-house.

There's only a couple of other loose ends, so I announce, 'Raids tomorrow then.'

'Why not do them in two waves?' Haywood suggests. 'The first main target in twenty-four hours' time to be Pepper, plus the bouncers who worked you over last night.'

Pepper, he speculates, will use the phone call that's usually granted to someone in custody to alert Ball. Ball may turn out his lawyer. 'Depending on what we hear and what you prise out of Pepper, we can take Ball later. We'll know precisely where to find him all the time.'

Good thinking, I think. 'Three police teams of three in the field at 11 a.m.,' I decree.

I return to the bedhead, phone the acting head of CID, and request him, his drugs squad inspector and a small hand-picked party of officers with the efficient woman information room sergeant to act as collator. 'All to attend a full briefing at Inspector Herrick's station at 9 a.m. tomorrow,' I add, not fully telling him why.

'Right, sir,' he says. Then: 'Seen the *Sun*?'

'Yes.'

'We've recovered our own copy. Want to see it?'

'Not particularly, at this time of a morning,' I reply rather tartly.

'Voss had a lucrative sideline going, it seems,' the superintendent goes on. 'Apart from the one the *Sun*'s got hold of, we've found three more on various top shelves in video shops. He sold them to an under-the-counter distributor, not under Voss Vision labels, naturally.'

Changing my mind, I ask for all of them to be delivered by hand to Herrick's office. 'Got the distributors' details?'

He gives them, adding, 'A back street warehouse.'

'Add half a dozen officers from Vice to your team for tomorrow to raid him, too,' I instruct him, suddenly finding myself with more players than on the staff at the Baseball Ground.

The phone rings soon after the receiver is returned to its

137

cradle. Sergeant Howard reintroduces herself, this time from Rotterdam.

The Dutch police have got all the warrants they require, she begins. On the list of the crew of the *Goud Wereld* appeared the names of skipper Johan Mulder and seaman Aron Veltman.

I sense myself grinning into the mouthpiece, can't help it. Such had been Pepper's panic at Scarborough a week last night that he'd simply pinched the names of two of the crew, the first that came into his head, and passed them off as his own and Tring's when he checked him into hospital.

Raids at eleven in the morning tomorrow our time on the exporter's office, the boat and its crew, I tell her. She can offer immunity to any crew member willing to travel here to ID the man who turned up in that stolen Rover at the harbour as they docked.

Gets better all the time, I think, feeling better all the time.

Something worries me as I crouch to read the cards on the squashed carpet of flowers in the alley where Clive Voss died. An uncomfortable feeling that has nothing to do with the physical pain that made me walk here slower than usual through streets crowded with shoppers.

Not the fear of someone sneaking up behind, because I know via Haywood the whereabouts of all my targets.

No second thoughts, either, about this charade of wreath-laying at the scenes of crime. How can you be charitable about messages like: 'You brought joy to our home – Denis and Mary'? Must be a joyless home then, poor Denis and Mary.

Not guilt at prying into private grief. This is a public display of emotion. Lines stolen from songs like 'Simply the best – Marj and Keith' are here to be seen.

I'm sad, I suppose, and angry at the knowledge that, on estates where Tring lived, the money could have been much better spent.

All the way from the city down south where Voss did his radio training have come mixed autumn flowers labelled 'Always Alive in My Heart, Helpmate' – a reference no doubt to his *Clive Live* confessional show which died the death. Would that they all had, I silently sigh.

Reading 'From your No. 1 fan – Flo', I wonder if she takes the

Sun and, if so, what she makes of the tabloid trend of demystifying celebrities and personalities. She'll probably dismiss it as a yellow press lie.

On a big bouquet of chrysanthemums that are lasting better than most, I read 'Amen with all my heart – Mandy'.

Must be from Amanda Ball, I deduce, because it's a line from *Othello*. My Em can't get enough of Shakespeare, drags me to the Playhouse or the Robin Hood Theatre every time they stage one. The thing I remember most about *Othello* is the dead and the dying scattered about at the end. I pray that *Murder Live* isn't going to finish the same way.

I browse on, find a less literary farewell that cribs his usual sign-off, 'Good-night and thanks for being there', and I cringe. Though he never made satellite TV, there's a reference on some pinks, dying of thirst, to the Great Studio in the Sky, and I smile to myself, can't resist.

All this money, all this thought and trouble and, because they are not in water, they are fading faster than flowers in a cemetery in the New Year.

Flick. The smile switches itself off. Got it now. Guilt is what I'm feeling.

All these well-meaning people, total strangers, have taken time to pay for and lay their tributes here and you, you shameless sod, take the mickey.

Yet, you aren't going to make it to the village cemetery in the Peaks to fill the vase in the small marble plaque over the ashes of your grandparents who raised you.

Shame. That's what this troubled feeling is, you smart arse, you clever little shit.

Weighed down by conscience, I read on and finally find the card I think I'm looking for. 'Everlasting love', it reads. Above is the name of the florist's shop from which a dozen red roses were dispatched. Beneath is no signature, just a row of Xs.

I slip it from its plastic holder and into a pocket, feeling like a grave robber.

'Carnations,' I request.

'Red?' asks the assistant in the florist's shop.

Every week I buy flowers, red normally, for Em. Not nearly often enough, I fill my grandfolks' vase; usually red, too. Today I

139

ask for pink. I pay the usual inflated price at Christmas, as if all shops like this one haven't made enough this week on ordered deliveries to death alley.

'Thank you, Mr Todd,' she says, politely confirming that she'd noted details from my warrant card which I produced with the shop's label.

'And thank you,' I say, patting a pocket with my notebook with the details I'd sought.

Outside, in the milling crowds, it doesn't feel right, carrying flowers for a woman who is not Em or grandma.

I wander aimlessly for a while on packed pavements that have dried in the cutting wind and weak sunshine, seeking my bearings.

Somehow I find my way back to the Shambles where I window-shopped with Cameron on Thursday night.

Pornography puzzles me, defeats and, to be honest, embarrasses me. Sometimes I wonder if I'm normal, because it never fails to have a steroid-style effect on me.

The ex-page three girl isn't my type anyway, wearing, as she does, a Biggles-style helmet, ear flaps buttoned down, and nothing else, in *Flying High*.

After twenty minutes of low jinks, she's gagged by a brute of a man who then takes her from behind, making her eyes roll in close-up and me, insensitive sod that I am, laugh out loud.

Maybe that's what I'm supposed to do, I think, changing cassettes. It's got to be some sort of sick joke, surely?

Feet back on the desk in Inspector Herrick's cramped office, dusty blinds drawn, I sit through *Detention* and find myself actually longing for a commercial break.

Anything – the ultimate party album, the wonder of Woolies, the mix that makes your pud rise and brown, even Bob Hoskins and 'It's good to talk', God help me – anything has got to be better than thirty minutes of a woman about a quarter of a century too old for school and five stones too tubby for a gym-slip enjoying six of the best; no laughs at all.

I get up again, wondering how the Rams are doing down at the Dell.

Take Away stars a scantily dressed oriental girl serving an extremely messy eater a six-dish meal. The service takes half an hour as one garment is removed per course. No prize for guessing dessert on a table-cloth that wasn't all that clean to start with.

No Chinese for me tonight; that's settled, I decide, changing over. Or sex, come to think of it.

Bartered Bride and *Sugar Plum* owe their titles to the classics, but nothing else. One is squirmingly sadistic, the other homosexual with lots of oil being sloshed about.

I fast forward through most of them. Nothing so far is producing the answer I am seeking. I'm going to take a break, have a little muse.

All the camera work is glossy, as it should be for a sideline from the professional Voss Vision.

Why did he do it? Can't be money. He was on a bloody good, well-paid thing.

Kicks, I suppose. Like parsons with boy sopranos for a bag of humbugs, Whitehall whizz-kids with call girls for a wad of notes. They lack control, never stop to think, totally block out any fear that they'll ever be exposed.

It's a madness and once you start to get away with it you can't stop. You're driven. More. More. More.

He'd been smart enough not to appear on screen himself, but what went on afterwards off-camera? He'd have been shopped sooner or later. And then what? A five-figure sum to tell his story, probably to the paper that turned him over so they could keep the scandal running; fat fees to appear on confessional shows, a bloody book even.

The modern media have changed standards from my grand-folks' time. You don't pay for your misdeeds these days. You're not ostracised. You profit. You're fêted.

And where, how did he get the women? Ply them with drugs or offers of stardom?

And what about the sad sods who buy or rent this rubbish? Can't get partners, I suppose, or, at least, get them to do what they want.

No inhibitions, see. Nowt wrong with inhibitions. They're what stopped me last night trying to find out if Amanda Ball's tanned legs were in tights or not.

One thing's for certain, I think, cheering up. If she's not a better actor and if Con Clarence doesn't produce a sharper script, *Fallen Angel* is going to be a bigger turkey than the Waltons order for Thanksgiving.

One to go from the collection the acting CID chief had delivered, so I'd best get on with it.

Sibling Rivalry features two good-lookers miscast as sisters. A blonde wears black bra, pants, suspender belt and stockings. A brunette has long hair and wears white bra and panties. There's lots of hair-pulling, arm locks, wrestling on a water bed I recognise, ripped underwear and lots of kissing better at the end.

Worth a second look, that.

I call in Herrick who brings with her the week of tapes she impounded from the security office upstairs at the Riverside Shuffle. She offers the top of the pile which she stacks on her desk. 'Start with last night?'

I shake my head, rewind the cassette that's already in the machine. 'This first.'

She pulls up a chair and sits primly by my side, not stirring, sighing, making no comment whatever, as *Sibling Rivalry* gets a second showing. As the screen flickers white, she's puzzled. 'I don't get the point.'

'You will,' I promise.

She stands and picks up the case on top of her pile. I shake my head again. 'Let's run with a week earlier.'

She goes to the bottom of the pile, then to the machine. Soon the TV screen is split into quarters, grainy black and white views as cameras range the Shuffle's front entrance, bar, stairs and dance floor. There's very little action anywhere.

The date, '13/12/' appears in white on a black block in the top left-hand corner. Next to it is the time: 20.00.00. The seconds in the last two figures are already on the move. I fast forward to 21.00.00 and sit through an hour watching the Shuffle filling.

Amanda appears twice, dressed in dark, tight hipsters with a lighter coloured top which reveals her midriff. There's a front view of her heading across the ground-floor bar in the general direction of the toilets, then a rear view of her walking back; both nice views.

She'd fibbed about the cameras. There's no soundtrack.

Elaine I spot a couple of times, in a check outfit, at a big table with her crowd.

142

The few black faces that appear are held and examined. Pepper's is not among them.

'Best film I've seen all day,' I declare as the white figures on the black block register 13/12/22.00.00.

20

The young duty doctor makes the introductions and Herrick hands over the pink carnations.

Head high on four or five pillows, Liz Clarence stares at them vacantly. She lays them, still in their wrapping, across the lime green bedspread that covers her up to the midriff.

Her dull black hair hangs lankly over the shoulders of a white knitted cardigan that looks too thick to wear in a side room of an overwarm ward in the district hospital. Her skin is ivory pale and flaking, her cheeks hollow, her brown eyes lifeless.

You don't have to be a doctor to tell that she's in one hell of a mess.

On the other side of the bed, Herrick begins, 'Your doctor says we can have ten minutes with you. OK?' She doesn't wait for an answer, small-talks, admiring a forced hyacinth in a moss-topped bowl surrounded by get-well cards on the bedside cabinet.

'From girlfriends at the office,' says Liz in a soft, noticeably rustic voice. The doctor backs out of the room.

Herrick looks across at me, nodding. It's not just an invitation to say my set piece. She's seen the point of watching *Sibling Rivalry*. We've identified the brunette.

Herrick lowers herself on to the edge of the bed while I pull a grey plastic chair away from the cream wall. 'We're inquiring into the death of Mr Clive Voss,' I begin as I sit at the bedside. 'Your husband worked with him and, of course, you knew him.'

A tiny nod.

'In circumstances like this, I'm afraid,' I continue with what I hope is a sympathetic expression, 'we've to go into personal backgrounds.'

'Con wouldn't, didn't do it.' She blurts it, eyes closed, rolling her head, screwing it deeper into the pillows.

'I know that,' I say, reassuringly. I won't add, 'because he

143

didn't have the time.' Instead: 'How well did you know Clive –
just socially or ...?' I let it hang there.

No response, eyes open again but on the ceiling.

Herrick finishes it for me. 'Or intimately?'

Liz looks sideways to her, almost talking to her pillows. 'Depends what you mean.'

I shouldn't really be here. This is woman-to-woman stuff. I'm
going to take a side seat and let Herrick take charge. 'Sex?' she asks.

'Not ...' Liz can't force the word out.

Intercourse, I'd have said, but Herrick uses, 'Love-making?'

Liz nods.

'Not the full act but romps, foreplay?'

'Some.' She closes her exhausted eyes. 'He liked to, well, see
me, you know.'

'And film you?'

'Yes.' Liz chews her bottom lip.

'I have to hear all about that, please, if you don't mind,' says
Herrick, seemingly oblivious to my presence.

Half-way through her story, slowly coaxed out by Herrick, the
impression I'm getting is of a simple young country girl, lonely
and hard-up in her bedsit when she came to the city. Clarence
was the first steady who treated her like a lady, who didn't want
to be forever rolling in the hay.

'He was nice, like, kind, and well ...' For the umpteenth time
she fails to complete a sentence.

Case studies like this aren't case histories because you only get
one side of the story. Even doctors can sometimes only best
guess. Mine is that back home in the Wolds she learned about
sex naturally (maybe, on occasions, unnaturally) and that she
was always more experienced and adventurous than the first
steady who became her husband.

Marriage was a mistake, it's plain to see now. To her, he was
company and security. To him, she was nice to have on your
arm so long as she didn't say anything silly at parties with
sophisticated media types around.

'I wanted to start a family, but, well, he wasn't sure we'd stay
here long and ...' She shrugs wearily.

I suspect that sex, love-making (call it what you will)
became routine, lessening with the passage of time as Clarence

144

worked longer hours. Maybe he wasn't that interested, very good at it, impossible to say until the shrinks have had a go at him too.

She started to complain about being left so often on her own. 'Even when he was home he was on his word processor till gone midnight running off that bloody script on his clattering printer.' A touch of resentment spurs her at last to the end of a sentence.

' "Go out with the girls from the office a bit more," he said. "You know I've got a lot on with *Fallen Angel* on top of everything else." '

'So that's his baby?' I put in.

In a very icy tone, she answers. 'The only baby he's ever going to produce, if you ask me.'

Confirmation, I think, of trouble in the marital bed. 'Have you read it?'

'Heard him reading slabs of dialogue off his screen. He's always having to change it.'

'What's it about?' I ask.

Unwinding a little, she answers with a question. 'Seen *The X-Files*?'

I reply with an enthusiastic nod.

'A bit like that. He spotted a short story . . .' She breaks off for a little whinge. 'When he's not writing, he's reading.' Then she gets back to her answer. '. . . thought it was a classic of its kind, talked Clive into taking up a film option. That's what he really wants to do – write for the screen.'

'Cost a lot to make, though, do films,' I commiserate.

'Don't I know it,' she responds with a sigh. 'He tried all over, no luck.'

'He, not Clive?'

'Clive is . . . was the front man. Con does all the work on it.'

'Is he still trying to raise funding for the project?' I ask.

She shrugs. As far as she knows, she's telling me.

I sit back again, satisfied I've got at the truth.

'Er . . .' Herrick resumes falteringly. She's in difficulties, can't disclose to anyone, certainly not an estranged and bitter wife, that Con Clarence shopped Golden Balls over the September drugs shipment.

'Three months ago,' she says slowly, 'I spoke to your husband. He expressed concern about the availability of drugs. I don't

145

know where he got his information. We don't always ask. From his journalistic work, I expect, but –'

'From me, sorry to say,' Liz interrupts. 'I, er, well, sort of, er...' She plucks up her nerve. '...took too many.'

'Ecstasy or what?' asks Herrick airily, as if everyone under her age took them.

'No. No.' Liz works her head in the pillows. 'I'm under the doctor. Depression. Have been for months.'

She looks helplessly at me and back again towards Herrick. 'I didn't want to tell him...' She can't face up to her suicide attempt, stops.

Herrick takes her hand, squeezing very tenderly. 'Don't trouble yourself with what you didn't tell him, luv. Tell us what you did.'

Liz blows out air, making her bottom lip tremble. 'That I'd been taking Ecstasy and other things.'

'And had you?' I ask.

'Just once.'

'Obtained from a bouncer on a girls' night out at the Shuffle?' I suggest.

A single nod. 'Made me sick.'

'What was your husband's reaction when you told him that white lie?' asks Herrick.

'Furious. The health risk, the addiction, the cost. He's very strait-laced, you know. He brought me in here and, well...' She's back into an old habit.

I help out. 'And here you eventually told doctors the truth about the drugs overdose, that they were medicinal, not anything recreational from the Shuffle?'

'And...' Liz stops to think. '...about a week later, I told Con everything.'

I have to cross-check this, make sure I've understood. I don't want to say 'suicide attempt' so: 'About the overdose not really being anything recreational or, even, accidental?'

'And about Clive, too.' says Liz.

'What about Clive?' asks Herrick in her matter-of-fact tone.

She'd known who Voss was from seeing him on television at home in the Wolds and got to know him at parties when he and Con worked at Ridings TV, better still when Voss Vision was formed.

'He came to our wedding. He was always friendly and amusing, but polite, just treated me as Con's partner, one of the crowd, until...' The sentence dribbles away again.

Herrick comes to her assistance. 'Until you started going out to the Shuffle without your hubby on Friday nights?'

A firm nod. 'And then he started coming on to me. You know, how lovely I was, how he'd always admired me.'

'And?'

'Well, one night, I'd had a bit too much to drink...'

Herrick anticipates another pause. 'Not mixed with drugs?'

Annoyed, Liz speaks hurriedly. 'No. Never take them. Not with tranquillizers and anti-depressants.' She thinks. 'Well, only that once and it made me bad.'

She relaxes into her pillows. 'We sneaked away early and...' She smiles very faintly to herself.

'Back to his place?' asks Herrick.

A warmer smile.

'And?'

'Well, there was some hugging and holding and he undressed me and...' She swallows. 'He took pictures.'

'Cine?'

'Ordinary camera first time.' Very quietly she adds, 'That came later.'

Between pauses and promptings, she describes how it became a regular thing, almost every Friday for three months last summer. He bought her all sorts of basques and frilly belts, filmed her with them on, then off.

'Did he ever get into bed with you?' asks Herrick, very bluntly.

'Never. No. I wanted him to. Would have loved him to.' A positive headshake. 'But never.' She sighs deeply. 'He said adultery would spoil a perfect relationship.'

Bullshit, I realise. He got his kicks another way. All she probably wanted after an abused childhood and a neglectful husband was some real affection. All she got was kinky sex.

'Did anybody else get into bed with you on those Friday nights?' asks Herrick.

'Not a man.' Her reply is defensive.

Cleverly Herrick draws out the facts without sparking an attack of hysterics by telling her we have seen *Sibling Rivalry* and so have lots of blue movie buffs.

The blonde in the film was already at Voss's place when

147

they got there. They sat around, having drinks. Voss said he wanted to witness something a bit extra, a bit spicy. Having already seen what they got up to on Voss's water bed I let my mind drift.

If Voss was still alive, what would he say? That she consented, co-operated fully, enjoyed it all and suggested some of the refinements herself, the usual pornographer's defence.

Yet it's rape, rape of the sort that never comes to court, pornographer's rape.

There he was – handsome, educated, famous locally, wealthy, smooth-talking, defender of the little man against big business and authority – and sexually perverted, a voyeur; a predator.

There she was – in a marriage of convenience to a sexually inadequate husband, more than vulnerable, already mildly mentally ill, unable to distinguish between love and sex because of her upbringing.

He'd tell her she was fabulous, marvellous, the most exciting woman he'd ever known. He'd buy her sexy garments. She'd do anything, anything at all to please him. And she'd convince herself she was enjoying it all. Seen it, heard it, a score of times before with prostitutes and their pimps.

She didn't do it for drugs. She's only taken one and that was bought from a bouncer. She wasn't seeking screen stardom. She loved him and she, poor betrayed girl, thought he loved her.

The making of *Sibling Rivalry* was the last time she went to his place, Liz continues.

Next time she saw him at the Shuffle he gave her the old conscience bit, how uncomfortable he felt about her being the wife of a colleague, like a married man brushing off a bit on the side he'd used and abused.

The Friday after that he was fussing around Amanda Ball and the week after that she stayed in and took the pills; a cry for help, I suspect, rather than a real try at ending it.

And what help did she get from her husband? He walked out on her when she told him the truth about Voss.

Clarence had undoubtedly overheard Ball setting up a drugs deal. At the time he'd been misled into believing his sick

148

wife was a junkie. He'd informed on Ball to Herrick as an act of revenge.

There was no recording of that call locked away in the safe. It never existed. Fearing for his life, he made it up when Pepper visited. In his panic, he named Voss as the police informer. Ball fell for it, used Clarence, not Voss, as his middleman in setting up Tring's release.

Had Tring succeeded in blowing the safe instead of himself, what would he have taken away hotfoot from the law office, if not incriminating evidence against Ball?

What would have been in Tring's hot little hand if he'd survived?

I break my long silence. 'Did you tell your husband you had allowed Clive to film you?'

'No, just that we'd been, well...'

This time I'm undecided how to help her out. Making love is inaccurate. Having a fling sounds too innocent, an affair too heavy. 'Playing around,' I suggest.

'It was more than that,' she says mournfully.

'But Con knows nothing, as far as you are aware, about the film Voss took of you and the other lady?'

'Nothing.' She looks aghast.

'But you did admit to him that you had formed a deep attachment for Voss?'

Her head comes down in a brief nod, then up, looking at the doctor re-entering the room. He comes up behind me.

'What was Con's reaction to that news?' Herrick asks.

'That it was over.' Liz starts to weep. 'Finished.'

'So where did you go when you left hospital?'

'My parents' place.'

The doctor is hovering anxiously and I hurry into my last question. 'And were you there last Friday night, doing what?'

'Watching TV, just hoping to see Clive on it and when I did...' Her voice cracks. Her face is screwed, tears flowing freely down both cheeks.

Herrick grips her hand tightly. 'And, afterwards, with the shock and everything making you so ill, who brought you back in here?'

'An ambulance,' she just manages to reply. 'My mum dialled 999.' She buries her face in her pillows.

The doctor places a hand on my shoulder. 'Best if you go now.'

149

Walking down the hospital corridor towards us is Elaine from the calculating agency. She is carrying a big bottle of lemon barley. Somewhere behind her in a stream of visitors will be one of Haywood's men.

She is wearing a long, thick black coat that almost sweeps the floor. When she is close enough to recognise me her face drops into a look of total disgust. As we pass, she hisses, 'Bastard.'

I don't stop, try to explain, just screw my neck into my shoulders, feeling smaller, and keep, on walking.

'A friend?' asks Herrick, chirpily.

'Was,' I say, glumly.

She looks at me with understanding. 'They are difficult to keep in this job, aren't they?'

No Indian tonight, no Chinese, and certainly no disco dancing, I think contentedly, climbing into bed after a soothing mid-evening bath. The cuts and bruises don't look any better, but some of the pain has gone.

Room Service delivers sirloin steak, medium well done, with all the trimmings and half a bottle of full-bodied red wine. I digest my day with the meal on a tray.

Liz Clarence has a watertight alibi, confirmed in a visit to ambulance control on the way back to the hotel. She was one of the two emergencies that lacked a police escort through remote and ice-bound countryside on Friday the 13th.

My problem now is Pepper. Got to get him to talk. How? The old way, I suppose. Frighten him before you get him into the police station, bribe him before you run the interview room tape; both highly illegal, of course.

So how? Well, if he's going around pretending to be from da Yard, what's to stop me? Witnesses, that's what. Don't have any then. Take him alone. Simple. Problem solved.

My mind moves on.

If Tring had survived the safe-blowing and returned from the law office without the non-existent recording of the incriminating phone call, how would Clarence have explained it away to Golden Balls?

Well, he's a budding scriptwriter, prefers fiction to fact, so he'd make something up again like: 'Voss must have moved it.'

150

And since Voss was dead and unable to deny it, he might have got away with it.

What did Voss have in safe-keeping then, if not the taped goods on Ball? Can't have been *Sibling Rivalry*. He wouldn't lock away a blue movie already available in local porno shops.

The phone rings after I've polished off the meal. Em wants to know what I'm up to. An early night after watching blue movies for most of the day, I tell her, and she laughs.

You? I ask. Shopping with Laura, she says. Was the city as packed as this one? I enquire idly, just needing to yarn for a while.

'Actually,' she replies, 'we didn't shop locally. Nipped up to Derbyshire. Took some flowers for your grandfolks. I knew you wouldn't have time to go.'

I close my eyes, only half listening as she gabbles on about this niece wanting a Blue John necklace and that aunt liking Denby plates for presents.

Nipped up? It's a two-hour round trip. And you can get Derbyshire-produced Blue John gifts and Denby pottery almost anywhere. She's spinning a cover story for a deeply touching and thoughtful act.

Though she hates me to tell her this outside the bedroom, she's just going to have to hear me out. 'Thanks. You know –'

'Thought you'd have phoned me by now,' she breaks in reprimandingly.

'Why?'

'Don't you want me to video anything?'

What's she talking about? I ask myself. *NYPD Blue* has finished its run. 'If I never see another video in my life it will be too soon.'

'That bad, eh?'

'Boring,' I sigh.

'Wonder if Derby County are any better?' she says brightly. 'They might be on *Match of the Day* in an hour's time. Know the result?'

I haven't bought a sports paper or listened to the radio. 'No. No. I'll watch it here.'

We natter for quite a while, about nothing in particular, me not mentioning what happened last night, because I never like to worry her.

151

She asks when to expect me home. I'll know for sure tomorrow, I reply.

She takes the hint that a showdown is planned because she says, 'Wear your lucky socks then.'

'I love you,' I finally say, and I put down the phone before she can rebuke me.

A little light reading until *Match of the Day*, I decide.

Not the case file. Light, I said. I need a diversion. I slip 'Jacko' Jackson's latest off the bedside cabinet. It seems so long and so much has happened since I picked it up (they're eminently forgettable) that I'll have to start again.

I turn all the way back to the inscription, smile, flip on through acknowledgements and blurb to chapter one.

I can't get into it. The words on the page become a blur. There's something at the back of my mind, lurking, nagging.

Suddenly, it bursts to the front.

I climb naked out of bed, find and rerun both Friday night tapes, do some rough maths on a sheet of hotel headed notepaper, phone the dog track manager at his home to double-check my calculations, miss *Match of the Day*, but find the answer I've been seeking for five days.

21

THREE DAYS TO CHRISTMAS

The Minster bells awaken me, a wonderful peal.

A quick shower and I move to the mirror. Not so wonderful. Bristles are sprouting thick and fast, blond to match my hair. The skin beneath is still too tender to shave.

Not wanting to go to the breakfast room looking like a baddie from a cowboy B-movie, I order a breakfast tray with everything apart from egg from Room Service and the *Sunday Telegraph*.

The lucky black-and-white socks are pulled on before my

underpants and there's no alternative to the brown suit. The curtains are opened on to a lovely day, ice blue sky and sunshine.

When the tray arrives, I turn to the sports pages before starting to eat at the table with a view of the city walls. The Rams lost 3–1.

Bill Shankley, the great soccer manager, once said, 'Football is not a matter of life or death. It's more important than that.' I look down at my socks, deciding, Bill Shankley was wrong. The Rams can bounce back. One mistake today and you can't.

Right elbow rests nonchalantly at shoulder height on the door frame, wrist limp, hand unclenched.

My feet are set apart, accurately balanced, left just ahead of right, knees slightly flexed.

Handcuffs are hooked by the last three fingers of my still swollen hand.

I'm ready. I take a deep breath.

The index finger goes to the bell on the white door of Pepper's apartment on the first floor of the riverside flats where Voss was a near neighbour.

Church clocks chime the hour.

In two minutes, timed by a stop-watch, the acting CID chief and the drugs squad inspector will come, as instructed, up the stairs from the private car-park. Every one of the next unwitnessed 120 seconds is precious.

I press the bell.

All I hear are more chimes.

On the eleventh I press again, anxiety mounting.

He's in there because Haywood's team say so. I don't know how heavily he'll be sleeping after getting home from the Shuffle at gone two.

A third ring.

'A minute. A minute.' A deep, fruity voice comes from the other side of the door some distance away. Then, closer, 'Who there?'

'From da Yard,' I call, managing to hold off a 'Yo'.

A chain rattles. A lock clicks. I firm wrist and clench fist.

The door is pulled open. Pepper's bleary face appears in the gap.

153

So much weight is thrown on my left foot that the right comes up to tiptoe as the fist flies fast and horizontally.

His nose is on the sweet spot, the flats between the first and second sets of knuckles; the perfect shot.

Crack. No pain, no jarring, not for me.

His head yanks back. His bulky body follows, staggering. Muscular legs judder but don't give.

'Jeez' burbles out very nasally through the blood.

I step inside, hold his chin up and hit him again, same spot.

I grab his right wrist, twist him as he sags, and cuff both hands behind his narrow waist. He falls to his knees. I walk round him, giving him a wide berth, and stand with my back to the opened door.

He is breathing in gasps. His head hangs. Blood flows freely through a matt of hair down his chest towards his white boxer shorts, all he is wearing. His head comes up. His look is spaced out. 'What the fucken... what ya want, mon? What's this?'

'Lookahere.' On his knees, Pepper contorts a bare shoulder towards his chin. 'Looka what he did.'

'Resisting arrest,' I tell the two local officers without looking behind me.

'He's puttin' it on...I...Damn straight, he did.' Pepper is so stunned he is stammering. 'Told me he was from da Yard.'

'With the Cameron Commission from Scotland Yard,' I lie effortlessly. 'You must have misheard.'

The door is closed to shut out the cold. The two plainclothes officers flank me. I look down on Pepper. 'Now don't mishear this.'

I flick my head towards the acting CID chief. 'The superintendent here is going to caution you and arrest you for ABH on me on Friday night –'

'You got the prob-lem, not me.' He glares up at me. 'I'm suing, see. Suing.'

'He will be taking you to the station –'

'Cum-on.' Pepper stretches some words out, hurries others. 'I wanna hospeetel. Now.'

'Oh,' I say evenly, 'you'll be going there all right – the one on the coast where a doctor and nurse and two orderlies will identify you as the man who took in Edward Tring nine days ago after he blew himself up.'

154

He sits back on his calf muscles. His chin drops. He watches gobbets of blood drip on to his thick cream hall carpet.

'Then, with your nose in a sling,' I continue, 'it's back here again by which time...' I look at my watch. '...members of the crew of the *Goud Wereld* will be landing at Leeds/Bradford airport to take a good look at you, along with the deputy boss from the pit where you pinched the dynamite for Tring's safe job.'

He shakes his head, making the blood flow freer. 'I'm saying nothin''

'We don't need you to say nothin'. We've seen Tring.' I pat the pocket with a notebook inside, hoping he'll assume he's made a statement.

Pepper looks up at me, sullen, puzzled.

I turn to my right. 'What have we got so far, chief?'

The superintendent fingers them off. 'Two counts of burglary – the pit and the safe. One count of conspiracy to pervert the course of justice with Nelson who, as I speak, is joining King in custody. They'll talk.'

'Bull-s-h-h-h-i-t,' drawls Pepper.

'Plus car theft,' the CID man adds.

'Plus, of course,' I say smiling down, 'breaking the speed limit on the A64 on Friday the 13th. Not your lucky day, was it, Christian?'

He looks back, taunting, almost snarling, 'Oh yeah. Oh yeah.'

I motion left to the drugs inspector. 'He'll be collecting up your clothes, everything you've worn for the last nine days, for Forensics and turning your Toyota inside out. Same with the car you stole and dumped at the racecourse.'

His face is plastered with blood and confusion, eyes darting between the three of us. 'Then we'll meet again, you and me, to talk about murder...'

'Shit, mon. I know nothin'...'

'Yes, you do.'

'Nothin' Nothin'...' Defiantly, he shakes his head. Blood sprays the white walls like drops from an overloaded paint brush.

'Well,' I say, easily, 'you're carrying the can for it.' I glance at the superintendent. 'How big's the bill?'

'Five for perverting justice,' the CID man speculates. 'Three for the burglaries. Consecutive, with a good judge.'

'All academic anyway,' I butt in, 'when he gets life for murder.'

Pepper arches his long broad back. 'I done no murder.'

'Think about who did then. And then do what all good Yardies do when the key's about to be turned and thrown away.' I pause, smiling. 'You'll talk about it to me, Christian, and, in return, I'll see what I can do for you.'

He sits back on his calves again, chin on his chest, its hairs more red than black now, saying nothin'.

At the station behind the courthouse, Pepper obscenely demanded what he claimed was his legal entitlement to a free call. Actually, it's a privilege but, being a decent sort, I granted it.

He insisted on keeping it private; a waste of time because, now, just a few minutes later, Haywood is playing back his opening line recorded on a miniature tape machine.

'Can't talk much but I need a brief. Now. Badly. Trouble. Big, big trouble.'

A Geordie voice asks, 'Where are you?' Then, 'Say nothing, not a peep, till he gets there.'

'They say they've nabbed Nelson,' adds Pepper.

'I see,' says Ball in a subdued voice. 'Say no more right now.'

Then Ball phoned the senior partner of a law firm, far bigger than McMichael's, and we listen to that bugged conversation, too. 'Get there immediately, represent him and report back,' orders Ball.

Five more minutes and the lawyer phones the station, wanting to know if Christian Pepper is being held. 'Yes,' says the acting CID chief.

By the time he arrives here Pepper will have gone to the district hospital to have his nose treated.

When the lawyer gets there, Pepper will be on his way back here again with an unnecessary stop at his apartment on the way; the old run around. His lawyer will not be the only one to miss his Yorkshire pudding this Sunday lunchtime.

Haywood walks, beaming, back into Herrick's office with two miniature machines. 'Listen to these.'

He thumbs on the first. Ball again: 'We have to talk...'

156

'Anything the matter?' a startled voice breaks in.

'...in person. Same spot. Fourish.' The line goes dead.

Haywood turns on the second machine; word for word the same conversation. 'He's phoned Con Clarence.'

His beam fades. 'We can track them, of course, but we may not be able to get close enough to monitor what they're saying unless we're extremely fortunate.'

'Yes...but...' My turn to beam as I recall my visit to the pit tip. 'It's our lucky day.'

So lucky that there's time for Yorkshire puddings filled with Cumberland sausages with Herrick, my treat, in that fine pub by the river.

Know what upsets me about mystery and suspense fiction, like TV police thrillers? The way the main character is always in jeopardy at the end. He's not.

Often, though he may supervise the show, he may not even plan the operation, like I've delegated this end to Haywood.

Certainly he doesn't lie in wait with a gun, shouting, 'Go! Go! Go!' He has marksmen from Special Ops for that.

These days, he has specialists for everything. He'll leave the routine taking of statements to them and float between interview rooms, listening to the tapes, dropping a question here and there.

The higher his rank, the further he's likely to be from the action. Back in my own force, I'd be superintending, like a chief superintendent should, sitting in my office, awaiting developments. At a weekend, ideally, I'd be by the phone at home.

The only reason I'm here in the cramped, equipment-laden back of this green Land Rover, borrowed from the Forestry Commission, is that I've no office to sit in and no home near enough to go to.

In my heart I know it's more than that. I got this leg on a stake-out when we were not armed, like we're unarmed this afternoon. The back-up was too far away to be of immediate help.

I just feel I should be here, that's all, close to the boys and girls of a force whose own chief has confused media management with leadership.

It's a bit like supporting Derby County or any soccer team. You ought to be there. Even if you get the wrong result, you have an understanding of how it all came about that no press report can ever give. You'll have seen with your own eyes, not heard or read it second-hand.

Crack this, and I'll bail out in a couple of days, back home. I'll make sure via Cameron that the TV and radio interviews are left to the acting head of CID, not the chief constable. Good for force morale, for one thing. Time to give the poor viewers a change of face, for another.

If this goes smoothly, my face will not be seen on TV, or even caught by the cameras Haywood's team have hung among the spiky green branches of thick fir trees. Nor will my voice be picked up on the mikes on cables that snake beneath the loose shale of the colliery's waste tip and the sandy footpath between it and these woods that block out any view of what promises to be a beautiful sunset.

Over my earpiece I hear the watcher Haywood assigned to Ball. 'Gold-coloured BMW turning on to track leading south to your location. Driver's dress: Green waxed jacket, green wellington boots, soft brown trilby.'

His disguise, I think with an amused smile.

'Abort task,' says Haywood, sitting at my side, an Ordnance Survey map spread over his knees.

Soon the woman shadowing Clarence reports in code. 'Three Vs north-bound' – which means the Voss Vision van is approaching from the opposite direction. 'Driver's dress: Dark blue anorak, lighter blue jeans, black boots. Hatless.'

'Abort,' repeats Haywood.

He turns a screw on the plastic mouthpiece of his headset and hinges it away from his face. 'Ball should park up here on this.' He taps his map with a finger. 'An old bit of runway, left over from a wartime RAF station.' His finger runs up a red dotted line that marks a footpath between the east end of the spoil tip and the wood. 'The Voss Vision van will come here, we think.' His finger stops at a lay-by. 'Five minutes' walk for both before they are in sight again.'

Unexpectedly, a third look-out reports from a hide among a thick bank of brambles alongside the footpath. 'Trilby is carrying a 12 bore shotgun, broken, but loaded.'

Haywood looks at me, urgently. Your call, he is saying.

Oh shit, I think, suddenly no longer a spectator sitting in a grandstand, but the manager on the bench, deciding the tactics. I shake my head.

Haywood twists his mouthpiece back into the place and speaks very calmly, 'Proceed to plan.'

No greetings are overheard when they meet. 'What's the trouble?' Clarence opens in a tense, tinny voice.

'Pepper,' replies Ball gruffily. 'They've arrested him and Nelson.'

'Oh, my God.' Then, even more nervously, 'Why the gun?'

'Pigeons,' says Ball.

Good cover if anyone walks down the path. Syndicates are permitted to shoot vermin on Sundays. He's careful, clever.

'Will he, er, like, er, talk?' stammers Clarence, barely able to himself.

'A good kiddo, he is. He'll say what I give him to say and no more.' Ball is making no attempt to moderate his broad Geordie.

'Told that superintendent all you told me to say, pointed him at Pepper,' says Clarence in an anxious-to-please tone.

'It's a cock-up, right enough.' Ball sounds deeply disgruntled. 'They should never have set about him. Asking for trouble, that was, stupid black berk.'

'How close are they?'

Silence. 'Been thinking. Er...' Ball stops. 'Let's get off this path. Stroll a bit.'

A grunt and a few huffs and the look-out comes on. 'Climbed the fence, walking westwards up the rough roadway between the lagoons.'

As I try to picture the scene, Haywood speaks away from his mouthpiece. 'They'll remain in range provided they don't go more than a hundred yards.'

Above the crunching sound of slow, heavy footsteps, Ball resumes, 'They must have worked out the Tring connection.'

'Where is he?' Clarence is talking so urgently that he asks another question before receiving a reply. 'How is he?'

Ball answers both. 'In hospital under an assumed name. Hanging on when we last heard from Holland.'

'Will he talk?'

'Why should he?' Ball raises his voice, offended, then lowers it. 'He didn't over his last job.'

Christ, I think, smugly, all but rubbing my hands. Ball financed the stately home raid and probably fenced the gems, too.

The crunching underfoot stops. 'The big question is...' Ball again, tone hardening. '... will you?'

'No.' Gasped. 'Never. You know that. Told that Commission copper all you authorised, nothing more.'

'You talked before.' Ball again, low, menacing.

'Look.' There's penitence in Clarence's tone. 'I've explained.' He sighs deeply. 'I thought she'd been hooked. When I discovered the truth about Voss, I came in, did all you asked. Took lots of risks.'

'To save yourself and fund your fucking film.'

Clarence is provoked enough to protest, 'It's not blackmail, never was. It's development money, an investment for the future, Mandy's future.'

'Then, why lock up that bloody tape?'

'Clive's doing,' Clarence protests. 'Security, he called it, in case you backed out.'

No words are exchanged for several crackling steps that sound like radio interference. Then: 'You playing around with her?' Ball again, more threatening than ever. 'Cos if –'

'No, Christ.' Clarence, distinctly panicky. 'No. Honest.'

'Was Voss?'

'No.' Pause. 'As far as I know.' There's doubt in his tone.

Silence again apart from audible breathing. Clarence resumes. 'Look, I played straight...'

Ball breaks in, 'After trying to shop me.'

'... did everything you said – the recce here, the shots of the safe, the signal. Everything. Saw that Todd, like you told me.'

'Talked too much, did you?' Pause, then: 'Again.'

'Only what you said to say,' Clarence gabbles.

'Run through it and make it accurate. I need to know.'

Clarence summarises our Thursday afternoon conversation, labouring the line that he'd heavily implicated Pepper. 'Stick everything else against Voss who can't answer back, you said. And I did.' He ends moodily. 'Not my fault it's not working.'

'It can still work,' says Ball, not too positively.

'Only if Pepper stays quiet,' Clarence points out timidly.

'He'll cough to what becomes necessary, to stitching up that policewoman and the safe job with Tring. All his own work, he'll say. He got bum info about a big pile of money or something.'

'He'll get years,' says Clarence, not sounding too concerned.

'Pensionable years. I'll take care of him. He knows the score.'

Clarence changes the topic. 'What about Voss?'

'What about him?' Ball sounds puzzled.

'The shooting?'

'What about it?'

'Will Pepper admit to it?'

'Why should he?' Ball seems astonished. 'Work that out for yourself.'

'Me?' Clarence is even more astonished.

'You had your reasons...'

'What are you talking about?' Clarence's voice is up several notes, approaching soprano.

'...revenge for your wife, to take over his business...'

'Me? What are you saying?' There's squeaky disbelief in Clarence's voice.

'My lads, none of 'em, are taking any raps for that. Got rid of the weapon, I trust.'

'Haven't got, never had, a bloody gun, any gun,' pipes Clarence. 'Look here. That wasn't me. It had to be you, your work. I'm not taking the blame –'

Ball butts in, quietly. 'Just keep us all out of it, that's all. Remember I can get at you wherever you are.'

'But it wasn't...' Clrence stops. '...and if it wasn't...'

A dozen egg shells appear to be smashed together. Then there's shuffling. Then a short silence. 'What's this?' demands Ball.

'What?'

'This.'

'Don't know.'

'Your work.' It's a statement, not a question, not a trace of doubt in Ball's voice.

'No. God, no.' Clarence is obviously horrified. 'Christ...'

'You again, trying to trap me...'

Oh God, I groan inwardly, someone has kicked up a cable.

'No. Listen.' Clarence tries appeasement, desperation in his tone. 'Maybe it's scrap.'

'Recording me again.' Ball isn't listening.

A dull click I've heard before, on the railway line when I got this leg, of a shotgun snapping shut.

'No. Honest. No, Alec.' Clarence, begging. 'Please, Alec.'

'Go! Go! Go!' I command, more of a scream than a shout, ripping off my headset.

22

'Armed police,' I scream again, with just about my last breath, breaking free of the needle sharp trees and the thorny thickets on to the footpath.

I reach a five bar fence, falling forward, leaning on it, steadying myself to catch my breath.

Clarence is in a tight ball on the grey shale, arms wrapped round his head, not moving, twenty yards inside the tip.

Too late, I think. He's shot him. Oh, Lord. He's dead.

Ball has his gun to his shoulder, ranging in a quarter-circle from me to one of Haywood's watchers who has emerged up the oily banks of the nearest lagoon seventy yards away, his boiler-suit so black he could be a frogman.

No whiff of smoke hangs on the air. No smell of cordite. No dark liquid seeps into the shale around Clarence. He moves, no more than a twitch, cries weakly. 'Help me. Please help.'

I've banked enough breath now to speak. 'The cable's ours, not his.'

'Bastard.' Ball trains the gun on me. 'First you.' He jerks the gun down, just slightly towards Clarence, and back again. 'Then him.'

All I can think of is Harrison Ford again in *Witness*. 'Enough,' I shout. 'It's over.'

What worked for Ford isn't working for me, I realise all too well as he eases his shoulder into the butt.

'You'll be dead before you can pull the trigger twice,' I say, quieter. 'You're surrounded.'

Another black figure comes out of the lagoon. Slowly they take up positions at each end of the bank. Dead wood cracks and splinters as Haywood and Herrick lead more watchers out of the trees and undergrowth behind me.

Ball looks about him, then back to me. 'At least, I'll have settled with you.'

162

'There's one too many dead already,' I say, rather feebly.

He shakes his head heavily. 'Nothing to do with me.'

'I know that.'

Ball isn't listening again. He flicks the gun away. 'Ask him.'

'Help me,' cries Clarence.

The gun stays trained on him. 'Up,' snaps Ball. Clarence doesn't stir. '*Up.*' Ball booms it. '*Up. Up.*'

'Do as he says, Con,' I call, climbing over the fence, sitting on the top rail, chin close to my knees, hoping to make myself a small target.

Clarence rolls on to his knees, scrambling in the shale. He pushes up, stooping double, as if trying to make himself smaller, too. 'Stop him. Please help me.'

Ball backs away, around Clarence. He hooks his left hand round his neck, The gun goes out of sight. My God, he's going to shoot him in the back. I drop on to the shale, take a few stiff paces forward.

The gun reappears over Clarence's shoulder, trained on me. Oddly, it's a sort of relief.

Slowly, Ball backs further away, dragging an unresisting Clarence ten yards with him, the gun resting on his shoulder. I walk on, just keeping pace and distance.

Ball waves the gun, unsteadily, with one hand. 'I'm warning you, laddie. I've got nothing to lose.'

'Please. You have to hear this.' I walk forward, slowly, carefully. 'We know it wasn't you who had Voss killed.'

He would have done, eventually, of course, when the heat from the safe-blowing had cooled down and it would have been done professionally, miles from here, a tragic accident, but you can't charge someone over a plan that hasn't been formulated.

'It wasn't me.' Clarence is staggering unwilling backwards, feet flapping, like a clown in a circus act. His chin is held so high under Ball's stiff forearm that he is speaking as much to him as me. 'Honest. It wasn't –'

This I'm not going to listen to, let alone debate. I put a finger to my mouth, then point it at him. 'Shut it. Just keep quiet.'

'You've got enough to put me away,' says Ball, still stepping back, dragging Clarence who has stopped working his feet.

'Not necessarily,' I say, as quietly as I can. 'Not with a good lawyer.'

For ten more slow yards I talk rapidly, almost a little legal lecture, raising the sort of questions a good lawyer should – did the police have reasonable suspicion for making an arrest earlier and therefore wasn't anything said on secret tapes inadmissible because no caution had been administered?

Ball hears me out, letting my hopes soar, then verbally shoots me down. 'Bollocks.'

'Worth a try,' I persist.

'Bullshit,' he repeats flatly.

Over the next few yards, I try a different approach. His car is surrounded. He's got no getaway vehicle. All his bank cards will be stopped. 'There's no escape.'

The back of Clarence's head has slipped down to Ball's chest. The heels of his boots have made twin tracks another ten yards in the shale. 'He's no protective shield,' I point out.

'At least you'll be dead,' he says fiercely. 'Me?' There's a change in his whole demeanour, body language as well as tone, impossible to fully analyse at this dusky distance with the pale light of a full moon behind and the afterglow of the sunset ahead. 'I don't care.'

Ten yards to go and I play my ace. 'And what about Amanda?'

'Leave her out of it.' He almost sobs it, slowing up, not what I wanted.

I speed up. 'Orphaned. Mum dead in a crash. You, a police killer, shot dead on a waste tip. A waste tip, for Christsake. Think what the papers will make of that. Waster wasted on waste tip.'

'Leave it be.' I'm near enough to see the glisten of sweat on his face, white and twisted.

He takes longer steps back, trying to put more space between us. Clarence, head close to Ball's stomach, is pulled with him.

'Is that how you want to be remembered?' I say, near enough to be talking almost normally. 'Is that how you want her to remember you?'

'Better than dying in jail,' he mutters, more or less to himself.

'Well,' I say, spreading my hands to demonstrate that there's nothing in them, 'if it comes to that, you'll be running the rackets in no time, baron of your wing, a cell with all the luxuries. You'll breeze it. It won't be life. Not the way it stands right now.'

164

'Yes, it will.' Less than a yard to go and he slows.

Don't want that, not this close. 'And Amanda will come visiting, a big part of your life, always.'

'Leave her out, I said,' he almost screams.

'You'll read about her stage and screen successes. You'll still be around, alive, to give her the benefit of your undoubted experience in the entertainment business...'

He lets go of Clarence, viciously kneeing the back of his head. Clarence flops with a groan on his face on the shale.

Ball swings his freed left hand towards the barrel, hunches his right shoulder. To firm himself in the aim position, his right leg goes back to set himself on ground that isn't there.

The barrel of the gun jerks from horizontal to vertical, discharging a brief puff, more white than orange, like a lighter going on and off, but with a thunderous clap.

I peer over the edge into the lagoon. Twenty yards below, Ball looks blacker than Pepper. He is floundering like a beetle on its back on the quicksand slurry round the edge of the deep, dark water on which his trilby floats. He is screaming the foulest obscenities.

Herrick cuffs a violently shaking Clarence behind his back and helps him to his feet.

Haywood appears at my shoulder, calling down to Ball, 'The more you struggle, the faster you'll sink.'

'Get me out,' Ball splutters through a mouthful of black slime.

'Let's leave him for a couple of minutes to soften him up,' I suggest. I'm going to delegate, like a chief superintendent should. 'Then fish him out.'

Haywood gives me a resentful look.

'Be fair.' I tug on my brown lapels. 'I've only got one good suit left.'

He looks me up and down, somewhat pityingly. My eyes follow his. Long threads hang here and there where the bramble thorns and the pine needles have snagged both jacket and trousers.

23

On the sheeted-down back seat of Inspector Herrick's car, north-bound up the A64 towards her station, sits Golden Balls; an extraordinary sight.

His hairless head reminds me of a shining black medicine ball. His oily hands are cuffed on his lap. His filthy clothes smell pungently of sulphur.

He turns to me. 'Make a note. No comment of any kind, not a single word, until I've spoken to my solicitor. Got that, dick-head?'

The whites of his eyes look like two drops of fat in a slice of black pudding. 'OK, Black Balls,' I reply, cheerily, winding him up.

I glance westwards. Horizon clouds have divided into jagged lines of crimson, grey-blue, pink and purple. 'Look at that sky,' I invite him.

He doesn't look and doesn't comment.

'Half an hour ago that was a perfect golden ball,' I say, with a dramatic sigh. 'Now it's all broken up. Symbolic, don't you think?'

'Bollocks,' he snarls ahead of him.

'That's your trouble, see,' I say, sadly. 'Unlike your daughter, there's no poetry in your soul.'

Back at the station, walking from a cell to an interview room, I throw an arm around Clarence's shoulder.

It sags. All of him sags, like a pudding that's not been made with that rise and brown mixture.

'Confessional time, Con,' I whisper to him. 'Put yourself in the position of one of those mealy-mouthed, whinging, moaning, not-my-fault, everyone-else-is-to-blame punters...' If I'm sound-ing like Inspector Grim in *The Thin Blue Line* it's intentional. '...on shows like the late lamented *Clive Live*. Let it all hang out. You'll bore the tits off everyone else but you'll feel better.'

I was half expecting Ball-like abuse, but he nods dumbly ahead of him, deep in some muse.

'I, er...' Clarence's official tape is off to a false, highly unprofessional start.

He stops, thinks, his left eye tic-ing ten to the dozen, then begins again.

To Herrick, he says with an expression of forced sincerity, 'Told you the truth as it stood three months ago, you know. I did overhear a drugs shipment being organised for Friday, 13 September. Liz was at death's door because, I honestly believed at the time, of drugs she'd obtained from the Shuffle.'

He turns to me, face apologetic. 'Lied about Ball's phone conversation being recorded by accident, I'm afraid. There never was a tape of any such call. Sorry.'

So far, so truthful, I think, as Herrick seeks to discover what happened to his sense of public duty between 13 September and 13 December.

After about a week in hospital, he answers, his wife admitted she had attempted suicide with prescription drugs, nothing to do with anything from the Shuffle, and then she confessed to adultery with Voss.

Technically, it wasn't adultery, but I won't correct him. 'So you changed sides?' Herrick continues.

'The decision was forced on me,' he replies with a note of self-justification. 'Ball got to hear of your inquiries. He suspected me of being your source. Pepper had me by the throat. Literally.' Clarence fingers his neck. 'It just came out, that's all.'

'What came out?' I demand, wanting it on the record.

He still addresses Herrick. 'I told him Voss must have tipped you, not me. What's more, he had a recording of the deal being struck over the phone which he'd lodged in his solicitor's safe. I knew he had something secret in his safe; never knew exactly what.'

His eye tic is no more than an occasional flutter, his growing confidence calming him. 'I made it up, there and then, to save myself. It was all I could think of in my panic. I was in genuine fear for my life.'

'A good idea at the time, you mean?' Herrick observes with a touch of scorn.

A mournful nod.

'Did Voss know you'd dropped him in it?' she goes on.

He thinks. 'All I know is what Ball and Voss told me afterwards. They'd come to an arrangement, both said. I wasn't

167

present, naturally. And Voss told me he'd negotiated development money for *Fallen Angel*, provided his daughter Mandy got a meaty role.'

'What conclusion did you come to over that?'

Clarence pauses for a second's thought. 'Pleased, I'd say, overall that my script was finally going into production after all those months of work.'

He's so immersed in that work, to the exclusion of duty even to his wife, that he's misunderstood the question.

Herrick puts him right. 'Wasn't that development money merely hush money?'

He looks quite shocked. 'Ball came to no financial arrangement with me, if that's what you mean.'

'What was your reward for saying no more to me?' asks Herrick.

'He'd let me live.'

'Provided you got pictures of the colliery ammo store and the safe at the solicitors for the Tring item?' I put in.

'No.' Definitely shocked now, or pretending to be. 'Voss organised all of that. He didn't tell me what it was all about and I didn't ask, but...' He pauses. '...of course, as soon as the safe was blown, I realised –'

I stop him. 'Before we go into Friday the 13th, didn't you realise, while making that *Cause for Concern* item, that something fishy was afoot?'

'Had suspicions, yes, but I couldn't work it out fully, and then, of course –'

I interrupt again. 'Let's keep things in chronological order, shall we? What other arrangements did you come to with Ball?'

'About what?'

'About drugs, for instance,' prompts Herrick.

None, he insists. He claims not to know if the drugs shipment had been put back from September to December and hotly denies making discreet inquiries about which was the safest landing place and passing on the information to Ball.

I get him back on track. 'You were saying that you began to have suspicions while making the Tring item and that, on Friday the 13th, after the safe was blown, you realised something. What?'

Immediately he picks up the thread. 'That Tring was got out

of jail under false pretences. But I didn't twig it at the time; only after the fire at the law office.'

'But you've already said that you knew Voss had something in that safe,' Herrick points out. 'OK, not a recording about any drugs deal, because one doesn't exist. But something very private.'

'Yes,' he concedes cautiously.

'So when your friend Voss –'

Clarence stirs. 'He was no friend. He was just a pretty face. He had no real talent.'

'And,' I add, 'you believed he had corrupted your wife?'

A brief nod.

'So you hated him?'

No response.

'That's a strong motive for arranging his murder,' I continue.

'I didn't.' He looks at me appealingly. 'I know nothing about that shooting, then or now. I disliked him, certainly, professionally and personally, but not enough to kill him or to have him killed. Ball must have organised it. Surely?' He raises his eyebrows.

'With Voss gone,' I suggest, 'you'd have taken over Voss Vision.'

'Never entered my head.' He shakes it heavily. 'Once *Fallen Angel* put a feature credit to my name, I was off to London, away from here and current affairs, into drama.'

His eye blinks normally now, in unison with his right. He's in complete control.

He knows we've got nothing on him for aiding the plot to import drugs. His defence against any conspiracy charge to pervert the course of justice over Tring is simple: Voss fixed it, not me. Our case at the moment rests on the admissibility of the tapes at the pit tip, touch and go.

We're nowhere near, and never will be, nailing him as an accomplice in the murder of Voss.

One last go, I decide. 'Did you know that Voss had a sideline in blue movies?'

'No.' He gasps it.

'And that your wife appears in one of them?'

'Oh God, no.' Groaned.

'Was it porn he had locked away in the safe?'

'How would I know?'

169

'If it wasn't Ball being recorded on the blower, what was it?'

'I don't know. How many times?' He closes both eyes tightly. 'I just don't know. That's the truth.'

I think the first and last bits are, but the middle is a pack of lies. I get up, picking up my file, leaving the rest to Herrick.

Alone in the office, I open the file and read this extract, highlighted in green, from the statement by the staff nurse from Scarborough Hospital: 'This is to confirm that I have just formally picked out the man who brought in a since deceased burns victim to our casualty department on Friday 13th of this month.

I recognised him in the line-up, despite the fact that he has since injured his nose. He gave his name to me as Aron Veltman.'

A cross-reference has been added for file: 'The two orderlies made similar positive identifications. The doctor was not 100 per cent sure.'

On I flick to this highlighted extract from the statement of Aron Veltman, seaman: 'This is to confirm that I have just identified a man who met my boat *Goud Wereld* shortly after docking.

He has a fresh nasal wound, but there is no doubt in my mind he is the same person. I talked with him on the quay while he waited to see our captain Johan Mulder. During that conversation he asked my name.

He and another man came on board to speak in private in the captain's cabin. They left with a bag I had seen the skipper bring aboard. Both got into a bronze-coloured car parked on the quay. A third man appeared to be sleeping across the back seat.'

There's another cross-reference for file. 'Skipper Mulder, his mate and his importer/exporter are held in custody in Rotterdam, refusing, as yet, to talk.'

There's no time to read on as a cadet pops his head round the door to summon me to Interview Room No. 2.

Ball, in white overalls, his bald head scrubbed surgically clean, sits at a table alongside a solicitor, the same lawyer who is representing Pepper. A busy man – according to the custody log, he has already had long private conversations with them both.

When the tape is turned on, the solicitor, a tubby, silver-haired man, does the talking, loudly and clearly, as if addressing a courtoom. 'My client has nothing to say at this stage, pending counsel's opinion on the validity of your actions, by which I mean your surveillance operation, today. He will answer no questions. Thank you. Please turn off now.'

I give the time and turn off the tape without another word.

'Right...' Pepper, in white overalls, sits in the chair Ball vacated, addressing the drugs squad inspector across the table. '...I'm talkin' to you, not him.'

He jerks his head towards me. A painful movement, I'd have thought. A thin strip of plaster, all the rage among sports stars these days, is across his nose. Swelling has made it so prominent that I can't be sure he isn't the spectator I saw at the soccer match on Tuesday.

He leans forward closer to the mike. 'I wanna state I'm lodging a complaint of assault. Right?'

'Noted,' says the solicitor gravely.

Pepper sits up straight. 'Right, then. I admit involvement in that safe-blowing and drug-smuggling.'

'Is that all?' I query playfully.

He ignores me. 'I was tipped there was lotsaloot in there. I'm not giving the source. A casual customer in the Shuffle. That's all you need to know.'

Some of the Caribbean sing-song seems to have left his accent. He is looking down at his hands which are rubbing rings on the desk. 'Didn't have the know-how, personally, to break into the safe. I was tipped that Tring had. Trouble was he was in prison.'

He stops, thinks, trying to remember the lines I suspect the lawyer had given him on Ball's instructions. 'Me and a couple of mates cobbled together that stuff about Tring drinking with us when he was doing the gems job. I got the jelly from the colliery and, a week last Friday, went with him to McMichael's office in the bank chambers.'

This bit's true, I acknowledge privately.

'He did the alarm OK,' Pepper continues. 'While I was on

watch outside, he blew himself up, er, yes...' He nods to himself. '...as well as the safe.'

From the disapproving expression on the lawyer's face, I judge that Pepper has added an unauthorised ad lib.

'I heard the bang and ran upstairs. Everything in the safe had gone up...' He frowns, then hurriedly corrects his earlier error. '...apart from ten grand in cash which was in a tin box.'

The lawyer grimaces his disapproval.

'Mr McMichael says there was no cash in the safe,' I point out.

Pepper stops and thinks over something not in his script. He waves a dismissive hand in my direction without looking at me. 'Then he's on a tax fiddle or something,' he tells the inspector.

'Must be the first time a fire victim has under-claimed on his insurance,' I interject sarcastically.

'Please let my client tell his story in his own way,' says the solicitor, irritated.

Before he forgets, I grouse privately.

'Tring was lying on the floor,' Pepper resumes. 'His clothes were smouldering. I gave him a fireman's lift downstairs, then walked him to a car-park.'

He is talking fluently, on much safer ground, sticking close to the facts.

'I couldn't take him to the district hospital. That would have been a dead giveaway. I nicked a car and drove him to Scarborough.'

I dart in. 'Why there?.

'Ain't finished yet.' In his anger at my interruptions, his accent is almost back home in his native South London.

'Had to go there, see, anyway, er...' Much slower now, not word perfect. '...to pick up some caine coming in. My first deal, a private job. The cash from the safe was to fund it. All gone now.'

He's over the worst, and speeds up. 'Tring lay across the back seat, shuddering violently now and then, but mostly he was quiet. At the port, I took delivery and then dropped Tring off at hospital under a false name. I'm admitting nothin' else, naming nobody I was with, not the boat, nothin' else.'

Not a bad performance, I think, unconcerned, opening my thickening file, looking down at nothing in particular. 'If you were too busy to watch TV, how did you know to go to Scarborough and not Whitby?'

172

'Is he deaf?' He shouts at the inspector as if he is. 'Can't he hear? I saying nothin' more.'

He goes silent for a second. 'Yeah.' He smiles faintly, another ad lib coming on. 'Yeah.' He screws himself contentedly in his chair.

The solicitor looks distinctly uncomfortable.

'Phoned a contact, didn't I, from that box near the car-park?' As if to convince himself, he repeats, 'Yeah.' Finally he turns to me, face triumphant: 'Buggered one of your witness statements, has it?'

He nods to the file in front of me.

Somewhere in it is a photocopy extract from the notebook of the officer who saw Inmate 415 King on remand in Wolds Prison, Humberside: 'This note is being made immediately after our conversation as the subject refused to make a statement and would permit nothing to be written down.'

'He stated that Pepper went to see him with a legal document he said had to be sworn in front of a commissioner.'

'The subject continued: "It said I was drinking with him and a bloke I've never met called Tring on this certain night. I wanted no part of it, but he said I'd get no more steroids for my gym if I didn't.'

'"On Friday the 13th I was supposed to go to the coast to collect a bag from a boat coming in – E mainly, and speed and some steroids for me." '

'"The drop was always on for Scarborough, but I had to watch that live programme on ITV for any last-minute change in instructions. If Jaffa Cake was favourite in the 9.45, no matter where it finished, Scarborough was confirmed and I was to go straight there." '

'"The day before, I was nicked selling pills and banged up in here, so I couldn't make it." '

'"I want this last bit clearly understood. If you are conning me and Golden Balls and Pepper aren't inside, you can forget this chat because to go into the witness box would get me killed. And, even if they are inside and I'm not out on bail, you can take a running jump. On the other hand, if I can get a deal, then maybe we can work something out." '

I close the file, deciding not to put King's off-the-record state-

173

ment to Pepper tonight. Or to disclose that a .38 short-barrelled Smith and Wesson had been found strapped beneath a mud-guard of his Toyota, not until Ballistics report back.

Save something for tomorrow, my old grandad always used to say.

Pepper mocks me now. 'No more questions then, Master Police-man?'

'Well,' I begin hesitantly. 'Did you go to a football match at Boothferry Crescent on Tuesday evening just past?'

He is completely relaxed. 'Never been there, thanks all the same.'

I nod acceptance. 'Earlier that same day, did you park your car at the Royal York Hotel?'

'What if I did? Went to the Tiles Bar for a drink. No law against that, is there?'

I wasn't being stalked, I realise, just thought I was. Bad luck, that, for Clarence. Getting it wrong made me wrongly suspect he'd tipped off Pepper about my presence here, focused my attention on him.

Pepper is still basking in the afterglow of his performance. He'll get a good review when the solicitor reports back to Golden Balls.

He'd talked himself into at least five years. He'd shopped two of his mates, but he knows we have them inside anyway. He realises we have him officially ID-ed for the job with Tring.

He's given away nothing we don't already know, nothing at all on Ball, who is more than a boss to Pepper, I guess. He admires and respects him, like a father.

'Anything else?' he asks, enjoying himself hugely at my ex-pense.

'Just tell me...' I pause. 'Do steroids wither your willie?'

'I say, I must...' The solicitor's spluttering is stopped when Pepper places a hand on his arm.

'Ask around,' Pepper brags. 'What's a matter, mon?' He's almost singing his responses. 'The old crow of a wife of yours complaining about size?' He laughs joyfully. 'Just ask around.'

'Oh, but I will,' I sing back. My face is switched to serious. 'Starting with the lady I saw you with on Friday night.'

All the sunshine sinks rapidly from his face.

174

24

TWO DAYS TO CHRISTMAS

Breakfast in bed, the full house, a last luxury before returning to the real world of cooking my own.

Em is up three mornings a week at four to get to the studios twenty miles away to present the breakfast news, regional, not national. She goes to bed so early that if I finish late, like last night, we don't speak. She's on today, which means our young sitter will have slept over.

Should have made time to phone home last night, I chide myself. Should have tipped her about the developments here.

She'll not be appearing this far north, but, out of habit, I flick on the news. Guilt is redoubled when the story leads, not the regional, but the national news.

'Several men are being held by police in York in connection with a live TV crime programme in which a journalist was shot dead,' announces an attractive fair-haired newscaster.

A male voice talks behind heavily edited film of the fire at the law office and Voss running from his truck towards the alley.

Unsurprisingly, there's not a glimpse of the dying scene. Apart from MPs grumbling that it sent the pregnant woman into labour and Liz Clarence back to hospital, the TV Complaints Commission has been inundated with continuing protests at the bloodbath being shown in the first place.

'Gruesome,' carped the critics. 'Tasteless.' As a result electronic newsrooms are now playing safe. Quite right, too. Who wants that when you're shaking tomato ketchup on your sausages?

The woman newscaster reappears. 'Over now to the officer in charge of the inquiry.' The acting head of CID comes on screen. 'What more can you tell us?' she asks in that superior way of theirs.

'The arrests follow a series of synchronised raids throughout yesterday in the city, Rotterdam and ...' The slightest of pauses. '... the Skipwith area.'

Wicked that, I think. He's all but telling the local underworld he's got Golden Balls. He won't have slept much again last night, but he's never looked better all week.

175

It was, he goes on fluently, not glancing at any crib cards, a major operation involving local CID, uniformed officers, Dutch police and senior specialists from East Midlands Combined Constabulary and London.

Like his style, I think; not just because he's mentioned my force and let my wife know I was busy last night. Unlike his chief, he spreads credit around.

'How many are you holding?' the anchorwoman asks.

'Upwards of a dozen.'

Either he's gilding the lily or they've knocked off more minions overnight.

'All in connection with the shooting?' she quizzes.

'We have never said that,' he corrects her. 'We are making wide-ranging inquiries into events before, after and during Friday the 13th.'

Newscasters don't like being publicly put in their place. 'Any developments imminent?' she asks off-handedly.

'More arrests are expected today,' he replies, wrapping up a dazzling début.

Two miniature tape recorders borrowed from Haywood sit on the desk next to the master machine between the drugs squad inspector and Pepper and the solicitor, who looks harassed already.

Feeling like Worzel Gummidge in my threaded brown suit, I sit down and pick up one of the miniatures. 'I'd like you to listen to this.'

Pepper folds his arms. 'I saying nothin' more.' His accent is back in da Yard.

'I'm not asking you to say anything,' I reply evenly. 'I'm asking you to listen.'

I thumb it on. A short extract towards the end of last night's taped interview with him is played, followed by a southern-sounding voice saying, 'Trouble at the Shuffle. Spilling out into the street. Looks close to a riot to me.'

I switch off. 'Our experts have been at work overnight. They say that's the same voice.'

He exchanges troubled glances with the lawyer.

'We're satisfied you made a call from the phone box at the car-park at approximately 9.45 that night. Not to any mythical contact. You were dialling 999, setting up Voss for murder.'

He tries to say something, fails, as the solicitor shakes his head at him severely.

'Further,' I continue, very formally, 'I have to inform you that my colleague here...' I incline my head sideways towards the inspector. '...recovered a Smith and Wesson from under the mudguard of your car. Ballistics confirm it is the weapon that killed Voss.'

Pepper tries to open his mouth. The solicitor kicks somewhere out of sight – his ankle, I presume – so hard that somebody's knee jerks, making the table jump. His lips purse shut.

I pick up the second small tape recorder. 'We're also inviting you to listen to this.'

The solicitor is shaking his head again, fiercely, at me this time. 'We don't have to listen to anything.'

'Then you listen.' I lean across the table, just managing to hold on to my temper. 'All last night you were scuttling between your other client and him...' I flick my head at Pepper. '...passing messages, briefing him on what to say, sitting there and letting him drop himself further and further into the mire.'

'I must –'

A lot's riding on this. Either out of anxiety or anger, I don't really know, I slap the table. 'Listen.' I pause. 'That, at best, is a major conflict of interest on which the Law Society might have a view. At worst, it's conspiracy to pervert the course of justice.'

Pepper's eyes are on me, wide and trance-like.

The lawyer tries again. 'You can't talk to –'

'Listen, I said.' I slap the table harder. 'I'm warning you now that I suspect you of conspiracy –'

'This is...' the lawyer blusters.

'Hold it.' Pepper is out of his trance.

'...monstrous.'

'Hold it.' Pepper is waving his hands down. 'Let's chill out now.' He looks at the lawyer intently. 'Let's hear him out.'

The lawyer sits back in a huff. So do I. Pepper leans forward, all ears.

What's played now is a version of Ball talking to Clarence on the pit tip yesterday afternoon, far more heavily edited than Breakfast TV's recap of *Friday the 13th Blues*.

Out has gone 'He's a good kiddo' and 'I'll take care of him.'

In has stayed 'He'll cough to what becomes necessary' and 'Stupid black berk' and Clarence saying 'Told that superintendent all you told me to say, pointed him at Pepper.'

The solicitor has gone deathly pale.

Pepper's eyes have closed. His face has the betrayed look of a loyal son disowned by his father. 'Er...' He clears his throat, looks threateningly sideways to ward off another kick. 'Would you mind if I spoke to this brief?'

This brief, I note. No longer 'my brief'.

'Privately.' Very politely, he adds, 'Please.'

Ball's face looks whiter and more creased than the boilersuit he's slept in.

The solicitor looks exhausted. Wearily he raises a hand as the acting CID chief lifts his to switch on the master tape. 'Before you do that, my client would like an off-the-record chat.' Both drop their hands on the table.

Ball sighs deeply. 'I'm prepared to admit arranging the death of Voss.'

I smile icily. 'And you're going to tell us you don't know the hit man's name because it was all arranged via a middleman. Or that he's escaped our jurisdiction on the *Goud Wereld* to the Continent. Or something like that.' I shake my head very sadly. 'It won't do.'

There's a worn, aged expression on his round face. 'I'm trying to help.'

I shake my head again. 'We don't need your help. We've got a timed video. We've got the gun.' I look hard at the solicitor. 'We're about to get the motive. We're home.'

Ball clasps his hands on the table, palms pressed together, fingers vertical, close to praying. 'Help me.' A begging look. 'You must understand.'

I understand all right. 'What's in it for me?'

'A full statement, a complete confession on all my activities,' he offers urgently. 'A guilty plea. I'll do the time, no problem.' A long pause. 'Please.'

I decide to fish. 'Give me a taster.'

He glances at the switched-off master machine and then the solicitor who gives him the nod.

Yes, he'd had to delay the September shipment. He'd

blamed Clarence for the leak. When confronted by Pepper, Clarence implicated Voss, claiming he had taped evidence locked away.

'A hundred grand for the film and there's a part in it for Mandy,' Voss said.

Ball decided on divide and rule, took Clarence to one side, suggesting a separate partnership agreement with him and Voss over the film which stipulated one partner took control in the event of the other dropping out. In return Clarence would assist in landing the delayed drugs deal.

Voss signed his end of the deal, but refused to hand over the tape immediately, wanting to hold on to it as collateral against any libel damages Inspector Herrick might win.

Blackmail like that could go on for ever, Ball decided, so he ordered Clarence to cook the evidence to get Tring out of jail to blow the safe.

I break in. 'Let me get this right. Voss and Clarence together used the tape to extract that hundred thou from you?'

'Yes.'

'But Clarence acted without Voss's knowledge in setting up Tring's release.'

'Voss hadn't a clue what was going on until the writ came in. Then he must have rumbled it, got cold feet. That's why he wouldn't hand over the tape until I'd also settled any legal bills.'

They both conned him, I realise, nodding him on.

On *Friday the 13th Blues*, he continues, Clarence gave the word that the delayed consignment should go in to Scarborough.

Again I have to come in. 'How did he let you know the coast at Whitby wasn't clear?'

'Easy,' Ball says with a little smile. 'If Clarence appeared on screen during the drugs raid on TV, speaking into camera, it meant the Customs watch was off. If he didn't appear, stick with Scarborough.'

Hmmmm, I think. Spotted that but hadn't worked it out fully. He confirms what I'd already sussed – he loaded money on Jaffa Cake to get the message across to his collectors.

Now Ball looks uneasy. 'And once I knew the safe was blown, I gave the word on Voss.'

'How?'

'I'm not telling you everything right now,' he says, smiling thinly.

I smile back, gleefully. 'And what if I told you that Tring, had he survived, would have returned empty-handed?'

His expression tells me he's totally baffled so I go on, 'There was no recorded evidence against you. There was never a tape.'

I expected him to explode like McMichael's safe. He takes it very calmly, thinks, then: 'Now there's a motive for you.'

'But it isn't true you had Voss killed,' I say.

Now he does explode. 'What's it to you? All you want is a clear-up, someone in the dock.'

'Yes, but I want the right one in the dock.' I also want Clarence there, too, and I'll not get him without Ball's co-operation, a statement in writing, his evidence in court, it occurs to me. I shake my head. 'I can't go along with it as it stands.'

'Look.' His eyes are pleading with me. 'I'll do the time, want to do it.'

'Sorry,' I say.

'Look,' he repeats. 'What do you think this is?' He runs a hand over his bald head.

The lawyer shakes his, mournfully. 'The prognosis is not good.'

He's dying from cancer, they are telling me. I'm lost for words, but not for mixed thoughts and a memory.

Explains his couldn't-care-less conduct yesterday, some of the things he said. He wasn't bothered whether he lived or died.

And I'm sorry, of course, sorry I let him struggle for so long in the lagoon, sorry for that flip remark in the car here.

Years ago, my grandad went to arrest a local vicar who'd been fiddling church funds to finance a chronic drink problem. 'I'm ruined. I'll kill myself,' the vicar sobbed.

'Well,' grandad reminisced, 'you can't not do your duty because someone may or may not die. That way, the world would come to a stop. So I said "Sorry" and nicked him.'

Both have their eyes on me, awaiting my reaction. 'Sorry,' I repeat, hoping he'll take it as an expression both of regret and of refusal.

'What then?' There is desperation in Ball's features. 'What?'

'Well.' Deep in thought, I tip the chair back on its two rear legs and clasp both hands on the back of my neck. 'Why not...'

I speak very slow, as much for the solicitor's benefit as Ball's. 'No guarantees, mind...but try, say, tragic and sudden death in the family...sexual blackmail...provocation at the scene. A walk in and a voluntary statement. It might win a hospital order, can't promise, though.'

Ball looks at the lawyer who nods very solemnly, then back at me. 'Do your best.'

'She's mad, fucken mad.' Pepper sits alone on the opposite side of the table. 'And I do mean fucken. At it all the time. Can't get enough. We've been at it on and off since her schooldays.'

Rehearsing for the Desdemona role in *Othello* even then, I think.

He sighs. 'Worried out my mind, I've been. Know what? This pisshead is supposed to have grabbed these one night.' A lifting motion with hands at chest height. 'Told her dad. Know what I had to do? Break both his hands. With an iron bar. Think what he'd have done to me if he'd found out.'

I prefer not to.

'Voss was always hanging around us at the Shuffle. Came back to my place one night. Watched us, the pervo. She didn't mind. Gave her an extra thrill.

'Next time he asked us to his place. Lots of booze about and he brought out some caine.' His face fills with disgust. 'And his camera. Both of us had been drinking and snorting and so . . .' He shrugs expressively. 'She thought it was all a big laugh. She likes showing off her body, loves cameras, being centre stage.'

'One quiet night at the club a few of the boys brought in some blue stuff for upstairs in the office. Some big fat tart in school gear up to something strange; can't remember.'

Yes, I agree privately. *Detention* wasn't so memorable.

'All I do remember is the bedroom furniture. Voss's. His name wasn't on the video label but it was his bedroom all right.' He wriggles in his chair. 'I shat myself.'

The memory makes him stop for a second. 'Told Mandy. She thought it was a giggle. Listen, I said, if he's putting this stuff on general release and your old man sees it . . . Let me put the frighteners on him, I said.'

'She'd handle it, she said, cool bitch. Fixed it, she said the next week. Daddy was backing a film. Voss would keep the video locked away at his lawyer's office.

'Last few weeks, ever since he ditched that potty Clarence bird, he's been sniffing around, all the more, wanting more of the same. Not for sale, he said. For his own private viewing. He was a pervo, real weirdo, the worst.'

'Even she was getting scared about him getting cained up and blowing it in the Shuffle. It was gettin' real heavy.'

'Midweek . . .' He stops to think. 'Week before last, she says, "I want a private word with him away from the club, not at his place or yours." '

'She's been to some meeting at the dog track with her old man, she says, and knew where Voss'll be and when on the Friday.'

'I knew there was going to be a live dog race plugging her dad's company, because I was under orders to watch it and wait for the signal to tell me which port to go to for the collection.'

'No one told me there'd be cameramen and policemen running about all over the place. It was fucken madness. But he's like that, likes to show off.'

Like father, like daughter, I think.

'She tells me where to dial 999 from and what to say. All she wanted was either a quiet word or to scare him off, she said. I didn't know she was going to kill him. I didn't give her the gun. She knew where I keep it 'cos she likes me to play with her with it sometimes.'

Instead of a vibrator, he means, and I grimace.

He notices. 'She's like that. Wild. Worse. Loopy. Come Friday, and the old man tells me I'll have to go with Tring because the look-out he's booked for the job had been arrested and was on remand.'

'He told me the safe job was to be done at dead on 9.30 at McMichael's office. Well, I couldn't tell him, sorry, I've got a little job on with your daughter that night to get hold of a blue movie featuring the both of us.'

'I can see you had a problem,' I sympathise.

'Not half. I knew from Clarence that the target was the office of Voss's mouthpiece. He told us, Alex and me, that Voss had stashed that tape on the phone call there. I thought that was Alex's target.

'I didn't want Tring opening the safe and running back to Ball with our bedroom antics, as well as that drugs evidence, now did I?

'So it suited me to go with Tring and look at what he took and snaffle the bedroom stuff. I thought we'd be in and out in five minutes and I'd still have time to make that 999 call at quarter to ten.'

He slows at a bad memory. 'Didn't work out that way and I had to make the call at the nearest box; no choice.

'When I got back from Scarborough and heard what had happened, I didn't know if Alex had hired someone to bump off Voss or what. She only told me last Friday when you were sniffing around. She was very frightened. She thought you were on to her. I went ape, panicked. Sorry. You OK now?'

I nod at his nose. 'You?'

'Yeah.'

'I want it on record,' says the lawyer, talking to the mike, 'that my client has come here of her own free will and wishes to make a voluntary statement.'

Herrick runs through the formal caution.

'I shot Clive Voss,' says Amanda Ball, very softly, not a touch of the dramatics. 'I didn't mean to, but I did.'

She looks countrified in a tweed trouser suit with matching waistcoat, crisp white shirt and brown brogues, but poised, as if there are cameras on her.

'The last year has been an absolute nightmare. With mum taken away so suddenly, there was no one I could turn to, confide in. I have one good friend, a soulmate, who has comforted me. We got close, too close, and while we were intimate Voss secretly filmed us.'

'He used it to blackmail me into securing financial support from my father for a science fiction feature he was producing and he insisted I appear in it. I wanted no part of it, but was given no option.'

'To add to my horror and humiliation, I discovered that he marketed home-made blue movies and feared that he would sell the video on the open market. For weeks, I have suffered sick migraines from the stress of the situation.'

'I knew that he was appearing on the live crime show and arranged through a friend to have him outside the club at 9.45. I borrowed his gun for self-protection, that's all.'

'Looking back, in the cold light of eleven days on, I don't know what was going through my mind, except that all I intended to do was talk to him, plead with him.'

'I was waiting in the alley where I knew he'd come. When he ran down, I pointed the gun but only to stop him just a yard or so short of me. "I'm going to expose you for what you are – a blackmailer and a pornographer," I told him. I was hysterical, I'm afraid.'

'He stood there and laughed in my face. "And what will your father make of that? And whither your glittering career then?" He actually said "whither".'

I smile to myself.

'All I remember is him reaching out for the gun and it going off in my hand and seeing him fall. I don't even recall running away, wish now I'd stopped and explained.'

'Everything else is a blank. I have not slept since. When I heard on TV this morning that innocent people had been arrested, I knew I could not let them go to prison for something I had done. I consulted my family's solicitor and, on his advice, I present myself here.'

She looks sideways at the lawyer, asking, in effect, have I remembered all my lines?

Not having had to prompt her once, he nods, satisfied. I'm impressed. The consummate actress, I think without admiration. She'll be the star of next year's Christmas panto in her jail or, more likely, a cushy mental home.

Herrick starts a series of obvious questions, all of which are met with the same response from the lawyer. 'My client will answer that in the witness box before her jury.'

I don't join in. It's less than half the story, of course. Voss and Clarence were blackmailing her father with a tape that didn't exist. As a failsafe, unbeknown to Clarence, Voss was blackmailing her with the blue movie.

The irony is that Ball would probably have coughed up the money willingly, just to buy her stardom. He loves her so much he would have gone to prison for what's left of his life for her.

In this business, you have to weigh up the odds. The odds are that without this partial confession no charge would stick.

Even if Pepper had told the jury what he'd told us, her QC would have torn him to shreds. And who would be believed? A Yardie, albeit a phoney one, with a record for perverting the course of justice, drug-smuggling, helping to blow a safe and dumping a dying man forty miles from the nearest hospital? Or this naïve, betrayed, sobbing sensation?

Add the full lowdown on her lowlife victim and a mostly male jury would set her free with a couple of quid out of the poor box.

Manslaughter on the grounds of provocation or responsibility impaired by a temporary breakdown is the odds-on favourite, the best bet I can get.

Much safer than her bet on the televised races. She'd seen the evens favourite, her father's dog, win the 9.15 and that would have doubled her stake. All of it would have gone on High Society because she liked its theatrical name.

It was even money when she left the TV in the office in the Shuffle. While she was out, it drifted to five-to-two. Her winnings would have gone up five-fold, not three. A girl with a holiday job in kennels making a mistake like that? I asked myself. She made it because she was away from the TV killing Voss, and missed the last-minute fluctuations in the prices. It was all downhill to the winning post from then on.

Herrick gives up, having got nowhere, turns off the tape.

Amanda stands, rather regally, beaming down on me. 'An honourable murder, if you will.'

I recognise a line from *Othello*. Another comes to mind. 'Alas, you are undone.'

25

ONE DAY TO CHRISTMAS

In the kitchen, the turkey is prepared, the boiled York ham is cooling. In the lounge, the gifts are wrapped and under the lit tree. A surprise extra for Em, an antique brooch, is among them.

Walking from the kitchen, she stops by the coffee table and picks up Jacko's book which I've unpacked. 'Read it?'

'Nar.' Stretched out on the sofa in scruffy cords and denim shirt, I yawn. 'Once you've put it down, you can't pick it up again.'

She laughs briefly. 'Will you give him your latest case?'

'Might. Should make a hardback for him.'

'It will never be adapted for telly, that's for sure.'

'Why ever not?' I ask, more upset for myself than Jacko.

'There's no sex in it.'

'What about the blue movies?'

'Just fleeting, aren't they? No bedroom scenes, I mean, bodies rising and rolling in soft focus, legs entwined in a twisted white sheet in the half-light.'

'That can be swiftly arranged,' I offer, no longer tired.

'Slowly, if you don't mind,' she says, walking slowly towards me, holding out her hand.

And, afterwards, in the half-light, I propose a younger Harrison Ford or maybe John Travolta, now he's matured, for the leading man.

Cruelly, she suggests Danny de Vito and, laughing, we roll into each other's arms again for the reprise, a lovely word.